LIFE
AMONG
THE
TERRA-
NAUTS

LIFE AMONG THE TERRA-NAUTS

CAITLIN HORROCKS

Little, Brown and Company

New York Boston London

Copyright © 2021 by Caitlin Horrocks

Hachette Book Group supports the right to free expression and the value of copyright. The purpose of copyright is to encourage writers and artists to produce the creative works that enrich our culture.

The scanning, uploading, and distribution of this book without permission is a theft of the author's intellectual property. If you would like permission to use material from the book (other than for review purposes), please contact permissions@hbgusa.com. Thank you for your support of the author's rights.

Little, Brown and Company
Hachette Book Group
1290 Avenue of the Americas, New York, NY 10104
littlebrown.com

First Edition: January 2021

Little, Brown and Company is a division of Hachette Book Group, Inc. The Little, Brown name and logo are trademarks of Hachette Book Group, Inc.

These stories originally appeared, sometimes in different form, in the following publications: "Paradise Lodge" in *American Short Fiction;* "Teacher" in *Arkansas International;* "The Sleep" in the *Atlantic;* "All Over with Fire" (as "Jan Palach in Prague") in *Colorado Review;* "Better Not Tell You Now" in *Crazyhorse;* "23 Months" in *Epoch;* "Norwegian for Troll" in *Glimmer Train;* "And Looked Down One As Far As I Could" in *Hayden's Ferry Review;* "On the Oregon Trail" in *Hobart;* "Murder Games" in *Joyland;* "Sun City" in *The New Yorker;* "Life Among the Terranauts" in *One Story;* and "The Untranslatables" in *Unstuck.* "23 Months" was also reprinted in *New Stories from the Southwest,* and "The Sleep" was reprinted in *The Best American Short Stories 2011.*

The publisher is not responsible for websites (or their content) that are not owned by the publisher.

The Hachette Speakers Bureau provides a wide range of authors for speaking events. To find out more, go to hachettespeakersbureau.com or call (866) 376-6591.

ISBN 978-0-316-31697-2
LCCN 2020941064

Printing 1, 2020

LSC-C

Printed in the United States of America

For my mother

CONTENTS

Contents

LIFE
AMONG
THE
TERRA-
NAUTS

THE SLEEP

The snow came early that first year, and so heavy that when Albert Rasmussen invited the whole town over, we had to park around the corner from his unplowed street. We staggered through the drifts, across the lawns, down the neat stretches of sidewalk where a few of Al's neighbors owned snowblowers. Mr. Kajaamaki and the Lutven boys were still out huffing and puffing with shovels. We waved as we passed, and they nodded.

Al stood that November in his family room, arms outstretched, knee-deep in a nest of mattresses and bedding: flannels and florals mixed with Bobby Rasmussen's NASCAR pillowcases, Dee's Disney princess comforter. The sideboard had a hot plate and an electric kettle plugged into a power strip. Al opened drawers filled with crackers, tinned soup, bags of pink-frosted animal cookies, vitamin C pills and canned juice to prevent scurvy.

"Hibernation," he announced. "Human hibernation."

This was before the cameras, before the sleep, before the outsiders, and the plan sounded as strange to us then as it would to anybody. Our town had always wintered the way towns do: gas bills and window plastic, blankets and boots. We bought cream for our cracked skin and socks for our numb feet. We knew how we felt when our extremities faded temporarily away, and we knew how much we hurt when they prickled back to life.

Al showed off a heater he'd built that ran on used grease and the filter that sieved out the hash browns and hamburger. Al had always been handy. He'd been the smartest kid in school, back when Bounty still had its own high school. He was the senior everyone called "college material" until he decided to stay, and then we called him "ours." Our Albert, Albert and his girl, Jeannie, who together were confident that everything they could want in the world was right here in Bounty. We went to their wedding, the Saturday after graduation, and then stood by, helpless, when Albert's parents lost the farm three years later. Maybe the family should have gotten out then, moved away and never looked back. Al might have found a job that paid better than fence repair, and Jeannie might not have been killed by Reggie Lapham, seventeen years old and driving drunk on Highway 51, eight months before this November invitation of Al's. Without that tragedy, Al might never have struck on hibernation, and we might all have gone along the way we'd been going, for better or for worse.

But they had stayed, and Jeannie had died, and Reggie had been sent to a juvenile detention facility downstate. The accident happened in early spring, when patches of ice were still dissolving on the roads, and what no one would say within Al's earshot was that the weather had killed her as much as Reggie had. Al needed something small enough to blame, and Reggie, skinny as a weed and driving his father's truck, served as well as anything could. Al had always seemed older than he was, had transitioned easily from high-school basketball star to assistant coach. Now, in his thirties, he looked twenty years older, bent and exhausted. We wondered if the weight on his shoulders was truly Jeannie or if he'd been carrying, for more years than we'd realized, some piece of Bounty, and he'd invited us over to make sure we understood that he was putting it down.

We'd all stayed in Bounty the way Al had stayed, had carried it as best we could. When our high school shut down, we bused our children to the next town over, then to the county consolidated when that school closed too. They came home with their textbooks about westward expansion, about the gold rush, the tin rush, the copper rush, the wheat farms, the corn farms, the feedlots. About land that gave until it couldn't give anymore and the chumps who kept trying to live on it anyway. Our children came home and told us that we were the suckers of the last century.

"But what if you love it here?" we asked them. "What if you don't want to leave?"

"What's to love?" our children asked in surly disbelief. What kind of morons hustled for jobs that didn't even pay for cable television? What kind of people spent twenty years buying beer at the Hop-In and drinking in the quarry, the next thirty drinking at the Pointes, the last sodden ten at the Elks Lodge?

Our kind of people, we thought.

"Sleep," Al said there in his living room and explained how in the old days in Russia, people sacked out around a stove when the snows came, waking to munch a piece of rye bread, feed the fire, slump back into sleep. Only so much food could be laid in, and the thinking went that unless a man had something to do in the cold and the dark that justified the calories, he was better off doing nothing. Those villagers would wake up skinny and hungry, but they'd wake up alive.

We worried that maybe Al and the kids were harder up than we'd thought. Times were tough for everybody, but other folks weren't shutting down their houses and lives and planning to warm their kids with burger grease.

"What do we do all winter?" Al asked, the kind of question we knew he considered rhetorical. "Why work like dogs all summer to keep the television on, the furnace cranked, noodles on the stove? Why scrape off the car to burn fuel to go to the store to buy more noodles? It's pointless."

Mrs. Pekola, of Pekola Downtown Antiques, opened her mouth for a moment as if she were going to point out that that routine wasn't much different from plenty of people's autumns and springs and maybe summers, in which case Al was saying that we might as well all blow our brains out and have done with it. But she stayed silent. There were many things we didn't need to hear.

"What about Christmas?" Mrs. Drausmann, the librarian, wanted to know.

"We're staying awake for it," Al said. "Just doing a two-month trial run this year, January and February."

"School," Bill and Valeer Simmons said. "Your kids."

Al shrugged. Both his kids were bright and ahead of their classes. At seven, Dee read at a sixth-grade level. Bobby was nine and the best speller at Bounty Elementary. Al had picked up copies of the upcoming curriculum: long division, suffixes, photosynthesis, cursive.

"We're having a sleepover instead," Dee said.

"You know what Mrs. Fiske has planned for February? *Fractions*," Bobby yelled, and the kids bopped around the room until Al chased them upstairs.

"They'll get caught up in spring," Al said. "I don't think they'll have difficulty."

He looked around at us, his old compatriots, the parents of the handful of children still enrolled at the school, and apologized. "I didn't mean anything by that," he said. "I don't think they're special. But they probably won't miss much."

We nodded. Being the children of a dying town had taught us that none of us were special. Whatever our various talents, whatever our dreams and aspirations, we'd all ended up here, in the Rasmussens' family room.

"Don't try to convince me," Al said, "that anything worthwhile happens in this town during January and February. I've lived here as long as you have." We could tell he meant to joke, but nobody laughed. "I'm not crazy. NASA studies this stuff. They're planning for astronauts to hibernate through long voyages so they don't go nuts and kill each other, bust out the shuttle walls." Al's fingers twitched a bit, and we looked at his walls: scuffed beige paint, three china plates with pictures of Holsteins, a family portrait taken at the JCPenney in Bullhorn when Jeannie was still alive, and a single round hole at the height of a man's fist, sloppily repaired with paint and plaster. Their walls looked a lot like our walls, and all of a sudden we were tempted to jam our fists in and pull our own houses down.

"You think we're like that?" Nils Andersen asked from the back of the crowd, all the way in the front foyer, and people parted to let him come closer. He'd been a point guard to Al's shooting guard on the old high-school basketball team. The two still sometimes took practice shots into the hoop on Al's garage.

"Like what?"

"Russians and astronauts. You think we've got two options, asleep or dead?"

Al started to shake his head, because we're not a town that likes to offend. Then he paused, ran his big hands through his hair, and let them drop to his sides. Fair and broad and tall, like his parents and grandparents and Norwegian great-grandparents, like a lot of the rest of us, he looked suddenly large and unwieldy. As if he could only ever fit in this little room curled up asleep, and we'd all been crazy to hope otherwise, to try to fit ourselves inside our own houses. He hunched his shoulders and looked down at the floor. "Maybe," he said. "This is about my family. I never meant any of you had to be involved. But maybe."

We'd thought our town's silence had been stoic; we glimpsed now how much we simply hadn't wanted to say. We rustled in the blankets but kept our mouths shut, put on our shoes, and drifted out into the snow.

Some of us drove straight home. Others took longer routes down Main Street, past First Lutheran, the Pointes, the Elks Lodge, Mrs. Pekola's antiques store, the single-screen movie theater with the marquee still announcing CLOSED, as if the closing were a new release, though it had happened years ago. The public library was housed in the old pharmacy building; we checked out our books at what used to be the prescriptions counter and bought our prescriptions thirty miles down the road. We looked at all the shuttered stores and tried to remember what each one had sold.

We cruised back and forth like bored teenagers on Saturday nights, watching the road run quickly from empty storefronts to clapboard frame houses and tiny brick ranches. We turned around at the Hop-In on the west end of town, near the park with its silent gray bandstand. We drove east until we passed the elementary school and empty high school, then turned into the parking lot of the old farm-supply store, the beams of its collapsed roof poking skyward and its windows like eyes. Bounty had never been a pretty town, but we'd tried to be proud of it. Now we examined it carefully, looking for new reasons to stay awake. One by one we gave up, peeled off, and drove home. We turned into our shoveled driveways in the tiny grid of residential streets or took spokes of blacktop and gravel out to scattered farmhouses in little islands of yard whose old acreage spread behind them like a taunt. Bounty was an assertion, an act of faith. It looked best when left unexamined.

A few of us met back at the Pointes that night for beer and darts. As the hours went by, no one said a thing about Al, but we were all waiting for it. "Fucking *grease,*" Nils finally said. "Like fucking *Russians.*" We were able to laugh then and walk out to the parking lot, slapping one another's backs and leaving trails of footprints in the snow. We felt better about ourselves, sitting side by side in our idling cars, waiting for the engines to warm.

On New Year's Day the Rasmussens made neighborhood rounds, dropping off house keys and perishables: a gallon of milk and some apples for the Lutven boys; carrots for Valeer Simmons; a bag of shredded cheese and half a loaf of bread for Mr. Kajaamaki, who had to be talked into accepting them. "This is a favor to us, not to you," Al assured him. We wished the family luck and hung the keys on pegs. We could have robbed them blind while they slept, but we knew they didn't have anything worth taking. We tiptoed inside in ones and twos to check on the family, to see how this hibernation thing was working out. The kids looked peaceful. The food disappeared in barely perceptible increments. The room was stuffy by late February, smelling of night sweat and canned soup, but the Rasmussens didn't seem to mind. Mrs. Pekola lit a lavender-scented candle on the sideboard and found it blown out the next day. All in all, they looked cozy.

In March the children woke first and bounded out the front door in their pajamas. Spring hadn't really started yet; dirty snow was still melting into mud. But the fiercest part of winter was over. Al looked rested for the first time since Jeannie's death. The terrible weight that had stooped his shoulders was gone and he stood straighter, his body again resembling that of the man we had known for years. But his eyes looked like a stranger's. No one could place the expression except those of us whose children or grandchildren had left Bounty, gone off for college or work. When the children came back, their eyes looked like Al's. Like departure. *Imagine,* we thought, *Albert found that look in his sleep.*

He asked for all the updates. A blizzard in early February had blown the roof off the old hardware store. Mr. Fiske had had a heart attack one morning in the barn with his livestock. One of the grain-elevator operators had died of cirrhosis, and half the town had applied for his job. The youngest Suarez boy had tried to hitch home from work at the rendering plant in Piric one evening, but nobody stopped; he'd decided to walk and disappeared into the snow. We drove poles down, walking across the fields in formation, bracing ourselves to strike flesh. We never found him; now that spring was coming, though, we probably would.

"Anything good happen?" Al asked.

We struggled. We hadn't thought about how dark the

winter was when we were in its midst. "One of the Thao girls had a baby," we said.

Al smiled, although only half the town thought the Thaos belonged to us; the other half wanted nothing to do with them. "That's something."

"What did *you* do?" we asked, and before he could say *I slept*, we specified: "What was it like? How did it feel?"

"I had these long dreams," he said. "Unfolding over days. I dreamed I was in Eden, but it was mine. My farm. I picked pineapples every day."

Al Rasmussen wintered in Eden, we thought. We started to feel a little like suckers for not having joined him.

Bobby and Dee had boundless energy and spent a lot of it recounting dreams to their schoolmates. Soon many of the children were planning for their own long sleep, and the ones who weren't were calculating how scary empty classrooms might get, how the forest of raised hands would thin and they'd get called on over and over, expected to know the right answers. They pictured how lonely the playground would be, all lopsided seesaws and unpushed swings, and soon all the children of Bounty were begging to spend the next winter asleep.

Come the next year, quite a few of them got their way. The Lutven boys later said they were happy not to have to catch the bus in the dark, standing around in twenty-below. The pudgy Sanderson girl, all bushy hair and braces, woke up with her teeth straighter and her belly flat. She showed off her new smile for Lucy Simmons, and Lucy confessed that her period had started sometime in early February. How easy, they thought; so much of the hard work of growing up had happened while they were asleep, when no one could make fun of them for it.

Mrs. Sanderson fit into clothes she hadn't worn since high school. The styles had changed, but she paraded around in her high-waisted, acid-washed jeans just so we could admire what sleep had done for her. Mr. Sanderson had started off awake, reporting to the John Deere dealership north of town at nine every morning the way he'd done for years. But suddenly he saw the unfairness, his creaking out of bed while his wife rolled over with a slack, content smile.

"Our food costs were way down," he said at the Pointes one night the next spring. "The heat bills. Gas. For once, my daughter wasn't pestering us for a new pair of jeans. I asked for a temporary leave. They said sales were down so far, I'd be doing them a favor."

A lot of us lived in houses our parents or grandparents had owned; mortgages weren't usually our problem. Just the daily costs of living, and the closer those got to zero, the less we needed to work. John Deere lost three more salespeople before the winter was over. Other folks didn't have any employers to apologize to. The families that still kept animals thought we were all a bunch of pansies, at least according to Nils, but then we imagined him slogging to the barn every morning at five for the feeding and the milking, his fingers stiff and snot frozen in his mustache, and we mostly just felt smart.

Mrs. Drausmann, the town librarian, hated the sleep even more than Nils. She cornered Bobby and Dee after story time, near the shelves that once held skin creams and now held paperbacks, and threatened: "This will be like Narnia under the White Witch. Always winter and never Christmas."

"After Christmas," Dee asked her, "what's there to like? What do *you* do?"

"I keep the library open," she said. "So everyone has books. They come and use the computers and get their music and their movies."

"If you're dreaming, you have your own movies," Dee said gravely, and Mrs. Drausmann sighed. We tried to make it up to her, registered for her summer reading program and attended fall story time. But Dee was right. Sleeping folk needed almost nothing—a little food, a little water, air, and warmth. They definitely didn't need DVDs.

That second winter the road crews had noticed less traffic, and some of the plow drivers' hours were cut. Several decided to say screw it and just sleep, and by the time the county and the drivers were done sniping at one another, the budget for next year's salting and plowing was half what it had been. The harder leaving your driveway was, the easier it was to stay home.

The third year a family died of carbon monoxide poisoning from an unventilated gas heater. An electric space heater started a fire at the Simmonses'. They got out, but the house burned. Al staggered into the snow bleary-eyed, called his neighbors dumbasses, and then invited them to pile on into his family room. When he woke up for real in March, he announced that if we were all going to do this thing, we should do it right. He didn't have enough old grease for everyone, so he charged hourly for consultations about different compact heating systems, then for assembly and installation, and soon he was doing well enough to quit his fence-repair job.

We were glad Al had the new business, because that October Reggie Lapham came home from the juvenile detention center. He'd been seventeen when he'd hit Jeannie three and a half years earlier, and as young as that was, as much as we remembered the ice on the road and the evenings we'd gotten behind the wheel when we shouldn't have, we weren't sure how to forgive him. Our hearts went out to Reggie and then to Jeannie and then to Al and Bobby and Dee and then back to Reggie until we couldn't keep our hearts straight and peaceful in our chests. These people were ours—all of them, not just Al—and we were too much like each of them. We needed men like Al to lead us and we needed young people like Reggie to stay. We looked to Al for permission to take Reggie back.

But Reggie seemed to know Al wasn't going to give it, at least not that autumn, because he walked from his parents' van into his house and wouldn't come out again. We spoke to Mrs. Lapham at the Hop-In. "He's looking forward to the sleep," she said. "That's really all he wants to do. I don't think he would have come back if he had to—"

She broke off and we wondered, *Had to what? Leave the house? Talk to people? Get a job?* The family went to bed a few days after Thanksgiving. Mrs. Lapham said that seemed like the easiest way to get through what had to be gotten through. Then we heard that Al had put his kids to bed early too, without Christmas, and then some of us started calculating the money we could save not buying presents. Those of us without small children or without extended families had to admit that the holidays were a downer as often as not. We knew that the Laphams and the Rasmussens weren't sleeping for the healthiest of reasons, but we understood the urge.

When everyone woke up the next spring, Mrs. Draus-mann called into *The Dr. Joe Show* to ask whether sleeping through four months of strife was sanity or just denial. She talked her way past the show's producers, but when she got on the air and explained the situation to Dr. Joe, he didn't believe her. "Sure, excessive sleeping is a sign of depression," he said. "But no one hibernates." Then he hung up.

Several of us heard the call and it prompted some soul-searching, both about why so many of us were listening to a radio psychologist to begin with and about what our town might look like to outsiders. We started to wonder if Reggie Lapham should maybe be talking to somebody. If Al and Reggie needed help, we weren't giving it to them, because sleeping was easier for us too.

A woman from the *Piric Gazette* heard *The Dr. Joe Show* that night and came to Bounty to ask some questions. We braced ourselves for the story, but the reporter apparently couldn't figure out whom to believe or what the heck was going on, and before she hit on the answer, the Gannett Company shut down the paper. We saw Al's old buddy Nils having a beer with him at the Pointes later that month, the first time they'd been social together in years.

"She came to interview me," Nils said. "I told her the hibernation business was bullshit."

"I know you think the sleeping's bullshit," Al said. "You don't need to tell me."

"I told her Drausmann was bullshit. I told her nothing was going on in this town that was any of Dr. Joe's business or the *Piric Gazette*'s. I told her to leave you alone." Nils shook his head and clinked the neck of his bottle against Al's. "I figure you've always known what you needed. Crazy fucker."

A few weeks later, as we prepared for the fourth winter of the sleep to bear down, we watched the grease heater leave the Rasmussen house in parts, the foam-taped exhaust pipe, the burger filter. The mattresses with Bobby's and Dee's sheets came out; they'd graduated from NASCAR and Disney to plain solids, navy and lavender. We worried Al was abandoning the cause until we found out he'd reassembled it all at Nils's farm. With more people to take care of the animals, Al explained, Nils could get some sleep too.

Others economized like this as well, throwing in their lots with friends, neighbors. The Simmonses rebuilt their burned house with a single large room on the ground floor, an energy-efficient heat stove in the center with non-flammable tile around the base. They went to ask Al's permission and then invited the Laphams to spend the next winter. They knew what a chill felt like, they said, as well as what it was like to be given shelter when nothing but cold was around you.

Mrs. Drausmann stayed awake. She had her books, her

own kind of dreaming. She and Mrs. Pekola would walk up and down the streets, Mrs. Drausmann's snow boots and Mrs. Pekola's orthopedic shoes leaving the only prints for miles. Mrs. Pekola's faith wouldn't let her sleep. She walked to the Lutheran church every Christmas Eve to light the Christ candle. "I'm sorry," she whispered to God. "They don't mean anything by it. They don't mean to disrespect You." She tried to tell us in spring how lonely our church looked, a single candle alight in the empty sanctuary.

In the first years, the reverend turned the electricity back on whenever the temperature reached forty-five, but then someone hit on the idea of Easter. We flipped the switch on the day of Christ arisen. "Alleluia, alleluia," we sang, uttering the word we had denied ourselves for Lent, one of the first words to pass our lips since waking. The Rasmussens and the Laphams stood in their old pews, just across the aisle from each other. They didn't embrace at the greeting-neighbors part of the service, didn't say "Peace be with you" or "And also with you," but they didn't flee. Al stood between his children with an arm draped over each of them, and we realized with surprise that Bobby was fourteen now and nearly as tall as his father. He would have been good at basketball too, if he'd been awake for the season. Dee's pale hair had darkened to a dirty blond, and her face was spotted with acne. The kids leaned into their father, facing forward, until Dee looked to her right and nodded at Mrs. Lapham. Just then, Reggie turned his head and peered anxiously over his mother, and Dee froze and then slowly nodded at him too. We all nodded our pale faces at each other, and that seemed like enough.

In the end the Hop-In is what brought the outsiders. Corporate couldn't understand why winter-quarter sales were down 95 percent from five years earlier. A regional manager came out, and then his supervisors, and finally news crews from Fargo. The satellite vans were hard to miss, and we stayed up that night for the eleven o'clock news. We hadn't expected the story they chose to tell, which wasn't a human-interest piece about ingenuity or survival. Our hibernation practice was horrible, anchors announced from up and down the state, then across the country. Horrifying. Another product of the recession. A new economic indicator: in addition to tumbling home prices and soaring unemployment, a town was going to sleep. A reporter in high heels and a pantsuit asked the Sandersons if they were making a statement.

"We get tired," they said. "Is that a statement?"

We were annoyed at how the reporters had filmed only the shabbiest parts of our town until we flipped through the newscasts and realized that together, they'd filmed nearly all of our town and it all looked equally shabby. We were used to our potholes and tumbledown barns, and now alongside those were cracked sidewalks and collapsing houses. The gray bandstand in the park leaned heavily to one side; the flat roof of the old high school had caved in under last year's snow. Raccoons and groundhogs hibernated in some of the downtown buildings and chased each other up Main Street in their spring excitement. A few had gotten into Mrs. Pekola's antiques store, either for burrow bedding or just to be troublesome, and we were plagued by a video clip of skinny raccoons bursting out the store's front door trailing gnawed-up christening dresses and crib quilts. A badger birthed a spring litter in the church basement on a pile of old Sunday-school workbooks. We told ourselves that none of this mattered. We weren't using the buildings anyway—the barns, the high school, most of downtown. We reminded ourselves that Bounty had never been a pretty place. It was built for function, not ornament, and as long as it functioned the way we wanted, we shouldn't be ashamed of it. We had never had any great architecture in Bounty, and the certainty that we would never have any didn't seem a sacrifice.

We might have become a tourist attraction except that getting to us when we were sleeping was so hard. The snow accumulated in giant drifts. We put a big stick out by the WELCOME TO BOUNTY sign and let it measure how deeply we were buried. People could come in on the highway as far as the county plowed it and then see a wall of snow taller than their cars greeting them at the entrance.

That was the establishing shot—a tiny car next to a wall of snow—when the documentary was released. On the tenth anniversary of the sleep, a public television channel contacted us and said they planned to take a more balanced approach than the news crews had. We liked that they promised to hold the premiere in Bounty, projected after dark onto the wall of the farm-supply store, since the old movie theater had been condemned.

They interviewed Bobby in his dorm room in the last weeks of the fall semester. The state university had offered him a small baseball scholarship. He was a one-sport kid. "I'm not sure where I'll go for Christmas break," he said. "I haven't had Christmas in years. My dad and my sister won't even be awake." He was broad like his father, a young man there in his cramped college room, and we wondered if Jeannie would even have recognized him.

The Lutven boys had already finished college; they'd worked for a year in St. Paul and then come home. They liked the pace of life here, they said. They liked the way winter gave you a chance to catch your breath. One of them married the Sanderson girl, who'd taken over the antiques store and chased the raccoons out. Even after having two Lutven babies, ten-pound Scandinavian boys, she could wear the shop's old clothes, the slim, fitted dresses. She liked the quiet way her boys were growing up, she said, polite and calm and curled up for five months like warm puppies at her side.

Mrs. Pekola had passed away, which we knew, but we hadn't known her family blamed us until we saw the film. Her eldest daughter was living in Florida, and the film-makers had gone down to interview her about how her mother had died alone in a church pew, frozen to death in a wool coat and orthopedic shoes. "No one found her till spring," the woman said, her anger fresh and righteous.

Mrs. Fiske had taught all the Pekola girls over the years. "Fractions," she whispered in the audience. "That girl just hated fractions."

Dee had never left Bounty, never expressed any interest

in going anywhere else. She was *ours,* like her father before her, despite her faraway look most days, her eyes the color of the ice that froze over the flooded quarry. Her dirty-blond hair had darkened to brown and her teenage acne had faded into a nearly translucent paleness. She volunteered at the library with Mrs. Drausmann and took over story time. The film showed her sitting in a rocking chair with books far too advanced for the children gathered cross-legged around her. "'He heard the snow falling faintly through the universe and faintly falling, like the descent of their last end, upon all the living and the dead,'" she read as the children squirmed. She wasn't very good at story time, but Mrs. Drausmann had grown hoarse and weary over the years.

One by one we tried to explain for the cameras. Why stay? What is Bounty worth? Three months? Four? Half your life spent asleep? Our people had moved to Bounty because the land was there and it was empty, and now all we had was the emptiness and one another. We had a wide sky and tall grass and a sun that felt good when you'd waited for it half the year. We had our children, the ones we'd feared for, feared their boredom and their recklessness and their hunger for somewhere else. We'd feared becoming Jeannie Rasmussen, and we'd feared becoming Reggie Lapham. We'd feared wanting too much and ending up with less than what we already had. Now Al and Nils dreamed the sound of a basketball bouncing off the warped, snow-soaked floor of the high-school gymnasium. Al dreamed of nights asleep in Jeannie's arms. Reggie Lapham probably dreamed his life differently too, but he seemed content with what he had; he was interviewed with his son on his lap, a boy who had never made a snowman, never opened a Christmas present. He spoke about that first year back, about how the sleep had saved him, and when his voice faltered, his wife, Nkauj Thao-Lapham, reached over to squeeze his hand.

Dr. Joe, interviewed, said that the sleep was profoundly unhealthy, that legislation should be passed before the custom could spread. The documentary included interviews with American history professors at the state university, experts on westward expansion, on what had happened to our county over the past two centuries. Someone in a bow tie said he was dismayed that we had lost our immigrant spirit, our desire to press on and out to something better. Our congressman pointed out that the immigrant spirit might have pushed us all the way on out of the state, farther west or back east, but instead, we'd found a way to stay. The census didn't ask if you were awake or asleep. It just asked where you lived, and now more than ever, we were proud to say we lived in Bounty.

"*Sisu,*" old Mr. Kajaamaki grunted for the camera with his hand held in front of his mouth; his teeth had fallen out, but he'd never bothered with dentures, and we felt a bit guilty that no one had insisted on driving him to Piric to get some fitted. Our people were shabby, like our houses, our streets, our ancient coats and boots. But our ancestors had come, and they had stopped, and we persisted. "'Persistence,'" Mr. Kajaamaki said, translating his old-world word for it. He looked annoyed at how lacking English was, how insufficient for the endurance of a people who had once starved and eaten bark and come across an ocean to a flat sea of snow to make new ways of life when the old ones seemed insufficient.

The film cut back to Dee and Al standing together on the shuttered main street of our town, the sky blue and endlessly wide. "But do you regret their decision? Your father's?" the interviewer, off camera, prodded. Dee squinted in the light, and Al squinted at his daughter.

He'd been quiet in front of the cameras, tentative to the point of taciturn, and as he watched the movie from a lawn chair in the farm-supply store's parking lot along with the rest of us, he fidgeted, turning his head to check the expressions on his children's faces, twisting around in his seat to look at the people he'd led into sleep.

"I barely remember what our life was like before," the on-screen Dee said. "I remember being cold."

"And now?"

Dee looked baffled, not able to find words sufficient to explain half her life, the happier, more perfect half. The camera turned to Al, but his face was unreadable. "Now?" Dee said. "Now I guess we're not."

Now we are the people of Bounty, the farmers of dust and cold, the harvesters of dreams. After the lumber, after the mines, after the railroad, after the interstate, after the crops, after the cows, after the jobs. We're better neighbors asleep in warm beds than we ever were awake. The suckers of the last century, but not of this one.

NORWEGIAN FOR TROLL

The car arrived late, crunching into the gravel drive and jolting Annika awake on the couch. The small wooden house sat hunkered in a clearing, and outside she found the cousins posed like miniatures in an out-of-scale diorama, heads tilted back to admire the bright channel of stars above the encroaching trees. The air was cool but gentle, summer newly enough arrived to still feel like a gift.

"You are Annika?" the younger man asked, turning as the screen door flapped shut behind her. "This is the place?"

"This is it," she said, stepping down off the front porch.

"Per," he said, holding out his hand. Annika shook it, hard enough that he blinked in surprise or discomfort. "Difficult to find, this house."

He looked down the dark road at the way he'd come and then up at her house. Without any neighbors to draw shades for, the windows glowed baldly, both welcoming and barren. Per's gaze moved from the windows to the peeling siding to the flower beds, empty except for weeds, and the handful of cracked, spindly shrubs. Annika thought about explaining how last winter's heavy snow had bent and broken the branches, about how deer had eaten her flowers and her mother's flowers and her grandmother's flowers until Annika had given up. But all she said was "It's easier to find the place in daylight."

She'd meant this as fact, not accusation, but it launched Per into a litany of the day's delays. Their flight had arrived late, and the rental-car clerk had been rude. They'd lingered too long in Detroit, ogling the ruins, the skyscrapers with sky visible straight through them. They'd stopped to eat at a place recommended on the internet for Coney dogs, the meat sauce dripping on their hands, then eaten more of them at the Coney shop next door, each restaurant founded by a Greek immigrant, brothers who were locked in a family hot-dog rivalry. There had been long toll lines at the Mackinac Bridge crossing into the Upper Peninsula. Past Marquette, the GPS had blinked out, and they'd gotten lost wending their way up the Keweenaw Peninsula.

"No landmarks," Per said. "Just trees, trees, trees."

"Welcome to the U.P.," Annika said.

The glow from the light of the open trunk lit the face of Per's father, Olav, who merely nodded at her. The two men removed their suitcases and rattled them across the gravel.

"He doesn't speak English," Per explained.

Inside, the house had distinct geological layers. The original rooms Annika's grandparents had built featured wide

26

yellow-varnished floorboards and a fireplace rimmed with green tiles; the back of the ground floor had been added later, successive strata of linoleum piled directly over the subfloor so that there was a small step up into the kitchen. There was a working stove from the 1940s, aluminum cabinets from the '50s, a red rag rug that Annika's mother had made. There were yellow curtains that Annika had been pulling down and laundering twice a year since she was a child. They framed and brightened the windows about as well as they ever had, so she hadn't felt the need to replace them. She didn't neglect the house, though. She'd bought a new refrigerator just last year, when the old green one died. The salesman had tried to talk her into French doors and stainless steel and she'd laughed in his face.

Olav tipped one of the suitcases flat onto the floor of the dining room and unzipped it.

"There are bedrooms for you both," Annika said. "Should I show you where you'll sleep?"

Olav ignored her, pulled out a crushed gift bag printed with Norwegian flags, tissue paper sprouting from the top.

"A hostess present," Per said.

Annika lifted the tissue paper, and a half a dozen little brown figures spilled onto the table, cheap ceramic trolls with matted artificial hair and maniacal grins.

"Norwegians believe in trolls," Per said. "I mean, not anymore. An old folk thing. Your grandmother, maybe she believed."

Annika nodded. "She told me to leave pine cones for the *nisse* on the back porch so it'd take care of the house."

Per looked at her quizzically, and she wondered what had

27

been lost in translation. He had contacted her out of the blue several months earlier, her grandmother's brother's son's first cousin. Something like that. Annika couldn't get it straight. Per had a passion for genealogy, and she trusted his research. He was planning a trip with his father, he'd explained in e-mails from Oslo. To Minneapolis, Chicago, northern Michigan—all the places that the Kristiansen descendants had ended up. Annika offered to host them for however long they wanted to stay. She wouldn't pretend Laurium was as exciting as Chicago, she'd written, but there was plenty of room and it would be nice to have the company.

In the dining-room light, Annika took a better look at her guests, searching for some family resemblance. All three of them were tall, and Per had her thick, unruly blond hair, but that was about it. Olav was solemn-looking and slightly stooped, a broad man eroding with age. Per was pale and beaky, younger than she'd expected, and wearing jeans so slim-fitting that Annika doubted she could stuff more than her ankle down one of the leg holes. He made her feel like a giant, powerful but lumbering in her flannel shirt and sweatpants. She'd never been a beauty, and now on the far side of forty she prided herself more and more on her strength, unambiguous and useful. She could ski for miles, hoist a deer into a tree to be bled. At the hospital where she worked, she could lift the patients from a stretcher to a bed, pull them up to get a look at their backs or buttocks. Her breasts she kept tucked away in sports bras. "Those may give lift, but they can't give separation," her mother used to warn her, as if separation were something to which Annika aspired. She didn't particularly like her body but she was proud of it. She saw no contradiction in this.

As she held up the trolls, Per pointed out details: The painted leg on the *tobi-tre-fot,* who supposedly sneaked up behind people and kicked them with its wooden limb. The *tusselader* carried little chisels and hammers, which Per said they used to chip away at sleeping people's teeth. The unarmed *tusse* might whisper in your ear to seed family arguments. The dolls were hideous, but Annika lined them up carefully, like a centerpiece.

"Thank you," she said. "You must be tired."

Per nodded, stretched theatrically, and translated her words for Olav, who nodded too.

"I'll show you where you'll sleep," Annika said and swept Olav's suitcase up off the floor before he could protest. Climbing the narrow staircase, she held the unzipped front panel closed. In her childhood bedroom was a twin bed made up with her old sheets, freshly laundered but ancient, patterned with stars and planets (including discredited Pluto), Saturn's rings gone fuzzy with wear. Olav said something that Per smirked at but didn't translate.

"Nothing fancy," Annika said apologetically.

"No, no, this is very much space. In Oslo, this would be a castle."

Annika led Per down the hall to the third bedroom. When she was young, the room had been kept nearly empty, a vigil for the other children who never came. Later it filled with flotsam; it became a craft room, an exercise room, a TV room, a sickroom, a junk room. Annika had tidied away the junk, unfolded the foldout couch. Those sheets at least were a plain navy. She told Per where the bathroom was, the clean towels, crept back downstairs to turn off the lights. Upstairs, she shut her bedroom door behind her and listened to the strange sound of someone else in the bathroom, flushing the toilet, running the sink. The shower came on and she thought she should have remembered to warn them how long it sometimes took for the water to turn hot. The first night Evan slept over, she'd woken to him shrieking like a girl, nearly tugging the curtain down from around the claw-foot tub after he'd hopped in without checking the temperature. She'd laughed almost immediately, as soon as she knew he was okay, and he'd joined right in. She'd felt like it had to mean something, how quickly they could laugh with each other. But things hadn't turned out that way.

There was a box of Evan's stuff still in one corner of the master bedroom, things she'd found around the house and kept meaning to mail to him. In her head she'd written and rewritten the note she'd send with them, something light-hearted, like *Didn't mean to steal these!* She mentally added two extra exclamation marks, mentally erased them. There was nothing very important in the box—a pair of thick, expensive wool socks, two bandannas, a metal water bottle. They'd gone hiking together one of his last afternoons in Laurium. At the bottom of the box was a set of photos she'd printed from his going-away party at a bar in Hancock, the guests mostly forestry colleagues from Michigan Tech and a few people from the hospital. He'd taken several photos of the two of them together, his arm held out, their heads squeezed close. He'd asked her to print and send these photos, which at the time she had chosen to interpret as a gesture of seriousness, a desire for their time together to have resulted in tangible objects and for her to know that he felt that way. But the longer she failed to make it to the post office, the more the pictures felt like an inconvenience and then like artifacts from a concluded epoch. What would he want with them now, when all that was over? And what was she still doing with his photo in her work locker?

She listened until Per's and Olav's doors were closed, the pipes gone quiet, and crept out wrapped tightly in a bathrobe. She wasn't used to guests, especially ones that weren't sharing her bed, and she hadn't realized how squirrelly they'd make her feel, tiptoeing down her own hallway, wincing when she dropped her own toothpaste, worrying about what they thought of her house, her refrigerator, her silly space sheets. There was a row of family photographs in the upstairs hallway, and as Annika tiptoed back to her room in the almost dark—a night-light left on in the bathroom—their faces looked shadowed and sinister. The house didn't feel livelier with the cousins; it felt threatening, full of ways to embarrass her, to make her life look like something other than the one she thought she was living.

Annika had owned the house and twenty acres of forest since she was twenty-four years old, managing the property taxes on top of her student-loan payments. Her father had left when she was a toddler. When her mother got sick, Annika finished nursing school and left her cramped apartment in Green Bay to come home. Her first night back, she'd stood in the driveway looking up at the same stars Per had admired, trying to figure out how she felt about them. She'd missed their milky brightness, and she'd missed the dark forest that made them possible, but when she thought about all that emptiness, she felt it wrap like a hand over her mouth.

Her mother had stood on the porch. "It's good to have you back," she'd said, tossing the words out into the night like pennies into a fountain, unsure whether the wish would be granted.

"It's good to be back," Annika had told her, choosing in that moment to mean it.

For over fifteen years now, it had stayed mostly true. She'd accommodated herself to the quiet, learned not to startle at her own reflection in the curtainless windows. In high school, she'd invited boys over for bonfires and ATV rides. Now she liked to walk or ski the property on weekends. She carried binoculars and heels of bread for the birds. She still, every so often, placed a pine cone on the back porch and felt the *nisse* watching over her.

Annika had taken the night off work to greet the cousins, but her body still expected some emergency or just the grinding boredom of a slow night at the hospital, and it took her a long time to fall asleep. She woke late the next morning and worried she'd been a poor host, but the cousins were still in bed. Some days she jerked awake worrying that she hadn't brought her mother her pills or remembered the glass of water her grandmother had wanted. *"Vann,"* the old woman would demand, *"vann,"* one of the handful of Norwegian words Annika knew. In waking, she had to float back to herself, remember the year, the generation.

When Per finally stumbled downstairs, Annika was drinking coffee burned from sitting on the heating plate too long. "Jet lag," he said, gesturing apologetically to the clock. He had a wad of toilet paper clutched in his fist, his nose red and raw.

"Are you sick?" Annika asked.

"I think I am allergic to something," he said. "You are all out of tissues."

Per woke Olav, and Annika drove them to Houghton for lunch. Per insisted on paying but didn't tip. Maybe Norwegians never tipped? Annika wondered. She sneaked a few dollars onto the table while Per was in the bathroom blowing his nose. They stopped at a drugstore for three boxes of Kleenex and two bottles of Benadryl and then headed for the Quincy Mine and the world's largest steam hoist.

"Do you want the full tour or the surface-only?" Annika asked them at the ticket counter.

Per shrugged but then insisted on paying for the full, brushing the top of his wallet like a fly had landed there. "Please," he said. "You are hosting. Besides, everything here is so cheap. It's like nothing. With the exchange rate, the money here is like nothing."

The woman at the ticket counter raised an eyebrow, and Annika shrugged apologetically. They watched the video tour of the No. 2 Shaft-Rockhouse, and then a guide took them to the Nordberg steam hoist, which had been powerful enough to pull ten-ton ore skips up a vertical mile. The bottom of the shaft had long since flooded, the guide explained, the groundwater rising and rising. As the tour group entered the mine itself, Per struggled to keep up with the increasingly esoteric commentary. "This was the first copper mine in Michigan to transition from fissure to amygdaloid mining," the guide announced. Olav waited for the translation and Per puffed out his cheeks in frustration.

"*I* don't even know what that means," Annika whispered. "Not all the guides are this technical."

"You have come here before?" Per asked.

"Sure. Everyone does. For school field trips or with visiting relatives. This is where we go."

"Underground," Per said. Olav had given up entirely and was staring at the rock walls in silence. Per turned back toward the guide, his head tilted like a dog's, as if his left ear were the one that might know *amygdaloid*. He perked up when the guide began to describe Quincy mine tragedies, most recently a local geology professor who had fallen two hundred and twenty-five feet while installing emergency ladders. "I understood that!" he said excitedly to Annika. "He died!"

An older woman on the tour turned to glare at them. Per began translating for Olav, presumably about the dead professor. Olav remained expressionless, which seemed callous to Annika, although of course what reaction was he supposed to have to some dead stranger?

Annika wondered idly if Evan had known the professor. Evan wasn't in the geology department, but Michigan Tech was a small university, the whole region a fistful of small towns between forest and lake. Evan had been at Tech only for the fall semester, working on an ash-tree mortality project during his sabbatical from his permanent job at the University of Michigan in Ann Arbor. He'd been married once, he told her. There were kids, now nine and twelve. His wife had primary custody, but he had the kids every other weekend and some weeknights. "Except this semester, of course, since I'm here." Evan liked camping and hiking; when the weather turned cold he couldn't keep up with her on the ski trails but he didn't fall embarrassingly far behind. He was a big man, and Annika liked the way they felt together, the way he never seemed fragile or outmatched. He said nice things about the family land, the overgrown trails threading through the woods, and he hadn't made fun of the space-patterned pillowcases that had ended up on her bed during laundry day. But the house was a complication, he allowed, because he needed to return to the U of M at the end of the semester. When he asked her to come with him, she'd started tabulating her own life in her head: Job, house, land. Lake Superior and the constant forest, oceans of blue and green. In winter, white and white and white, trees bristling from the earth like a porcupine's quills.

"Ann Arbor's still Michigan," he offered.

Ann Arbor, she thought, was an expensive, stuck-up college town a full nine hours south. It might as well have been another country.

At the house, Annika cooked dinner, family recipes that Per and Olav were polite about, although she couldn't really tell how authentic or tasty they found the meal. Per chatted about how happy he was to take this vacation from his work writing software for photocopiers. It was a good job, he said, and it paid for a two-bedroom apartment in a nice Oslo suburb, but still—a bit dull. They needed the second bedroom because his wife was expecting, he confided. No one knew yet, not even Olav, because Per's wife wouldn't let him tell people. "But I can tell you," he said. "You will tell no one." Annika made a toast to this next generation of Kristiansens, then glanced guiltily at Olav as the older man dropped his fork and lifted his beer to join in whatever they were celebrating.

After the dishes were cleared, she retrieved a single box from the basement, hoping to create a show-and-tell activity Olav could participate in. She unpacked it slowly: a pocket watch, a prayer book in Norwegian, a hand-tatted wedding veil. "Did she make this? My grandmother?" Annika asked. "Before she came here?"

Olav laughed when Per translated. "He says he is not *that* old," Per said. "It was from your grandmother's grandmother. No one makes lace for very many years."

Annika's grandmother had described Norway as a land so vertiginous and un-arable that children played with ropes tied around their waists, the other ends wrapped around the boulders that made the plowing crooked. If they slipped over the cliff edges, they could be hauled back up, their waists rope-burned and their sides scraped, but alive enough to die slowly of hunger. Still, the siblings had thought she was a madwoman for leaving, for surrendering what she had on mere rumors of better. A ship passage like a dice roll, a lady gambler. Already, in that way, an American.

"Perhaps her family thought a *tusse* put the idea in her head," Annika said, picking up the little gift troll. "Goaded her into leaving."

"Perhaps," Per said. "In old times, *tusse* took the blame for many bad decisions."

Annika wasn't sure she'd understood him but didn't ask him to repeat himself. Olav took a photo from one of the albums, removing it from the black cardboard corners: Annika's grandmother as a young woman, with round cheeks, careful hair, a dotted dress.

"'Milwaukee,'" the old man read when he flipped the picture over in his hand.

Her grandmother had taken the train there after landing in New York, Annika told him, chasing some cousin's cousin's offer of work. She had met Annika's grandfather there and fallen in love with the young man; he'd brought her north, where the mines were already starting to close.

"Milwaukee?" the old man repeated.

"A city," Annika explained. "In Wisconsin."

"A city. Mistake number two," Per said.

Annika didn't know what mistake number one was. She tried to style the *tusse*'s hair, but her fingers were too big, the head too delicate. "Tell me more about trolls," she said.

"Norwegian trolls are big," Per said. "Bigger than other trolls, because they can hide in our mountains." His voice swelled with patriotic enthusiasm for his oversize trolls. He talked about how, tradition had it, light turned them to stone, so many geographical features in Norway were really troll corpses. Trolls were afraid of both church bells and lightning and thus predated two religions. Trolls were older than Jesus, Per bragged, but also older than Thor. Then Per sneezed.

"I should get to work," Annika said. "I'm really sorry about the allergies. I wish I knew what it was."

"Don't worry about it," Per said. "Don't be late."

Annika changed into her scrubs but hesitated in the kitchen; she didn't like to leave the dishes unwashed, as if she expected her guests to do them.

"Go, go. We won't steal anything," Per joked.

"There's nothing here you'd want," Annika said, not liking the appraising way Per looked around and agreed.

She'd worked in the emergency room for a full decade after nursing school and never thought she'd be back. Diabetes counseling had regular hours, no on-call. The job was easy but demoralizing; she passed out pamphlets all day and later found them wadded up in the trash can down the hall—outside her office but before the main doors. The patients didn't want to offend her, but they weren't going to change. Laurium was a small place, and it was hard for Annika to watch people let themselves go. There'd been more hard-eyed men in her office than she could count who said, "If this is what kills me, that's okay." She monitored their gait so she could schedule them for foot care, trim the hard nails, sand the calluses, check for sores. After a few years, they'd lose toes anyway, and she'd see them limping into the diner, still ordering pie after their cheeseburgers. State funding for the counseling program had been cut four months ago, a few weeks after Evan moved downstate. She went back to the emergency department, asked her old supervisor about openings. "We only need nights," he said apologetically.

The first several hours of tonight's shift were steady—stitches required for a mishap with a bread knife, a feverish baby, a vomiting teen stinking of booze—but then it quieted, and Annika retreated to the break room. Most of the other staff who worked nights were younger, people without enough seniority to pull better shifts. They shared a camaraderie, but Annika hadn't made any particular friends. She'd been close with plenty of girls back in school, but they were scattered now to Wisconsin or downstate, or they just had families that kept them busy, jobs that kept them hustling. Annika peeled the foil top off her yogurt container, silently let the break-room conversations wash over and around her. She wondered if this was what it felt like to be Olav and then remembered that in his own country he might be a chatterbox, a sparkplug. He might be someone entirely different.

A receptionist poked her head into the break room. "You have a visitor," she said, and Per bounded in.

"Surprise," he said.

Annika kept stirring her yogurt, although it wasn't the kind that needed to be stirred. It was the same consistency all the way through.

"I thought I would come see where you work. Is it okay?"

"Sure, I guess," Annika said.

"Also my allergies are better here." In his arms was a tray of supermarket cookies with a bag of what turned out to be Norwegian candies perched on top. He opened them both on the break-room counter. "Eat, eat," he urged everyone.

He wasn't unkind, Annika thought, just oblivious. She took a cookie. They did the round of introductions, a tour of the building. "I can examine your photocopier," Per said, and he looked at it gravely. "QuikImage L2940. Very old, very old. No one writes software for these anymore."

They finished the tour back in the break room. Annika wanted to check her phone before resuming her shift, but when she opened her locker in front of Per, she winced—she'd forgotten the picture of Evan she'd taped inside, like he was her middle-school boyfriend.

"Oh-ho," Per said. "Who is that?"

"Nobody in particular," Annika said, although as she pulled her phone out, she noticed that she had a missed call from Evan.

"Whoever it is called you late," Per announced, looking nosily down at her screen.

Annika shrugged. "He calls when he gets bored grading exams."

"He told you that?"

Annika shook her head. "No, he's very tactful. He tells me he misses me. He doesn't live here anymore."

"Call him back," Per said.

"I'm working. I should be working."

"Right. I will leave you alone."

"I didn't mean it like that. Thank you for coming. It was a nice surprise."

"But I really should go. I don't want my father to wake up and worry."

She didn't tell him how she liked to save her phone calls for evenings home alone, how the silence that had never bothered her before was expanding, filling the house like a gas leak. Evan always greeted her by asking if this was an okay time to talk, if she was alone. "Just me. Only me," she'd tell him, imagining the trees watching her, her body trapped inside the lit windows like a puppet show. He ended most calls by asking her again to come to Ann Arbor, and she both hoped for and feared the day he'd stop asking.

The first night of the new year, Evan gone just days before, she'd stood in her clearing under the stars, knee-deep in snow. When her feet had gone numb in her boots, she staggered into the trees. She'd knelt and scooped steadily with her hands, digging through the snow until she felt damp pine needles. Her hand closed around a pine cone and pulled it free. She blew the snow from between the spines, melted it with her fingers. She put the naked pine cone on the porch. Not for luck, she told herself, but for wisdom. *Tell me what to do,* nisse, she thought. And then: Nisse, *how could I leave you?*

The next day Annika woke late to find Per and Olav playing cards on the back porch in a cloud of insect repellent, the bug zapper crackling. They'd carefully put the deck chairs in the middle of the porch, leaving unmolested the ring of pine cones around the edge. Per filled her in on their morning, how they'd driven the rental car along the Brockway Mountain scenic drive and taken a tour of the Copper Harbor Lighthouse. "How'd you like it?" Annika asked, dreading the answer.

"The mountain drive is not much of a mountain," he said. Then, relenting: "But if I want to see mountains I can stay in Norway. Lake Superior is very nice. Like the sea."

41

He slapped at his forearm; a blurt of blood appeared and his cards fanned briefly open. Annika saw Olav look.

"They must like Norwegian blood," Per said. "We sit outside because I think I am allergic to your house." He went inside for more repellent, and Annika sat silently with Olav. She picked up Per's cards and thought about playing his turn but couldn't tell what the game was.

They ate dinner outside, pizza with plenty of beer. Olav stared out into the forest as if the English conversation were only some unnecessary, inscrutable soundtrack to a narrative in the trees. Annika noticed for what felt like the first time in years her mother's old truck up on blocks in the yard, still there partly because she hadn't been able to bring herself to get rid of it and partly because of the expense of having it taken away on a flatbed. There was other junk in the yard, and rusty shovels and rakes propped against the tar-paper shed. It had all looked routine to her, but now she worried that the story Olav saw was about how her family had had three generations to make the property into something, and this was what they'd ended up with.

They sat out until they could hear the rising whine of mosquitoes, eddies of bats rustling above the trees. They took refuge inside, and Annika put on coffee. Per opened a new box of tissues and placed it at the ready beside his elbow. Last night's photo albums were still sitting on the dining-room table along with the trolls. Olav examined another picture, Annika's exhausted-looking grandmother holding a screaming newborn.

"She left before the oil," Per said.

"*Olje,*" Olav agreed.

"No one knew about the oil then." Per took the photo from his father, sighed, and placed the picture back in the album. Not in the cardboard corners, just facedown on the page as if she were dead. *She is, of course,* Annika thought. *She has been dead for many years.*

"When they found the North Sea oil. Everything changed."

"The oil," Annika echoed dumbly.

"Money for roads, for tunnels. Money made the mountains go away. You just sit in your car and drive, and when you come to a fjord you drive the car on a ferry and then drive away at the other side. You should come to Norway sometime."

Annika noticed that he did not say, *You should come stay with me.*

"Money for people. The government would have paid your grandmother just to keep living in her village. *Distriktspolitikk,* to maintain the rural population. To keep people in the places people want to leave. Like this."

"Like this?"

Olav looked at her, then said something to his son. "*Små kommuner,*" Per added hastily. "Small towns. Not for everybody. For some, okay, just not for everybody."

"Mistake number two?" Annika said.

"Mistake number one, to leave before the oil," Per said. "Mistake number two, to come here after the mines."

"They weren't quite over," Annika said, "not when she came. It wouldn't have seemed like a mistake." She heard the disloyalty couched in her defensiveness. Is that what it had been, a mistake?

43

"She should have stayed put."

"In Milwaukee, or Norway?"

Per blew his nose, added the tissue to the cluster of damp wads on the table.

Annika brought a trash can from the kitchen and set it pointedly beside him. "I'd never have been born, then. You realize that, right?"

Per shook his head. "I am speaking only of income. Standard of living. Nothing personal."

Annika took the photo from the album. She held it too tightly, the scalloped edges bending inward.

"I'm sure Americans don't talk about this kind of immigrant," Per said.

America, then Milwaukee, then Michigan. A bad roll. Snake eyes. Annika's grandmother had lived in this house until the end, when the only language left had been her mother tongue. She'd kept crying out, asking for things that Annika and her mother could neither understand nor provide. Her mother had cried out the same way; in English, but Annika's helplessness had been just as great.

"She was happy here," Annika said. "She said the house had a *nisse*. Its very own troll."

"Troll is not *nisse*."

"A little household troll. She's the one who taught me to leave it pine cones."

"Ah," Per said. "The pine cones on the porch?"

"She said it was traditional."

"*Nisse* is different from troll. And they do not like pine cones. It was tradition to give *nisser* porridge, with butter. A *nisse* is good luck, but also very...choosy? There is one

44

old story, a farmer who gave porridge with no butter, he woke up and his milk cow was murdered by the *nisse*." Per laughed a little. "Families who had nothing to spare, the *nisse* just left. Giving pine cones, I think you are lucky the *nisse* did not get so angry it burned your house."

Annika felt herself flush. "If *nisse* is *nisse*, what is 'troll' in Norwegian?"

"*Troll,*" Olav interjected emphatically, rolling the *r*, and Annika looked at Per.

"'Troll' is *troll*," he affirmed. "It came from us."

Annika had the night off, but she didn't tell the cousins. Instead, she got into her car and drove to Houghton, to the duplex Evan had rented on a quiet residential street. There were no pines, just a tidy maple in the front yard. She cut the lights and engine and rolled into the spot where she'd always parked, up on the grass along the road. She wondered what Milwaukee tenement or rented room her grandfather had been living in when her grandparents first met. She imagined peeling wallpaper, grimy light from a single window, a few shirts hanging from pegs. Still, her grandmother had been sure enough of him to try. She'd been sure enough to follow him here. *Or desperate enough,* a voice added in Annika's head.

The lights on Evan's side of the house were out, but she didn't know if it was the late hour or if the unit was vacant. There were empty homes throughout the region. A thousand miles of mined-out tunnels unwinding beneath her feet. The cousins had not needed to visit Detroit to see ruins. To witness a bet gone sour.

"Nursing," her grandmother had once told her. The woman's hands were knotted in her lap, her feet bruised-looking and bulging out of her shoes, a result of her diabetes. "It's a good profession. You can take it anywhere."

She'd thought her grandmother had meant as a backup plan, for emergencies. But maybe she'd been saying, *Get out.* However much you love this place, it isn't your problem. Unwind the rope from your waist, slide down the cliff face, trust that something better will catch you. Let the forest take the house, let the winter take Laurium. Let the trolls come.

Annika's own house was dark, not even a porch light left on for her. This made her feel lonelier, and then it felt infuriating. At the back of the house, her bug zapper was still glowing. She hadn't meant to let her world get so small and silent. It hadn't felt small until Evan had entered and left. Until the cousins arrived, two men who traveled all the way from Norway to make their family, their world, bigger. She swept up an armful of the pine cones and began throwing them at the house as hard as she could.

Olav's light snapped on, and she saw his silhouette standing in the window. He disappeared, but then another light went on in the stairwell, and then the kitchen, and then Olav was stepping onto the back deck.

"Sorry I woke you," Annika said and then threw two more pine cones that landed just below Per's window.

Olav watched her and shrugged. "Benadryl," he said, pointing upstairs. "Per, Benadryl." He made a pillow with his hands and laid his cheek down.

The bug zapper crackled furiously. Someday it would short out, Annika thought. Someday this house would burn. It would take the photographs with it, the prayer book, the wedding veil.

"Zzztttt," Olav said, like he was conversing with the zapper, the one thing in this country that understood him. Someday he would die, and Per would cry at his funeral, perhaps remember to send Annika an e-mail about it months later.

"Zzztttt," Annika replied. Someday she would die. If she could do it over—no. Best not to think of it. If her grandmother could do it over—no. Best not to think of that either.

Annika jumped onto the low deck of the porch and climbed on a plastic chair. She switched off the zapper, and in the sudden dark she could still see the filament glowing before her, superimposed on the house, the forest, Olav's face as she turned. In the silence they could hear the wind high above, at the tops of the pines. Something snapped a branch in the forest.

"Troll," the old man said, pointing toward the sound, toward the troll-riddled forest she'd thought she loved more than any person. Now she was no longer sure.

It was very late, but her phone began to ring, programmed to sound like chiming bells. The screen lit up, and the glow showed through her pocket. A moth landed lightly there, then fluttered away as she pulled the phone out and saw Evan's name.

"Is this an okay time?" he asked. "Are you alone?"

As if sensing her need for privacy, Olav went into the

house, from which there soon came the faint sound of a beer tab popping and the low click and giggle of the television. She filled Evan in on the cousins' visit, obtuse Per and the mockery of the family artifacts. He talked to her about ash trees, mentioned his kids: school play, concert band. She waited for him to ask her again to come to Ann Arbor. The conversation trickled down awkwardly to weather until her chest was so tight and panicked it squeezed the question out of her: "Is there someone else?"

"What?"

"Are you seeing someone else? Is that why you called?"

"Huh? No. Why?"

"There's no one else?"

"Do you care?"

"I care." There was a long silence. With the bug zapper off, Annika could hear a truck drive by in the distance. She thought of the dark road leading out of the forest, the way Per and Olav's car would crunch down the gravel and leave her. She looked up through the tunnel of trees into the stars and felt like she was standing at the bottom of a drain, already washed away. "Look," she said. "If I hate it, I can come back here, right?"

"If you hate it? That's not really comforting."

"I'm trying."

"Are you saying you want to come here?"

"Do you still want me to?"

There was a long pause, and her breath curdled in her lungs before he finally said, "Yes. If you're sure. If you're sure about trying."

"Then ask me again. Please, ask me again."

★　　★　　★

Inside, Olav was sitting on the couch watching an info-mercial, the volume nearly silent. "Okay?" he asked her.

Annika was grinning despite herself. She left the back door open, and the summer breeze followed her in through the screen. She looked around the house: the rag rug, the strata of linoleum, the family photos, and the ceramic trolls. She felt like she was seeing it clearly for the first time in many years. "Okay," she announced, and she held up the phone, still smiling.

"Okay," Olav said agreeably, smiling back. He'd apparently brought an extra beer with him into the living room, and he offered her the unopened can on the coffee table. She took it, snapped it open.

"*Skål,*" Olav said.

"I know that one," Annika said. "*Skål.* Cheers."

"Cheers," Olav said.

She watched them drink in the reflection in the dark window. She could keep the house or try to rent it, come back for vacations. Let the deer eat the flower beds. She could leave a bowl of buttered porridge in the shed and hope for the best. There was a rustling sound outside—a chase of leaves in the wind, or a light-footed troll, a soft-hearted *nisse.*

Through the screen doors a breath of wind came, moving the yellow curtains. Annika heard it like a voice. *Go,* her parents whispered to her. *Go.*

Gå, she imagined her grandmother murmuring. *Gå.*

"Yes," Annika said. "I'm going."

SUN CITY

They floated into the afternoon in their little stucco submarine, blinds shut against the sunlight and the swamp cooler whistling on the roof. In the artificial air the two women wrapped jewelry in tissue paper and placed it in the compartments of egg cartons. Bev sat on the couch, Rose knelt on the matted carpet, and Cline, Bev's guinea pig, wandered under the coffee table. Rose had had this idea, the egg cartons, on the plane to Arizona, and it had made her feel organized. In the aftermath of her grandmother's death, at least there were omelets to be made. When she'd realized just how much stuff her grandmother had owned and how little of it Bev wanted to keep, Rose should have come up with a new plan. Instead, they just kept eating eggs.

"It's Cline after Patsy Cline, you know," Bev explained for the fifth time that week as her cassette tape clicked to silence on the stereo in the hallway. She heaved herself off the couch and over the child gate that confined Cline to the living room. Bev was majestically huge. The lift of her legs over the gate reminded Rose of dockyards, cranes and I-beams, vast weight swinging dangerously free. If the house weren't a concrete box laid flat on the dirt, the floors would shake. Rose, solid herself, envied this size; Bev looked armored, untouchable, as if nothing could come at her that wouldn't bounce straight off. Grandmother Vera's death, the dispersal of her possessions—at the end of the week, Bev would step over it all and disappear into some other hallway of her life. She'd step straight over Rose and never look back.

"They eat these, you know," Rose said, scooping Cline off the floor. "In South America."

"That's disgusting." Bev swung herself back into the room, and Patsy Cline went walkin' after midnight on the tape deck.

Rose moved Cline's front legs in a little dance. "It's a delicacy. There's a painting of the Last Supper in some church in Peru where Jesus eats guinea pig."

Bev lifted Cline onto her shoulder. "No one's going to eat you here, sweetie. We aren't savages."

"They roast them whole, eyes and toenails and every-thing."

"Why are you telling me this?" Bev cuddled Cline defensively.

It was a real question and Rose felt sheepish. "Sorry," she said, and she held up a pair of clip-on silver birds, still on the plastic store backing. "Are you *sure* you don't want these?"

"I don't need Vera's old costume crap. I've got enough junk of my own."

Rose agreed with her there. The house bulged with it, cowboy figurines and Kokopellis and lots of monotonous Southwestern art, cheerful brown children in brown pueblos. Bev's own cheerful white grandchildren smiled from every wall, the frames shaped like hearts or guitars or kitten heads, the pictures cut off at awkward angles inside. "This pair's real silver," Rose offered.

"Take 'em for yourself. Take anything you like. We've been through this."

"I wear pierced, not clip."

"I noticed. Five times in the one ear, four in the other." Bev peered closer at the pair of bird shapes. "She never wore those. Your mother sent them to her one Christmas. She hated them."

"Okay, then. To the consignment store." Rose tried to tuck them in an egg cup, but the plastic backing didn't fit. The birds eyed her resentfully, protruding from among the coiled necklaces, quiescent little serpents.

Bev wore almost no jewelry, just a tiny cross with a diamond in the center. The gem caught the light and blinked at Rose like a beacon from Bev's oceanic chest.

Vera had lived here for eight years, a long quiet twilight filled with card games at the neighborhood clubhouse, a bowling league, classic-movie channels. Vera and Bev were both retired and didn't seem to miss their jobs. They'd both been widowed and made it known that they didn't miss their husbands. Vera had been a secretary for a company that made plastic garbage cans. Bev had been an electrician. She wore her hair short and played softball and, in the photos Vera sent, wore overalls until her weight ballooned and she switched to housedresses. They cowrote their Christmas letters, trading off every paragraph to crack jokes about each other. They included pictures of themselves at the botanical garden or a Diamondbacks game, their full names—Vera Beasley and Beverly Morrison—written on the back. They filled the frame, these two old ladies, one large and one lean, smiling and pressing their cheeks close.

Say hi to Bev, Rose wrote in every note to her grandmother, the postcards or the thank-you notes for the five-dollar bills that still came on her birthday. Each time she felt like she was winking, their eyes meeting over the decades, seeing something true in each other.

Rose had once dated a woman who'd had a whole other life, a marriage, two kids. "You've always known who you were," she'd said when Rose had talked about mixed spin the bottle in seventh grade, high-school girlfriends, coming out to her mother while high on painkillers in the car going home after a tonsillectomy. Her mother just pulled into a drive-through to buy her a milkshake and said, "Oh, sweetie, I know. We've known for a while, haven't we?"

"I envy that," the old girlfriend had said. "It must have made life so much easier."

"It's never easy," Rose said, referring vaguely to life in general, or romance, or sex, or relationships. She'd realized only later that the woman had simply meant self-knowledge, and that *had* been easy for Rose; it had come plainly and she'd never wanted to deny it, never felt she could. Vera's story was beautiful and sad to her, how long it had taken her to find Bev, to find herself. After Vera died of a heart attack, about as suddenly as a seventy-three-year-old woman can die, Rose flew in from Portland for the week. Partly because she knew her mother wouldn't, and she thought Bev would need somebody's help, and partly because that story had allowed Rose to love her grandmother less complicatedly than her mother had ever managed. Probably to love her better, Rose thought.

Rose had rented a car at Phoenix Sky Harbor and driven to the house in Sun City. Bev showed her to Vera's room, but there was only one person's clothes in the closet and a tightly made single bed with rough white pillowcases. "I'm across the hall," Bev said, then peered closer at whatever expression was on Rose's face. "She didn't actually die in here, you know. It happened at the hospital." Bev explained that she'd already paid for a booth at a local consignment store; Vera's stuff had to be out of the house by the end of the week. "I'll need another roommate," Bev said. "The HOA fees out here are something else." Vera herself was in a brown box on the dresser, blank and cardboard and dangerously like part of the pile of mail left sitting beside it, the sales pitches and charity pleas that had arrived after her death. "I suppose you'll be taking this back to Portland," Bev said, holding the box up for inspection. Rose hadn't realized a crematorium would even let you walk away without an urn, with an entire person contained in a fragile paper box.

"Unless you want it here," Rose offered carefully.

"You're family and it's yours. And why would I?"

Roommate. Rose had assumed in those Christmas letters that it was a euphemism. But maybe it wasn't.

The other bedroom door had been closed since Rose arrived. Bev disappeared into it every night after dinner to listen to the most miserable country album Rose had ever heard. A woman's lone howl crawled out from under the door, singing about love and death, and Rose thought if she listened hard enough she'd eventually hear Bev crying along. But Bev popped out each morning clear-eyed and so brusque Rose couldn't imagine just asking her, putting her question into words that Bev could laugh or take offense at or just deny.

Bev gave up on a tangle of necklaces and pushed the clot of metal across the coffee table. "I'm going for my swim," she announced. "You said you'd call U-Haul about her furniture." Rose picked at the clasps until she heard the sliding door to the backyard open and shut. Then she sneaked to the kitchen window. She hunkered down, her arms in the sink, her head as low to the windowsill as she could get it.

Bev couldn't actually swim. She got from one side to the other somehow, but with wild movements of her arms, great gasps of breath. Sometimes she turned onto her back and shot a plume of water into the air like the spray from a whale's blowhole. At each side, she pulled herself up with an elbow, the flesh of her upper arm spreading against the concrete. She caught her breath, practiced a stroke one-armed, hung on to the edge, and kicked her legs. Put her face into the water and blew delicate bubbles. Then she set off back across and it looked exactly the same, her strokes a broken windmill, her hips swiveling, water spraying three feet up on the concrete deck. It was the worst swimming Rose had ever seen, worse than she had imagined possible without the swimmer drowning, and it was the best entertainment of the past three days.

After fifteen minutes Bev climbed out of the pool and Rose ran back to the living room, dropped to the carpet, and grabbed the necklaces. "Doesn't look like you've made much progress," Bev said, closing the sliding door behind her. A gulp of outside air came in with her, hot enough to reach Rose in the living room but already dissipating, a flame thankfully snuffed. Bev stood in her swimsuit, dripping a puddle onto the tile floor. Rose shrugged, listened to the water drop and the swamp cooler straining on the roof, and realized the Patsy Cline tape had stopped. Bev tucked her towel around her waist and stood, arms akimbo, outside the child gate. "The swimming. Can't ever stop learning. That's when you die. Anyway, you going to make us some dinner? Something other than eggs."

Rose wanted to protest—why was it her job to make dinner?—but Bev was already down the hallway. Behind the bedroom door, the miserable country album started up again. A banjo twanged and the singer howled. Rose thought of her first girlfriend. She'd left lyrics in Rose's locker written out like poems. Some were about love but most were about suicide. They'd put on a CD and smoke pot and try to feel more than their lives at the time had given them to feel. They thought listening to the right song might let them squeeze themselves so tightly, something ugly would come welling out. Rose listened and pretended she was the girl her mother must have envisioned, giving her the name she did. She imagined the beauty, imagined the thorns. Dark things were deepest. Every teenager knew that, gay or straight.

The singer in Bev's bedroom shrieked like something was biting her. "I'm going to the store," Rose shouted.

Bev had the single track on repeat, too loud to hear or answer, and Rose thought that if she'd owned this album as a sixteen-year-old, she might have hurt herself for real.

Rose's mother worked at the U.S.A. Dry Pea and Lentil Council trade group. She was the kind of lifetime admin who prided herself on being able to merge five distribution lists, kick the vending machine in the right place to free a stuck soda, and fix a paycheck all at 4:55 p.m. on a Friday. Iris had worked fifty weeks a year for thirty-five years and counting. One week of her two weeks of vacation she used to take Rose somewhere edifying, a national park or historic battlefield. One week she would go to Cabo San Lucas alone. There were plenty of men in her life, usually one at a time for a few months each, but they never went with her. Rose wondered sometimes if she'd modeled this part of herself on her mother without realizing it. The series of women, a few months each. Iris had used Rose as her excuse—single parenthood, the need not to let her little girl fall too hard for men who might not last. But Rose never fell too hard, not so hard she couldn't walk away when she wanted, and she usually did.

During Iris's solo vacations, Rose stayed with Grandma

Vera, who took her bowling and made cookies with ingredients seemingly left over from the last time Rose had visited, the brown sugar crusted into jagged points at the bottom of the bag.

"What does your mom *do* all week in Cabo? I mean, the same vacation every year. If I had the money to go somewhere, I'd try to actually see something. I'd see the world."

Vera handled the dough like she was annoyed with it, rolled it into balls, and pressed them on the baking sheet so firmly Rose knew they'd spread too much and burn. The first batch was already out of the oven, brown and crispy. Rose ate them anyway.

"Your mother's wasted her life," Vera said. "She was a smart girl and she's wasted it with those pea people."

Rose went very still, chewing her cookie as quietly as she could. She felt like a wild animal was coming into view, a shy specimen her mother knew but Rose rarely saw. She imagined the hushed voice of a nature-program narrator excitedly announcing the find. The old Vera had been a drinker. The old Vera had been sharp-tongued, quick to insult, frequently cruel. Iris avoided talking about this angry version of her—she could acknowledge Vera's newer self without quite wanting a relationship with it or believing they could manage one. When Iris shared her memories of Vera, she described howling fights, words that sliced true, and wounds that never quite scabbed over. Rose would watch them float from her mother's mouth and settle like spores on the car dashboard or kitchen table. She imagined her mother saw them too, because she always changed the subject immediately, deny-ing them soil to root, to darken Rose's mind against the grandmother she adored, the one who baked her cookies, even though they were burned, who called like clockwork on Sundays. It was only later that Rose real-ized that Vera called punctually, predictably, so that Rose would be the one waiting at the phone, no need for her to talk to Iris, no obligation to try and fix something broken.

"Don't you waste your life too," Vera used to tell her. "Not like your mother." And Rose just nodded.

She didn't think she was wasting her life, but she suspected Vera might have thought so; Rose was in her mid-twenties, tending bar, no college degree, no marriage, no children. Her mother had sent Vera the reviews of all the places Rose worked. They almost never mentioned the drinks, but her mother would find something, like "attentive service," to run a pink highlighter across. They had all figured out a way to live around rather than directly with one another—the restaurant reviews mailed to Vera, the notes of congratulations that Vera then sent to Rose, the careful dance around one another's loyalties. The most recent review was in a still sealed envelope on Vera's dresser with the rest of her mail. Rose was mentioned by name in that one, as the "mixologist and mastermind behind the exquisitely crafted cocktails." Rose opened the envelope, stuck the review in the mirror frame, and pretended her grandmother had had the chance to read it. Looking at it, posted above the blank brown box, she felt both vindication and disappointment.

Whatever big goals Vera might have had for herself remained a mystery. She didn't seem especially proud of any one ability or accomplishment, her family included. Her moving in with Bev had seemed like an explanation: transgression, courage, forbidden love—that was a story that might justify everything, misbehavior and devotion both. But if Vera was alone at the end of her life, surrounded by Kokopellis and pictures of someone else's grandchildren, a roommate, a guinea pig, an estranged daughter, then what was her excuse? How angry was her life, and how small, there at the end, if it was without love?

In late afternoon, the heat was a blast furnace, every possible cliché: oven, kiln, campfire, house fire. Rose's jeans were swampy before she'd even pulled out of the driveway, and at the Safeway she lingered as long as she could, buying food and a two-dollar pair of flip-flops. Her feet were suffocating in sneakers.

Her mom called while she was stalling in the magazine aisle, actually reading *Us Weekly* instead of just flipping through the pictures of celebrity baby bumps. "I still don't hate myself," Iris announced as soon as Rose picked up. "I'm still not coming."

"Okay."

"How are things?"

"Weird."

"Is Bev there? Can you not talk?"

"I'm at the grocery store. Did you know they didn't—"

"My therapist says he thinks it's fine if I don't go. He said people grieve in their own way. Or don't. I don't know yet if I'm grieving. But I'm not coming down."

"I wasn't asking you to."

"You don't know what she was like."

"No." Rose put *Us Weekly* back on the rack. "I didn't. I really didn't."

"I just wanted to check in. I have aerobics. I'm outside the studio right now."

"Then go inside."

"Okay, I'm going. I'm going," she said, and hung up.

Rose, delaying, looked for a circuitous route home, which wasn't hard. Sun City was a giant suburban hamster maze. In one of the strip malls Rose spotted a giant red sign reading BEVMO. She turned into the parking lot. She could get Bev something with the name, even just a labeled bag or business card. Maybe Beverly Morrison would find it endearing. Maybe she'd tell Rose the truth. The store turned out to be a giant liquor emporium, and Rose felt foolish asking for a bag alone, so she grabbed a bottle of vodka. There was no liquor in Vera's house. Rose had looked.

At home, Rose saw Bev had pulled all the dishes out of the cupboards, wrapped half of them in newspaper, and stuffed those in boxes on the counter. Rose had three bags of groceries and had to put them all on the floor. "I thought you were hungry," she said.

"I am."

"Should we do this later, then?"

"I've already started. No point in putting them all back just to pull them out again."

"Do you want me to help?"

"You don't know what was whose."

"I'm pretty hungry."

"So order in if you don't think you can wait." Bev's hair was wet from the shower and Rose realized how much longer it had gotten since all those pictures of her with a blunt cut and wearing overalls. It spread across Bev's shoulders, the damp gray strands soaking the fabric, saturating the colors and pressing the pattern against her skin. The combination of thin hair, dark pink peonies, freckled skin, looked vulnerable in a way that the rest of Bev didn't.

"I brought you this." Rose unfolded the BevMo bag and snapped it in the air like a matador's cape. "It reminded me of your name." The bottle of vodka was in the glove compartment of the rental car.

Bev looked at it a long time. She was holding a beige mug labeled CARDIO FUN RUN '89, and Rose tried to imagine what possible incarnation of either Bev or Vera in any decade went running. "What'd you buy?"

"Nothing. I just got the bag."

"Too bad," Bev said. She wrapped the fun-run mug in a piece of newspaper and then put it in the BevMo bag, consignment-store-bound. She picked up a plastic Hamburglar cup and tossed that in too. Rose took the hint and let her clatter around by herself until there was enough room to cook. The meal was the quickest one she could make, broccoli and instant mashed potatoes and two chicken breasts. She was just waiting on the chicken when her cell phone rang.

"I'm done with aerobics," her mother announced.

"Headed home." Rose could hear the murmur of Top 40 radio and pictured the dusty dashboard of the ancient Honda Civic, purple travel mug in the cup holder, sunglasses elasticked to the visor, Juicy Fruit in the door pocket, and felt nostalgia so strong it was like she'd lived there, like that car was a home a person could go back to. "Can you talk?"

"No." Bev was in the living room. The news was starting, sweeps for illegal immigrants, and Bev talked out loud to the television: "About time."

"Bev's there?"

"Yup."

"Sorry I couldn't talk earlier."

The tick of the oven timer sounded hoarse as it slipped into its last minutes. Rose held the phone between her ear and shoulder and thumbed through the give-away box. At the bottom there was a melamine plate with her own face on it, age eight. She was wearing a Care Bear sweatshirt and fluffy bangs. She remembered her mom having the plates made and then her grandmother talking about how tacky it was that she'd worn a branded shirt for her school picture. "You should make those animals pay you," she'd said, "if you're going to wear 'em across your chest."

"You're sure there's nothing you want?" Rose asked. "There's nothing I should be saving for you? Grandma had a lot of stuff."

"For the millionth time, no. Let Bev take whatever she wants, you take whatever you want, and get rid of everything else."

"She doesn't want anything."

64

"What?"

"She—never mind. I'll call you later." Bev came back into the kitchen and got them two glasses of water straight from the tap, water that tasted so foul the city distributed brochures with tips for drinking it. Add lemon slices, they recommended. Rose pulled a water bottle from the grocery bags and carried it with the plates into the living room. She ate off her own portrait, uncovering it bit by bit. There was Brave Heart Lion from the Forest of Feelings. There was her toothy smile. She arranged the last of the potatoes into a white hat on her head and waited for Bev to apologize for just dumping this plate in a consignment box without even offering it to her, the one person who might conceivably want it. But Bev seemed determined to ignore her completely. They ate in silence until the news had dwindled to the dangers of leaving pets in hot cars and the weather—it would cool off later that week, the weatherman said, down to 109. Bev ate with Cline in her lap, passing shreds of broccoli to him. Finally she put down her fork with a clank and waited for Rose to look at her. When she did, she didn't understand why Bev looked so angry. "Your grandmother knew, you know. She knew what you were."

"Excuse me?"

"She didn't mind. I wanted you to know that. She forgave you." Bev handed the last of the broccoli to Cline and then fingered her necklace, rubbing the little cross, the gold disappearing between her fingers.

"What I am?"

"She didn't hate you or anything."

"For being a bartender?" Rose tried to joke.

"Oh, she hated that you were a bartender. Said you were wasting your life. Those stupid reviews your mother sent. But that's not what I mean. You know what I mean."

Rose ate the last few bites of potatoes, thinking something would come to her. Nothing did. She climbed over the guinea-pig gate and threw her plate in the sink so hard, it shattered.

She grabbed her bag and two-dollar flip-flops and headed out the front door, Bev calling after her. It was dark and the air was cooler but the heat still radiated from the sidewalk, birthing itself off the pavement. She sat in the rental car and opened the warm bottle of vodka. She thought about where she might go, what she could do, and decided that what she really wanted to do in that moment was drink so much she shouldn't drive anywhere. She got back out and started walking. She wandered the development's endless curves, the wide streets, the low, sunbaked houses. People went to bed early here, and the homes were dark and quiet. The cheap flip-flops rubbed her feet, and when she came to the development's golf course she cut across the seventh hole, deserted in the dark. She tried to take her shoes off, but the grass was deceptive—dyed green, it was nearly dead underfoot, brittle and so sharp it hurt to walk on. Rose sat in a sand trap and buried her feet to soothe them. The vodka was an obscure brand she'd decided to try, but it turned out there was a reason she'd never had it before. It tasted like a mouthful of dirty glass, and she wished for tonic or vermouth, olive brine, a shaker. She wanted to be back behind the bar, where the problems were always everybody else's and all she had to do was listen. She wanted someone right now to listen to her, a row of old customers who could be made to return the favor. She wished she weren't between girlfriends just so she'd have someone to call. She'd always let go of people so easily; it had made her feel strong but now it made her feel like Bev, careless, callous, inscrutable.

Her phone rang and she got sand all over it trying to answer. "Should I come down there?" her mother choked out. "Just tell me. You'd tell me if I should, right?"

"Do you want to? You should come if you want to."

"Don't give me a choice, because I'll say no."

"I can't tell you you need to come."

"It matters. Of course it matters. I don't want to pretend like it doesn't."

"Mom."

"I didn't realize—I didn't realize until...I should be there."

"You don't need to be. It's fine."

"I hated her. I hated her for a long time and I can't take that back."

"I know."

"I was picturing you doing to me what I'm doing to her. When I imagine you not caring, it's the worst feeling in the world."

"Mom. That won't happen."

"Your father's the one who...he said, 'If the two of you make each other that miserable, why keep doing this?' And that made so much sense."

"Then don't apologize for what made you happy."

"But she's family, Rose. Sometimes you aren't supposed to be happy."

"Maybe that's not healthy."

"I just— When you asked if there was anything I wanted. There *is* something. There was this necklace she used to wear. Real delicate, just a little gold cross with a diamond in it. She'd had it since I was little, when Daddy was still alive. I remember that. Have you seen it?"

Rose pressed her palm into the sand like she could leave her print behind. Her face on a plate. The phone was sweaty in her hand, hot against her ear.

"If you see it, can you take it for me? I don't think she would have gotten rid of it. It'll be in the house somewhere."

"I'm sure it is," Rose said. She pulled her feet out of the sand; grains stuck to the raw places. She could see the dark lines in the moonlight, sandal straps of blood and grit.

As Rose opened the door, she steeled herself for Bev's awful sad song, but there was only silence. The swamp-cooler air hissed through the sealed house, raced out the open door. Rose shut it and stood still, breathing deeply, sobering up slightly in the cold. A strange animal noise scrabbled somewhere, like Cline grown to enormous size. Rose kicked off the flip-flops, winced at the fresh blood between her toes, and went padding through the house. She found Bev in Vera's room, lying on the bed. The hem of her peony housedress was hitched above her knees, her body curled tightly above her pale, dimpled legs. She was crying. Cline wandered over the coverlet down by Bev's feet, having no interest in comforting his mistress or no idea how. The Hamburglar cup was on the nightstand, full of soda. No, whiskey and Coke, Rose recognized after lifting it and smelling. Bev looked up at her and Rose felt powerful.

Bev took one of the pillows from under her head and held it across her face. "Your grandmother was a good friend to me," she said. "I know she could be sharp but she was a good friend." Rose pulled the pillow off and dropped it on the floor, but Bev grabbed the next one and curled it more tightly over her head. "I never did," she said. "I never slept here before. In this bed."

Rose sat beside her, and the mattress creaked. She reached out and touched the necklace with a single finger, the pendant so slight she couldn't help but touch Bev too, the warm skin beneath. Bev flinched and lifted the pillow long enough to take the Hamburglar cup. She tried to drink flat on her back and coughed. Liquid spilled into the gullies of her neck and ran down the gold chain. She pushed the cup back into Rose's hand and replaced the pillow. "You should ask me," she said, her voice muffled. "Just ask me what you want to know."

"Was she happy?" The question came to her as a kindness, a way of easing Bev into greater confessions, but as she asked, it felt like something she needed very much to know.

"I don't know. I wish I did." Bev curled on her side, lifted the pillow enough to reach for the cup again. "Ask me if I'm happy."

"Are you happy?"

"No."

Rose took the drink from Bev's hand. "You're cut off. Robble-robble." She set it on the nightstand clumsily, drunk enough herself that the liquid sloshed in the cup.

"I should have said something. But she could be so hard. You know how hard, your grandma." Bev's fingers closed around air. "Give it back."

"Where did it come from?"

"My bedroom. Vera didn't drink. Said she used to like it a little too much."

Rose could feel Bev's warmth against her back. "That's what my mom always said. I don't know. I didn't see that part of her. She'd stopped before I came along."

"You never really know. The things a person doesn't want to show you."

"Even the things they do," Rose said, and it felt wise but sounded helpless. Tucked in a corner of the mirror was a snapshot of Bev and Vera at the zoo. She wondered if Bev had noticed it, if it made her feel better or worse. She wished it were framed. She wished there were a heart drawn around it in lipstick, something irrefutable. The brown box sat mutely beneath it.

Bev braced her arm on Rose's thigh and worked herself upright, then leaned back against the headboard. "I took—" She gripped the necklace. Then she noticed Rose's feet. "That has to hurt. You should wash them."

"I will. Later."

But the moment was gone. Bev took the Hamburglar cup again, and Rose didn't stop her. "I didn't want to tempt her," Bev said. "But I'm not a woman who likes to do without."

"I like that about you," Rose said honestly. Bev grabbed the bottle of vodka from the nightstand and poured some into the cup. "That's going to taste disgusting," Rose said.

"I don't care."

"I care. Shut up," she said as Bev opened her mouth to protest. "Let me make you something." She got up and walked unsteadily across the hall into Bev's room. There were more grandchildren pictures on the dresser, a music stand, and an accordion. The bed was unmade, the sheets pink with a nubby chenille coverlet. A cardboard box filled with bottles was halfway out of the closet. Rose hefted the whole thing up and then heard the CD player hissing on top of the dresser. It was cued up, paused at the beginning of a track, the disc whirling, waiting. She pressed Play. *Blood calls to blood, calls to the wound*, the singer howled. *Bones long to be broken.*

She went into the kitchen. Bev had cleaned up the supper dishes and the giveaways. Rose set the box on the counter with a satisfying clank. She pulled out every bottle to see what she had to work with. Some were nearly crusted shut, but she wrenched them open, one by one. She pulled every bottle of juice, every soda, every can of frozen concentrate, from the fridge. She pulled every glass, every mug left in the cupboards, and placed them all on the counter. She began to pour.

The sliding door opened and shut behind her. She looked out the sink window and saw Bev with Cline under one arm, Vera's box under the other. Rose worried they were all going in the pool, but Bev set the box down gently on the patio table, Cline on the concrete rim. She turned

71

on the pool lights and then leaped into the water with a splash that hit Cline like a tsunami. He just squeaked and stayed loyally put. Bev threw herself across the water over and over. Rose mixed. They could toss drinks down their throats, down their cheeks. They could throw them into their eyes and weep bright tears. Bev paused at one end, her housedress ballooning around her. She looked like a magnificent pink squid. The cross glittered at her neck. Rose opened the sliding door. The heat rushed in like wind. Bev had opened her bedroom window, and the sad song circled the backyard.

"You can have it," Rose said.

"What?" Bev gasped, out of breath.

"You can have it."

Bev shook her head, confused, water flying from her hair. She pointed at her ears. "Water," she said and stuck her index finger in one like she was popping a balloon. "What are you making?" she called.

Rose held up a finger, meaning *Wait,* although in a loud bar it would just mean *One,* and you never told customers to wait. She chose two glasses and carried them out, jewel-bright, showy with floating, separated layers. If you looked closely, you could see them already collapsing together. The heat wrapped around her, a living, tireless thing, laughing at the dark. Sweat sprang from her face, her neck, under her arms. She stood on the concrete edge, and Bev surged toward her. The splashing felt like relief.

"Get your feet in here," Bev said, and Rose sat, legs dangling.

The chlorine burned the raw spots on her feet, and they

both watched the blood and sand lift into the blue and drift away. "Medicine," Rose said, handing Bev a glass.

They nearly toasted in silence, helpless for the right words. Bev held the edge with one arm and treaded water, her legs churning.

"Bottoms up?" Rose finally said, raising her drink toward the patio table, the box.

They clinked their glasses together. The song ended, and in the few beats before it began again, Rose opened her mouth.

"Don't say anything else," Bev said. "Don't spoil it."

Rose swallowed and drank. *Let it find the illness,* she thought. *Let it bring the answers. Let it be the cure for something.*

TEACHER

Nine years after he was a student in my fourth-grade class, Zach Nowak threw a brick off an I-75 overpass. It smashed straight through the windshield of a white Subaru and into the face of the driver, a mother piloting her family toward their summer vacation. She lived long enough to be brought to the hospital where my ex-sister-in-law was a nurse. I'd been divorced for almost five years, but Helen had stayed closer to me than to her brother. "He was a jerk," she'd say. "The new one's dumb as a box of rocks. Even he knows he made a mistake." I was skeptical on that count—he'd never tried to come back to me, or even apologize. But I appreciated Helen's lie.

We met up for dinner every few weeks, mostly at the Thirsty Sturgeon, the only restaurant worth eating at anywhere near Walleye Lake. No one lived here for the food. Or the walleye, really. Or the sturgeon. Mostly, we lived here because we'd always lived here, in the forested swath of north-central Michigan that the rest of the world drove straight through.

The family in the Subaru had been pressing north, planning to stay overnight in Mackinaw City and take the first ferry over to the island to do the usual: horse-drawn carriages and bike rentals and fudge. The brick came down at nine thirty p.m., not long after sunset.

Our first dinner together after the brick, I thought Helen was bringing it up the way any of us in town might: a terrible thing had happened in a very small place, and we worried at it like a rash, the scratch of "What was he thinking?" and "That poor family." I hadn't realized that Helen had been working in the ER when the family was brought in.

"We're not a level-one trauma center," she said. "We're not supposed to see things like that." And after we ordered, she told me just a little of what she'd seen, how the husband, who'd been in the front passenger seat, had had pieces of his wife's face on his clothes. Their kids had been strapped in in the back seat and were unharmed except for what they'd witnessed. I understood that she wasn't saying any of this to horrify me or impress me but because she needed to say it to someone.

When the server came with our food, she ordered two whiskey sours, both for her, although she usually nursed one beer all evening. "Was he in your class ever?" she asked me, doing the math.

Zach Nowak was eighteen, barely, when he threw the brick. I'd taught at Walleye Lake's only elementary school for fifteen years, and I admitted he'd been in my class.

"What was he like? If you remember."

"I remember." He had seemed like the kind of kid who might someday throw a brick off an overpass, was what he'd seemed like. But I didn't know how to say that without sounding either flippant or irresponsible for not doing something to stop him.

I was sure we all remembered him, every single teacher who'd ever been in a classroom with Zach Nowak. But we'd also known crooked kids who'd turned into straight arrows, or at least into adults who held down jobs, went home and watched TV, and didn't throw bricks off overpasses. We'd known sweet kids who went the other way. Life is long and strange and none of us sees what God does.

But what I'd seen in Zach had scared me. When other kids angered him, he didn't yell or hit. He waited until they were distracted and then he took his revenge. It wasn't always violent. He liked to piss on things—people's backpacks, books, faces. One winter, when the hallway was lined with snow boots, he'd walked along spraying the whole row of them. "Honestly, he was creepy," I said. "But—kids. You have to believe in them. You have to assume there's time for them to turn out okay. If *you* can't reach them, maybe someone else can."

Once Zach had flagged me down during a math test. I'd laid one palm flat on his desk while we spoke. He stabbed me in the back of the hand with his sharpened pencil as hard as he could. When the principal asked him why, he said I'd made the test too hard. Zach got a week's suspension. After the week, he was back.

"What did you do after that?" Helen asked. "Help him

via megaphone? I wouldn't have been willing to get within arm's length."

I mostly hadn't helped him, was the real answer. I'd ignore his waving arm as long as I could. I had thought that at parent-teacher conferences I might discover that his parents were neglectful or cruel in some obvious way that I could report and then whatever was messing this kid up could start to get fixed. But when the parents came, they were tidy and polite and kind. Which doesn't always mean anything, of course, but then they'd started telling me everything they'd tried, every kind of therapist they'd already been to see, driving three hours down to Lansing for appointments. "Don't give up on him," they begged. "We know he's a difficult kid. Just please don't give up."

Of course I wouldn't, I said. He was just a child. And maybe if I'd managed to be kinder to him, he would have risen to the kindness, turned toward it like a plant and flowered. I watched Helen demolish her napkin, tearing it into small strips, and felt like maybe I could have spared her this, like she was one more person Zach had managed to hit with the brick I hadn't stopped him from throwing.

Speaking to the police, Zach didn't pretend he hadn't understood what brick plus overpass plus windshield plus driver might mean. He was just curious, he said, just messing around, but he said it like a toddler who looks straight at you before pouring his milk all over the floor. A toddler is old enough to understand overturned cup plus milk plus floor; he just wants to watch it happen. Zach was arrested when he drove back to the same overpass that same night to do it again.

"It was probably for the best," Helen said, "that the woman didn't make it. I'm not supposed to say that. I'm not even supposed to think it. But the injuries she'd sustained..."

"Zach was scary," I said. "From the moment he started school. Before, probably. We weren't supposed to think that. But he was."

The last time I spoke to Zach he was thirteen and buying a yellow pouch of Sour Patch Kids at Walgreens. He was ahead of me in line, and I hoped he wouldn't look back; I was buying tampons and a bottle of dandruff shampoo. When I went through the sliding doors, he was waiting for me outside. "Hey, Ms. Z.," he said, the name I'd asked the kids to call me. My married name was very long and Polish and had never seemed worth it.

I said hello and he asked me what dandruff was.

"Not really your business," I said first, then felt childish. *You're an educator,* I thought. I wasn't going to be a wife much longer by then, and after four miscarriages I knew I might never be a mother. But I was still an educator. "Dry scalp," I explained. "It gets itchy."

"Where's your itch, Ms. Z.?" he asked, and smiled like he was ten years older.

I shook my head and started walking.

"You don't have your car, Ms. Z.?"

I'd walked, because it was autumn and the weather was going to turn cooler any day but hadn't yet, and I was grateful for the warmth. My house was a quick trek through a patch of woods behind the drugstore. It was township land, the trails no more than deer paths. A track spit out at the end of my street, so familiar it didn't occur to me that I should stick to the road. But then Zach was following me through the trees with no one else around.

"Ms. Z., are you still Ms. Z.? Or are you something else now?" My husband had left me three months earlier, and Walleye Lake was so small that everyone had heard the news.

"I'm still Ms. Z. to you."

"You sure? Can I call you Trisha, Ms. Z.? Since I'm not at your school anymore?"

I'm still not sure how he knew my first name. "No, you can't call me that."

He kept following me. At first it was just his footsteps on the path, crunching through the autumn leaves, and then it was "Hey, Trisha." Over and over: *Hey, Trisha, hey, Trisha, hey. Hey. Hey. Hey, Trisha, hey. Hey, Trisha, hey, Trisha, hey. Hey. Hey. Hey, Trisha, hey. Hey, Trisha, hey, Trisha, hey. Hey. Hey, Trisha, hey. Hey, Trisha.*

This went on for half a mile. I didn't see or hear anyone else. My lungs got tight, my breath fast and shallow. Sweat trickled down my sides. I wound the plastic drugstore bag tighter around my left hand. Finally I stopped dead on the path. I'd seen a gray rock half covered in leaves and bent to grab it with my other hand. I'd planned to rise in one smooth motion, rock raised, but it was almost too heavy, almost too big to hold in one hand, and I staggered a little before hefting it up and over my right shoulder like a baseball.

For a moment he looked startled, and then he grinned. "You're not going to throw that at me," he said. "You're a teacher." Puberty had barely gotten started on him. He was still shorter than I was and probably fifty pounds lighter. His voice was high and thin. Was I really going to aim a rock at a child like he was some stray dog? It would be an admission that I was afraid of a thirteen-year-old boy. A boy with his whole future, supposedly unwritten, still ahead of him.

I didn't throw the rock, but I didn't put it down. All the rest of the way home I carried it, cradled it in the crook of my elbow as I unlocked the front door and dived inside. He waited at the bottom of the drive, as if politely making sure I'd gotten home safely. He stood out there a few minutes longer, then walked away.

"You can't save everyone," Helen said. I could tell she was still thinking about the woman in the driver's seat with the obliterated face. She'd shoved the napkin strips aside and started tearing the red-and-white-checked paper underneath her fish and chips.

When she said it as a nurse, it was true, but if I said it as a teacher, it would be sacrilege. Yet it's true, it's true, you can't save everyone. For years I thought that if I'd been the sun, the rain, the patient breath of kindness itself, maybe I could have brought him into flower. But now when I remember that moment in the woods, all I can think is that I should have thrown that rock. I should have thrown it as hard as I could, straight into his smiling face.

23 MONTHS

I met this guy at a party, is what happened. But that seems like a lousy way to start a story. I don't want anyone to get the wrong idea; the juicy part's not all that juicy. I arrived at the party alone and he told me about the pod people and I told him something I had never told anyone else and then I was home alone before two thirty. That's pretty much the shape of the thing.

The party. I counted twenty-one people when I got there. It was a funny number because you could tell Miranda had expected a lot more, and I felt a little embarrassed for her. A little glad too, because it was a new thing to see Miranda embarrassed. But twenty-one was enough to spread through the house and spill out onto the back patio with at least a few people in every place, so it didn't look so bad. I'd meant to show up at ten thirty, two hours late, so people would have had some drinks and be easier to talk to. But I got lost when I got off the freeway and ended up pulling in at eleven.

Miranda gave me a tour of the house, low and stucco with huge bathrooms. She had two roommates and it made me wish I knew people to move in with, to afford to rent a house like this. She introduced me to some of her friends. How brave, a few said, you came here on your own, how brave. And of course what they meant was *How sad*. How sad that you don't know anyone and had to come alone, a woman alone at a party, all dressed up and sipping half a glass of wine and is there anything sadder than that?

One of the bedrooms was almost bare, nothing but brown cardboard boxes and a double bed with a green comforter. "One of my roommates," Miranda said. "He's moving out next week."

"Where's he going?"

"Prison. For a while." She'd paused before saying it, but not too long, because it might be rude to tell tales on your roommates but it was also fun to have a great story, to be able to say, *My roommate's headed to prison*.

"What did he do?"

"He was in a car accident. He caused a car accident. But he hadn't been drinking."

"You go to prison for that?"

"His girlfriend died. They'd been driving to Tucson to visit her parents. He was speeding. A lot, I guess. Her parents asked for jail time."

I'd never been in the bedroom of someone who had killed someone else. "Is he here?" I asked.

"Out back, last I saw," Miranda said. "On the patio."

Isn't that something, I thought, *to be at a party with a guy who killed his girlfriend. Everybody eating and getting drunk and making nice, and there he is, that guy with the glass of Chianti, he killed his own lover.* I wanted to go find him. Talking to him seemed like a good way to spend the party, knowing a secret about somebody and that person not knowing you know and maybe telling you about it just because he wants to, because you're a girl he wants to tell things to.

"Thanks for the tour," I said, and Miranda asked me if I'd be okay schmoozing around on my own. She wasn't so bad, really. I could see that she'd let me stick close by her the whole night if I wanted to and she wouldn't try too hard to ditch me. It made me wish more people had come to her party.

Miranda and I weren't friends. We both worked for the Arizona Hospital and Healthcare Association. I had my own cubicle where I researched funding opportunities for member hospitals. It wasn't interesting. I had a cousin who had put in a good word for me at AHHA and I'd been hired over the phone a month earlier. The job hadn't been worth coming halfway across the country for. I wasn't all that good at it, and they probably wondered why they'd bothered to bring someone like me all the way from Minnesota when there were people like Miranda here in Phoenix who could do my job twice as well and who made sure everyone knew it. I don't care all that much about public health, really. I kind of feel like people should just look after themselves.

My cousin had me over to his house in Scottsdale when I first arrived. He's got a wife and two kids and a big house. After he'd gotten me a job and fed me dinner, I think he figured he'd pretty much done his duty by me, and I guess he had. He worked in a different part of the building and I never saw him. I checked the weather in Minneapolis online every day: 22 degrees, 17, 2, −5. It made me feel better about being where I was.

I walked back through the living room and kitchen and passed the food by. If you're the girl alone at a party, you don't want to be the girl alone at a party eating. The patio was just a long rectangle of concrete covered by a wooden roof with Christmas lights tacked all along the edge and a porch light on the wall beside the back door. Other than that, it was dark. Just beyond the edge of the patio the light gave out in an almost perfect line. Concrete and a few inches of grass and then darkness. There was no moon and I squinted to see the bodies standing out on the lawn, smoking. You could catch the lit red ends of cigarettes moving up and down. It was February and the weather was soft and warm and it was still strange to me, the way winter felt sweet in the desert. It had rained that afternoon and the air had a spiky, gray smell someone would finally tell me was damp creosote the week I left Arizona for good.

On the far left side of the patio, this guy was standing by himself, and I knew that it was the roommate, the accidental murderer. Nobody else came near, like he was quarantined. He had a quiet face, black hair. He was wearing jeans and a green T-shirt. If he'd been lying on his bed, he would have matched the comforter. The T-shirt was too big—the shoulder seams falling partway down his arms—and while he was probably just wearing an oversize T-shirt, it made me wonder if he'd been heavier once, if there was less of him now than there used to be. I was wearing a black dress and felt stupid. It was too formal for standing in a backyard with a plastic cup of wine.

I'd been a fat kid, which made me notice certain things, like the way people wore their clothes and the way the other white girls at the party were thin and hard and all one color, a tanned orangey brown. It made me notice people who were fat like I used to be and that made me feel good but also embarrassed, because I would think: *That's the way I used to look, that's the way I used to move, taking up too much room in the world.* I was glad I wasn't fat anymore. I liked being able to walk up to some guy, a nice-looking one, and stand beside him and feel like I had a right to be there.

I walked over to the roommate and said, "I'm Leah. I work with Miranda."

"Sasha," he said, which I'd always thought was a girl's name. He was leaning against the house, looking out at the yard.

I thought about saying, *I hear you killed your girlfriend.* Instead I said, "It's dark out there." I say a lot of dumb things.

"Yeah," Sasha said. "It's dark."

"How do you know Miranda? Or did someone else invite you?"

"I live here," he said.

"So you can tell me what the yard looks like," I said. "When it's not dark."

He thought about this for a while. "We have a trampoline."

"Yeah?"

"Yeah. You can't see it from here, but it's out there."

"Does it work?"

"Sure it works. It's a trampoline."

"The springs could be broken."

"They're not," he said, and I wondered if he was annoyed because I'd implied that his trampoline was all busted. He took a drink of his Newcastle. "There's a grapefruit tree too," he added. "Behind where they're smoking."

"Really," I said.

"Do you want some grapefruit?"

"No, thanks."

"Sure? Miranda and Sam don't like them. I've juiced some but the rest will just stay on the tree."

"Why not juice the rest? Shame to waste them."

"There's only so much grapefruit a guy can eat," he said, which wasn't what I was going for. *I know why they'll go uneaten,* I wanted to say. *I already know about you.*

"So holler if you decide you want some grapefruit. I'll grab you a plastic bag."

"Okay."

We stood there awhile. For a guy who had killed somebody, he wasn't very interesting. Someone had attached a phone to some little speakers on the patio picnic table. People kept walking by and changing the song.

"There's a garden out there too, or a place I think used to be a garden. The dirt's all turned under but none of us planted anything."

"You could plant stuff now."

"I don't think you're supposed to plant now. It'll get hot soon."

"I forget. The seasons are all backward here. Spring comes and everything starts to die."

"Where are you from?"

"Minneapolis."

"So I guess you got a lot of snow," he said.

"Yeah, I'm used to snow." I put my cup to my lips and tipped it back but it was empty. I swallowed anyway to make it look like I'd gotten something, but I forgot that the cup was clear.

Sasha was watching me and he seemed glad that my drink was so visibly gone, that I had to leave now to get another if I wanted something to sip on like a normal person.

"I'll just go get some more wine," I said. "You need anything?"

"I'm okay."

The back door opened into the kitchen, and the wine was lined up along the counter. The bottle I'd brought was half empty, the plastic cork stuck back inside. I poured a cup and read the magnetic poetry on the fridge. They seemed to have two sets of magnets, dog poetry and French poetry. *Dobermans sont grandes,* I read. *Vous mangez chew toys.* I wondered if there were poems they'd taken down, if they'd taken words like *car* and *road* and *girlfriend* and hidden them in a drawer somewhere until the day Sasha left and they could stop watching the things they wrote. If I'd taken Spanish in high school instead of French, I'd be in a whole different salary bracket with the AHHA now. *Je suis stupide.*

"I tried to mingle," I announced when I returned, even though I hadn't. Sasha was still standing where I'd left him. "It was a bust. I tried to take myself off your hands but I don't know anybody. Sorry."

"That's okay," he said in a tone of voice like it wasn't, really. "But I thought you were Miranda's friend."

"We just work together. Do you have a dog? You have magnetic dog poetry on your fridge."

"Miranda has a Lab. It's probably around here somewhere but it doesn't like crowds. It usually hides in the bathtub." He said it like he was jealous, as if he were tempted to go fight the dog for its bathtub and be alone.

The patio was getting crowded—people arguing over the music, a bunch of girls wanting to dance, and Miranda trying to keep things mellow. I was hoping Sasha would suggest we go somewhere else.

"You want to see something?" he asked.

"Sure."

"Follow me," he said, and stepped off the patio into the grass. I followed him, keeping his back in front of me, the person-shaped darkness that showed up against the dark of the yard. He didn't go far, just to the high wooden fence at the back of the property. We passed the trampoline, the smoking people, and the grapefruit tree. When the yard matched his description—trampoline, tree—I felt weirdly as though he'd confided in me, that he hadn't just been making small talk. It was quieter away from the house. "Wait here," he said and went behind a small shed that stood in the corner. He came back with a stepladder, kicked its legs out so it stood flush against the fence. "Climb up, look over," he said, and I set my wine down in the grass beside the ladder. I thought he'd maybe take my hand, touch my arm or my back to steady me, but he didn't.

There was a narrow dirt alley behind the house, black

trash cans and blue recycling bins lined up along either side. It smelled warm and dirty, food softening in plastic bags, animals staking out their territories. The only light came from a streetlamp at the end of the block, dim and orange, and a floodlight in the yard across the alley. Sitting behind the neighbor's fence was an enormous silver pod, like an old Airstream trailer but slicker, no seams or antennas or visible doors or windows. Just smooth metal walls, a trailer-size lima bean. It had a circular hole in its top left side. The branches of a tree poked through, lit from underneath. The tree was green, not just the leaves, but the bark, the funny green-skinned trees they had here.

"What is it?" I asked.

"The neighbors are architects, built their own pod. There was a thing about them in the paper and a whole feature in some architecture magazine."

"They live in it?"

They slept there, he said. They used the kitchen and bathroom in their regular house, but they'd knocked out the remaining walls—anything that wasn't load-bearing—to make an enormous studio.

"It doesn't seem very comfortable. Living in a pod."

"I think you'd either bake or freeze. And then when you wake up, you have to go outside just to take a piss and start some coffee."

"What's the point?" I asked.

"Search me," he said, and he smiled just a little.

"They make cool neighbors, at least. I should come to more parties here."

"Miranda and Sam are moving when the lease is up.

They're looking for a place for just the two of them. No more pod people."

"You could find new roommates." I was still on the ladder, fingers hooked over the tops of the fence boards. They were rough and smelled damp and I knew I'd have the smell on my hands, of soaked wood and splintery fence.

"I won't be here when the lease runs out."

"Where will you be?" I asked.

"Prison," he said, but he looked so sad to say it that coaxing it out of him wasn't much of a victory.

"What did—it's none of my business."

"Reckless driving. Someone died. Twenty-three months."

"I'm sorry," I said.

"I'm sorrier. But then I guess that's the point."

"When do you leave?"

"Day after tomorrow. Yesterday was my last day at work. I drop my stuff by the storage place tomorrow and then report Monday morning for—whatever."

I asked if he was scared and he said he was. "I'm sorry," I said. "For being so nosy."

"I don't want to leave," he said. "Is that wrong? That I don't want to go?" He was staring straight ahead into the fence, the cracks between the boards seeping light from the pod planet onto his face.

"No," I said. "I don't think so."

"I think I'm supposed to welcome it. I'm supposed to do my penance and be graceful about it, but I—I feel like I've already been punished. And she's gone, regardless. She's just gone."

I was a little disappointed in him, that my murderer was

so selfish, that what he really wanted was just his life back. It didn't seem like a very worthwhile confession. I wondered what I should say to him next, if it should be comforting or something sharp, to remind him of his crimes.

"And Miranda's having a goddamn party. She said she'd had it planned for ages when my reporting date got pushed back. Then she said she wanted to throw me a going-away thing, but it's not like I want everyone Miranda's ever met to know."

"So it's a secret going-away thing where no one knows you're going away."

"They probably know. They probably all know, everyone at this party," he said, and he looked at me like he was so thankful, so grateful that I was a stranger. "They're out of town, the pod people," he said. "Asked us to pick up their mail for the weekend."

"You guys? All the way around the block?"

"There's a gate. We're the closest neighbors if you cross the alley."

I waited for him to offer to take me, because why else had he told me the pod people were gone, but he stayed quiet. "I'd like to see it up close," I said finally. "The pod planet. If you don't think they'd mind."

"I think it would be okay. Wait a minute." He headed back to the house and all of a sudden I felt silly standing on top of the ladder at the edge of the yard by myself. I could hear someone being sick near the grapefruit tree. Sasha came back with a bottle of wine, two cups. He held his right hand out flat and bounced his palm up and down so a set of keys jingled.

"For the gate?"

"The house and the pod. I can give you a tour."

We crossed into their yard and shut the gates behind us. The door frame of the pod was marked with puckered ridges of welded steel, and it had a little round, flat lock like a car door. Inside was a single room with curving silver walls, a futon mattress on the floor beside the palo verde tree. The bedding was all hospital white, blinding; Sasha and I sat on the end of the mattress and I took up fistfuls of the duvet while he poured the wine.

"Down," I said. "The comforter and pillows. Real birds in the bedding."

"Architecture must pay okay," he said, and we got drunk for a while. We were pod people in our thin-shelled home, the walls shivering a little with the noise from the party. We owned a green-skinned tree and bedding so full of feathers it could fly off on its own. At some point we put down our cups and lay down on our backs, side by side.

"Are you seeing anyone?" Sasha asked me, and I thought it was kind of a weird question, because in two days it couldn't matter to him whether I was or wasn't. He wouldn't be in a position to see anybody.

"Not really."

"What does that mean?"

"Someone in Minneapolis. But only sort of."

"We don't have to do anything."

"I know. I'd like to," I said, and reached my hand out so it touched his, and our arms made a V on the bed between us.

"Why?" He didn't sound like he was fishing for a

compliment. He sounded tired and confused, like I was one more thing at this moment in his life that didn't make any sense.

"I don't know. Give you a send-off?"

"You've got a guy in Minnesota."

"He hit me," I said, and in that moment, Sasha, the sad-sack murderer with the grapefruit tree, became the only person I'd ever told. "My cousin got me a job out here. Just to get away for a while."

"You're going back?"

"Maybe."

"You shouldn't."

"You're saying that because you're supposed to. You've watched a bunch of domestic-violence PSAs."

"Still. You shouldn't go back."

"What if I deserved it?"

"I'm sure you didn't."

"You don't know that. I'm not a very nice person."

"I'm sure that's not true," he said, and he pulled his hand out from under mine so he could pet me with it, just brushing over my knuckles, down my wrist, smoothing the little staticky hairs on my arms.

"It is," I said, and I rolled toward him, closed the V of our arms into a long straight line.

Neither of us said anything else for a few minutes, just did the usual things, the kissing and the fumbling with each other's clothes, and before Sasha pressed inside me he asked, "Is this okay?" and I nodded.

I waited for a couple more minutes, his forearms under my shoulders and his face a little sweaty and his ear right above my lips and then I whispered to him that I'd known all along. "Miranda told me," I said. "When I got here. She told me about your girlfriend."

Sasha raised his head and stared at me, betrayed, and for an instant I wanted to brush his sad hair out of his sad eyes and take it all back. Then he closed his eyes and kept moving, hard, like he couldn't let go or didn't want to, and he went on so long I started to hurt. "You knew," he said, pushing, angry. "The whole time."

"The whole time."

"Maybe you did deserve it. When your boyfriend hit you."

Sasha finished and rolled away from me so that our heads were on separate pillows. I turned to look at him but he was staring at the ceiling, and his nose was longer, sharper in profile than I'd thought it was.

"I think I did," I said. "And if that's true, then it means he didn't do anything wrong."

"Maybe you should go back."

"Maybe I should," I said, but I was still lying beside Sasha when he said, "I meant you should leave."

"Oh. Okay."

I got up, started pulling my dress back on. He tugged the duvet up over his legs and watched me. I stacked the empty cups beside the bottle and found my left shoe beside the tree, the toe edging over the hole in the trailer floor above the spreading roots. I was standing at the door, my hand on what looked like the stainless-steel handle to a refrigerator, when Sasha asked me, "Do you still love him?"

"I think so. I want to."

"Then maybe you do go back. To Minnesota. Maybe you shouldn't fuck things up."

"Thanks," I said, and pushed my way out of the pod and down the steps to the yard. The door fell shut behind me and as soon as my eyes adjusted to the light I was walking through the grassy yard of the pod planet to the driveway, down to the sidewalk, and around the block to my car. The party drifted in and out of earshot, snatches of music and laughter and conversation. I was scared to be driving, worried about cops and the way the world spun a little when I turned my head, how the lights along the freeway were haloed with a furry glow. I was glad to make it home.

I woke up with a bruise in the middle of my forehead, plum round and tender to the touch, and it took me until Sunday evening to realize it was from pressing my head too hard against the tap while being sick in the bathroom sink.

Two months later I quit my job with AHHA, and two weeks after that I moved back to Minnesota. Miranda and I never became friends, and we didn't pretend we'd stay in touch. I never knew Sasha's last name or the names of the pod people, and I wouldn't be able to find that house again if you flew me into Phoenix and gave me a rental car, Google Maps, and a month.

When Sasha got out of prison I was shoveling snow, sharing a bed with a man I told myself I wasn't afraid of anymore. I told myself everything was fine again, and it became mostly true and stayed mostly true for four mostly good years. I never told him about Sasha. There were a lot of things I never told him, which was maybe part of our problems, but someone told me once that I seemed like a better person when I kept my mouth shut. It sounds mean, but it was pretty good advice.

I figure it works the other way too, though—that if you *are* going to tell a story, you should try to make it good, make yourself look nice. So the pod-people story, I've already decided if I ever tell it to anyone how it should go. How I arrived in Phoenix unattached and outgoing, brought bagels and coffee to the girls in the office my first week and made friends with them all. How Miranda even asked me to come early to her party to help set up and how I brought little hors d'oeuvres from Trader Joe's and warmed them in the oven and they were a big hit. How I'd already read about the pod people in *Architectural Digest*, because I read that kind of thing. How I didn't even get tipsy before Sasha and I went to the pod planet and how the sex when we got there was lunar. And then we didn't say anything afterward, nothing at all, didn't try to be funny or mean or smart. Just slept all wound up together in our own private cell, my head on his shoulder and his arm not even tingly when he pulled it from under my waist in the morning. We woke up together on the pod planet, I'll say, and it was fine and happy and fearless, to be a pod woman with her lover, woken by the sun slanting through the branches of a palo verde tree.

And then I'll say, "The end," and it'll be a story sweeter than the truth.

BETTER NOT
TELL YOU NOW

Daisy picking daisies, is how it all started. We were sitting outside the cafeteria, early spring, and wildflowers sprinting out of the overgrown soccer fields. Goldenrod and Queen Anne's lace and daisies, white with soft-boiled yellow centers. We finished our sandwiches and fidgeted in the grass. Daisy dismantled a flower, playing he-loves-me, he-loves-me-not. The final petal was he-loves-me-not, so we told her the stem could count too, that she should toss the flower over her shoulder to end on he-loves-me.

We didn't think the stem really counted, but we also really thought he loved her. Daisy and Brett were one of those high-school couples who seemed to actually mean something, like each of them might, at sixteen years old, have stumbled on the person they'd be twenty alongside, and forty, and eighty. We'd seen the way they looked at each other, heard how they said "Love you" unselfconsciously in the hallways. "That flower," we told Daisy. "It doesn't know what it's talking about."

But that afternoon, during fifth-period U.S. history, he stopped loving her.

As quick as that. There was a test on the Spanish-American War that they'd studied for together, divvying up the questions and arranging a system to share answers during the exam. As the teacher patrolled the rows of desks, Daisy tapped Brett's shoulder with her pencil, increasingly desperate for the date of the Battle of San Juan Hill. Finally he passed her a folded scrap of paper, but all it said was to meet him in the parking lot after school. "I think we should be friends," he told her there, leaning against the Econoline van where they'd had sex for the first time. The very first time, for both of them. "If you want. But I don't think we should see each other anymore."

"I love you," she said nakedly.

He shrugged. "I loved you. I just don't, anymore. I don't know what happened, but I don't."

We spent days trying to analyze Brett—his heartlessness, his sudden, mystifying cruelty. "I just can't believe it," Daisy said, and we shook our heads in commiseration, as if shock and heartbreak were emotions we could simply refuse. But we felt foolish for talking about *belief* when we spotted Brett's varsity jacket in another girl's locker two weeks later. We broke the news to Daisy during lunch, while we sat in the grass outside the cafeteria; Brett was just an ordinary cheater, it turned out. We thought she'd be relieved.

"I don't understand when it would have happened," she argued. "We were together every day after school." The last of the wildflowers were all around us, crinkling and browning in the sun. Daisy kept her hands in her lap.

We tried to find other things to talk about during lunches. We bought sodas from the vending machines and brought sandwiches from home, and we worried about Callie, who ate nothing all day except a single piece of fruit. One day, bored, Zora twisted Callie's apple off its stem. I started to count the twists. "A, B, C, D"—we chanted nearly all the way through the alphabet until the stem gave way, at X, and we groaned—the worst letter, almost impossible, the odds astronomical that Zora would ever marry anyone whose name began with X.

"Well, I'm named Zora," she said. "So anything's possible."

In sixth-period biology that day, her teacher introduced a new transfer student named Xavier and assigned him to be Zora's lab partner. She met us that afternoon by our lockers, her eyes as wide as petri dishes. "I can't hang out today," she said. "I have a date."

They went to his house in the afternoons and to the movies or the mall on weekends, and we disliked him a little because we almost never saw Zora anymore. But she seemed happy. Then she asked us to skip class one morning and meet her in the third-floor bathroom, where she had a pregnancy test shoplifted from CVS. She didn't want to do it at home. She wasn't sure how to hide the box from her parents, and she didn't want to be alone when she found out what she already knew.

"You don't have to marry him," we told her. "You don't have to have the baby. You don't have to do anything you don't want to."

But they got engaged during finals week. For Zora's bridal shower, her mother requested practical, if depressing, gifts—bottles and diapers and rash cream to prepare for the baby. Nothing for Zora. "Xavier didn't even want me to keep it," she told us when her mother went to the kitchen to cut slices of cake. We didn't know what to say.

We left her house and drove to the Dairy Queen to be girls again, to sit on the picnic tables and sing songs from the spring choir concert. We played would-you-rather and truth-or-dare. Isabel had a notebook in her car, and I wrote out a MASH game. I left off the traditional categories predicting the husbands we'd grow up to have and the number of children. To a list of possible houses, I added jobs, pets, luxury possessions. We wanted ridiculous, impossible futures. We drew numbers, calculated the results.

"Ugh," Isabel said. "I'm supposed to end up as a janitor in a shack."

"But at least you have a swimming pool." We pointed it out on the page.

She called us that night in tears. Her parents had met her at the front door, sat her on the couch to talk. Her father had lost his job months ago, and there'd been no year-end bonus. He'd finally found new work, but it paid a third of his old salary. They'd been hoping not to worry Isabel, hoping the numbers would all work out somehow, but they hadn't made a payment on the house since January. The bank had come today to take photos.

"But where are we supposed to go?" Isabel asked.

"Your grandmother," they said. She had a guesthouse in her backyard. Isabel knew the place. Peeling paint, leaky roof, bushes so overgrown the branches had reached under the siding and started to pry it off. As children, she and her cousins had dared one another to peer inside the scummy windows. The guesthouse sat beside an old empty swimming pool stained green with algae and mildew. "We told her you'll help out around her house this summer," Isabel's parents added. "You know it's hard for her to keep things clean anymore. She's being very good to us, to let us stay."

On the phone, Isabel didn't even have to say it. *Swimming pool. Janitor. Shack.*

One night in July, we picked her up, since her car had been sold, and went to the county fair. All of us except Callie ate elephant ears, and then all of us went on the Vomit Comet, even Zora. Daisy saw Brett there with his new girlfriend, so to distract her we paid extra to see the Beast, which turned out to be just a mummified goat. Next to the Beast was a trailer painted to look like an old gypsy caravan with LADY LUELLA'S TAROT written on the side. We dared Callie to go in.

We'd refused to learn our lesson, because to be afraid of fortune-telling meant that we really believed our fortunes could be told. It meant that our futures were somewhere waiting for us, traps already baited and set. It meant that when I sat in my bedroom at night and asked my Magic 8-Ball if I would get into Dartmouth and it said, *Outlook not so good,* that was the truth. Or when I asked if there was anyone at school who liked me, and it said, *My sources say no,* those sources were correct. "Boys *or* girls," I whispered, either girls who knew they liked girls or girls like me who weren't sure of what they wanted. *Very doubtful,* it still said. "What *do* I want?" I asked, but that was not the kind of question a Magic 8-Ball could answer.

I'd asked the same questions over and over, collecting replies so I wouldn't put too much faith in any one answer. I'd twisted the 8-Ball back and forth so often that bubbles had appeared in the dyed liquid, collecting against the window, nearly obscuring the fortunes. I squinted through the foam, and then I churned up more. I wanted to know everything, and I didn't.

"Don't be a wimp," I dared Callie, and I gave her the ten dollars for the tarot reading so she had one less reason to say no.

She was inside the trailer for what felt like forever, and when she came out she wouldn't speak. She had tears running down her face, and Daisy had to bring her tissue from a Porta Potti. "I just want to go home," Callie said, and since she'd driven us, we all went with her. She dropped off Isabel, and Daisy, and Zora, and that left just me. Callie and I had been friends since elementary school, before we met the other girls, back when she still ate Pop-Tarts and French fries and wore oversize T-shirts. I hoped she'd tell me what Lady Luella had said. But after Zora got out, she didn't even give me time to climb from the back seat to the front before speeding to my house. She pulled into the driveway and waited for me to get out.

"Whatever the woman said," I told her, "it's not true. It's not real."

Callie made eye contact with me in the rearview mirror, and her stare looked like an animal's, stunned still in the middle of a road. Whatever was coming would crash straight into her, and she wasn't going to do anything to try and stop it.

That fall Callie was still eating nothing but fruit, and she was cut from the field hockey team when she didn't have the stamina to make it through practices. Her calves were sticks, her knees swelling like apples above the high, white socks. Her parents took her out of school and put her in a clinic. We visited and asked her again what Lady Luella had told her. She folded her arms across her chest and shook her head. Her lips were cracked and dry. Over winter break, when her parents brought her home for Christmas, she swallowed an entire bottle of sleeping pills. They didn't find her in time.

In my bedroom, I held the Magic 8-Ball until it was sweaty in my hands. "Are you there?" I asked the hard, opaque top, pressing my forehead against the plastic. The central heat kicked on, and air whistled out of my bedroom vent, a lick of hot breath. "Did Lady Luella tell you this would happen?" I slowly turned the 8-Ball over.

Reply hazy, try again

"Did you make it happen because she said it would?"

Reply hazy, try again

"Is this my fault?"

Better not tell you now

★   ★   ★

We met in January in my basement, Daisy and Isabel and I. Isabel's family had moved out of the shack and into an apartment, but it was in a different school district, and we didn't see much of her anymore. We'd invited Zora, but the baby was just a few weeks old, and she didn't feel she could leave for an evening. Plus, she said, she was done with the witchy stuff, the fortunes. She didn't want her baby touched by any part of it.

We got a Ouija board out of the closet. Isabel tore three sheets of paper from her notebook. We each wrote a question.

"It's your Ouija board," Daisy said. "You choose what to ask first."

"You're guests," I said. "You choose."

"You," Isabel said. "You always liked this kind of stuff."

I opened the folded papers. Daisy had written, *Are we making this happen?* Isabel had written, *Can the future be changed?* I couldn't imagine showing them what I'd written: *Dartmouth? Girlfriend?* My selfish, private, fragile future. I crumpled all the papers together and set them aside.

We put our hands on the plastic planchette. Isabel and I accidentally brushed knuckles and we both jumped. The room was vibrating. I thought about what I most wanted to know. "Can you promise us we'll be happy?" I asked.

The planchette shivered but did not slide. In silence, we stared at the board, at our own fingers. We looked into one another's eyes. We knew how this game worked. We waited, hoping the planchette would slowly creep toward *yes*. We waited, wanting one of us to begin to lie.

CHANCE ME

J ust," his son corrected him at the airport. "Just 'Just.'"

Bond, James Bond, Harry thought. Like they were starring in a rip-off action flick and not the road-trip buddy comedy he'd been hoping for. "Harry, Harry Krier," he said, holding out his palm for an ironic handshake.

"*I know,*" Just said, horrified. "I know your *name.*"

"I know! I know you know. It was a joke." Harry had insisted on meeting his son at baggage claim rather than at the curb outside, but now he was dismayed at all the witnesses. Also, Just didn't have any luggage. Only a ratty backpack slung over one shoulder. Harry went in for a hug instead of the handshake. Just raised his arms, awkwardly returning the embrace, and Harry caught a whiff of body odor. His son had grown tall enough that Harry's nose was armpit height. Willow had been tall, Harry remembered. Willow had been an Amazon. Maybe she still was.

After fifteen years without seeing Just, Harry had steeled himself for almost any physical manifestation of his son, for Just to look exactly like his mother, Willow, or exactly like Harry himself. He was ready to be bludgeoned with memory, or guilt, or joy. But Just was a nearly blank slate—brown hair and eyes, a body that gave no hint of what its occupant used it for, no swimmer's shoulders or runner's wiriness. Jeans and sneakers and a plain black T-shirt. *Such an ordinary boy*, Harry thought, and the words seemed heartless, but not the emotion. Whole and healthy and ordinary. He could deserve no better fortune. He didn't even deserve that.

"Sorry," Just said, breaking the hug. "I probably need to shower."

"You're fine," Harry said. "You're perfect."

Commentary on the flight (okay), the autumn weather (chilly, gray), and the traffic (heavy) got them out of Logan and onto I-90 heading toward Brookline.

"There are a lot of Dunkin' Donuts here," Just observed, looking out the car window.

"Do you want to stop for anything?"

"No. I was just saying. There's a lot."

"I thought we'd have dinner at home, if that's okay. Miriam's picking something up."

"That's fine," Just said, and he asked Harry how he and Miriam had met.

"I sold her a condo." After closing, they'd gone out for a celebratory drink. Six months later he'd moved into the condo with her. There was no stipulation against this in the National Association of Realtors bylaws. Second marriage for her. First for him, technically.

"Do I want to know what *technically* means?" Miriam had asked.

"I was very young," he'd said, and the truth of this had hit him with unexpected force—a load of bricks, a piano out a window. He'd been very young when he was living in Arcosanti with Willow, and he wasn't any longer, and he never would be again. Wherever else his life might take him, it would not take him back there, to the red desert hills and the bleached sheet of sky snapped open every morning above them, their baby squalling in a hand-painted cardboard box. Now that baby was sitting in his Lexus, six feet tall and applying to Harvard.

On the phone, Willow had rattled off names like she was reading an online list of Boston-area colleges, not just Harvard, MIT, Tufts, but the off-brand schools out-of-staters never applied to, like Lesley, Suffolk, Simmons. "I thought Simmons was a girls' school," Harry had said. "I mean, women's. A women's college." Was his son transgender and no one had bothered to mention it to him?

"He's still narrowing down the list," Willow had said. "There's a school counselor who helps."

Harry hadn't realized that tiny Jerome, Arizona, even had a high school. After Arcosanti, Willow had ended up in a mining town turned vertiginous ghost town turned artist colony / tourist trap. She'd bought a house and a metalworking studio for almost nothing because it was at geologic risk of sliding off the mountain. Uninsurable, but she hadn't cared. She'd sent photographs of Just posed with the lawn ornaments she made and sold; birdhouses on sticks were popular.

"He buses to Cottonwood," Willow said, like she could hear what Harry was thinking. "It's a good school. Pretty good, I guess."

"It'll have to be if he's applying to Harvard," Harry said, pointlessly.

"Look, everyone understands how competitive it is. Can he stay with you or not?"

Harry hadn't wanted the conversation to go this way. He felt like no conversation he'd ever had with Willow had gone the way he'd meant it to. "Of course he can stay."

"He just needs a place to sleep. He can get himself to the campus visits on the subway. Right? I think that's right." Her voice was suddenly uncertain.

She'd never lived in a town with more than five hundred people, he remembered. Neither had their son. "I'll show him around," Harry said. "I'll take time off work."

"You don't have to." Willow never told him he *had* to do anything. She hadn't made him the bad guy. He was the no-guy. Not the villain, just written out of the script entirely, and he'd let her do it. Miriam had rented that movie with Daniel Day-Lewis, the one where his character screams, "I abandoned my child! I abandoned my boy!" *At least that guy abandoned the little deaf boy to become an oil baron,* Harry thought. *I abandoned my boy to become a real estate agent.* The saddest movie never made. Or maybe it was a road-trip buddy movie after all, now that Just was finally here, and the real movie of Harry's life had simply had a very, very long setup.

Harry had first encountered Arcosanti as a single slide in a darkened college classroom. The freshman course was a year long and quixotic, lectures three times a week on subjects like "the urban consciousness." Paolo Soleri's work came after images of Babylon and Alexandria, Levittown and Detroit, and immediately after a slide with a big question mark on it, symbolizing, the professor felt the need to explain, how no one knew what the future of cities would hold. The next image was an architectural drawing of insane complexity, a palace of tunnels and arches, pencil lines so fine and densely clustered, the city looked woven. Harry felt an immediate sense of loss when the instructor clicked it away. The drawing felt like the maps that appeared on the frontispieces of all his favorite novels, a key to an alternate world, its promise of transport. He used interlibrary loan to get hold of all Soleri's books, even *The Omega Seed: An Eschatological Hypothesis* and *The Bridge Between Matter and Spirit Is Matter Becoming Spirit*. At a copy shop, he had the drawing made into a poster, blown up until the lines bled, the city an unraveling skein of wool. No, not a city—an *arcology*, a system that functions so perfectly with and for its inhabitants that the place and people become a single living organism. "Like a snail in its shell," an acolyte explained on the first day of the summer workshop Harry signed up for at Arcosanti, an experimental arcology being built in the desert north of Phoenix.

Soleri lived south in Paradise Valley, coming to Arcosanti only for master classes, which sometimes felt like the only class; most of the workshop turned out to be manual labor, digging foundations or pouring concrete or repairing the buildings that had already stood long enough to start crumbling. Arcosanti had been founded in 1970, and a quarter century later the future had not materialized. The towering arches from Harry's drawing were covered in peeling paint. The round, porthole-style windows, a Soleri trademark, made the buildings look like concrete ships, a fleet that had set sail for the future and run aground in rough weather. The nicest building was the cafeteria, where tourists could join the residents for communal meals. Upstairs was the gift shop, where tourists could buy metal wind chimes forged on-site. This income, plus workshoppers' tuition fees, financed the city.

"But isn't arcology also about humans taking responsibility for our own relationship to the natural world?" a girl asked that first day of the workshop. She did not bother to raise her hand. "I feel like a snail's not the best metaphor. I mean, a snail's got no *agency*."

She was white with blond hair braided into cornrows that left pale furrows of scalp exposed and rapidly reddening in the sun. Despite this, Harry thought she was beautiful. She was wearing steel-toed boots, overalls, and a sports bra, her body underneath rangy and tan. She was sexy, although this was a word Harry's brain gained the confidence to use only after they'd actually had sex, after the miracle of Willow choosing him out of all the architecture students and career-changers and spiritual seekers in the workshop.

Miriam had picked up sushi on her way home from work. Harry knew it was meant to be a treat—it was from the best place in the neighborhood—but seeing how carefully Just observed them mixing wasabi into soy sauce, Harry guessed that Just had never had sushi before.

"If you don't like it, we'll get something else," he assured Just.

"It's fine," Just said and gamely thrust a raw shrimp in his mouth.

Harry felt proud, then ashamed—nothing his son did was anything Harry could take credit for.

"So why Harvard?" Miriam asked.

"That's the one school nobody ever asks that about," Just said. "It's Harvard."

"But what makes it somewhere you want to go?"

"It's Harvard?"

Miriam gave him a confused look. "You need an answer to that before your interview."

"It's a group thing. Like, an informational presentation. Individual interviews are with alumni in your region."

"There's a Harvard alum living in Jerome?"

"Prescott. About an hour."

"Still. They're everywhere."

"Like roaches," Harry contributed.

"Preparing Earth for the alien invasion," Miriam said, "when they'll team up with our new extraterrestrial over-lords."

Just looked at them as if this conversation were causing him physical pain. Harry supposed it might be. He tried to remember being eighteen.

"You should have a question ready to ask," Miriam said. "If there's time for Q and A."

She was really throwing herself into this college-counseling thing, Harry thought. He wondered if she were wishing she had her own child to go through this. But no kid of theirs would be anywhere near college age. If she'd gotten pregnant the very first time they'd ever had sex, the kid would still be learning to read. And Miriam had talked about it that very first time in her direct way—not just pills or condoms but how she didn't want children, then or ever. "Me neither," he'd said. He'd omitted mentioning that he already had one.

"What majors are you interested in?"

"Miriam. Leave the grilling to the admissions people."

"I wasn't grilling, I was making conversation." *Making* it, manufacturing it, because it wasn't happening naturally.

"Not everyone's born knowing what they want to do. Just you."

"What do you do?" Just asked her, *making* conversation, except that now Miriam would think Harry had never bothered to tell Just one single thing about her.

"I've told you that," Harry protested.

"I'm a lawyer," Miriam said, and Harry knew the fact she didn't specify what kind meant she didn't think Just was savvy enough to understand or care.

"That was what you always wanted to do?"

"My parents watched a lot of TV-lawyer shows. I thought I'd get to make lots of speeches."

"So you're in litigation?" Just asked. Miriam nodded, surprised, and Harry wanted to cheer.

"Knowing what you want out of life, it's a superpower," Harry joked. "Rarer than radioactive-spider bites."

"So in the absence of spider bites, you joined a cult?" Miriam sniped.

"You were in a cult?" Just asked with sudden interest,

not understanding that Miriam was talking about the place his parents had met, the town he'd been born in.

"It wasn't a cult," Harry said. But it had been, a little. The least effective cult in the world, making you dig holes and eat generic peanut butter until all your illusions were crushed. He'd been looking for the jobs that weren't on television, he thought. He'd been looking for the secret options he was sure existed. But there weren't options, not really. TV had it pretty well covered. He didn't want to think the world was like that for everybody, but it had been like that for him.

"I don't see how he's competitive for Harvard," Miriam whispered that night in bed.

Harry flicked the sheets aside before he got in, to see what she was wearing. Nothing, as usual. She wasn't going to let Just's presence in the guest room change that. Hopefully, Just wouldn't change anything else between them either. Harry stripped off his own pajama pants.

"It's cold," Miriam complained and pulled the covers back up as he climbed in.

"You've only known him for four hours," Harry protested.

"Four long, monosyllabic hours."

"He's a teenager. They're all like that," Harry said with false authority.

"Not the ones who get into Harvard or MIT."

"Look, I can't say whether his mom's had a realistic conversation with him about it, but there's no way to ask without making everything worse. I'm not proud that I don't know enough about my own son to tell whether this whole college-visit trip is deluded, but I don't."

"Okay," Miriam said. They were both still whispering or her voice might've lowered with surrender. With tenderness, Harry thought as she brushed his hair off his forehead. He reached for her hip under the covers. She was bony in a deliberate way, sleek as a greyhound. They didn't even try to work out together because he couldn't keep pace with her on her runs. He wasn't soft, exactly, but he was softer than her.

He'd been softer than Willow too. Even after his summer of hard labor, she'd looked like she could break him. Willow was his first, and it took him years to understand that much of what he thought he'd been learning about sex, or about women, were things unique to that summer: the layer of concrete dust their sweat lacquered to their unshaved bodies; the calluses over her hip bones where her tool belt rubbed; the challenge of fitting themselves onto the bunk beds in the plywood dormitories or behind the shelves at the wind-chime foundry; lying on a blanket in the desert at night, stars flickering above them as the temperature dropped and they both pretended they weren't cold. Maybe Willow hadn't been. She'd seemed superhuman, impervious to discomfort or doubt. This was why he hadn't believed her when she'd told him she was pregnant. It seemed like a mistake her body wouldn't make. He'd thought she was joking.

"Are we naming it Paolo? Or Soleri?"

"Fuck you. This isn't fucking funny."

"Oh. No, it wouldn't be."

"Wouldn't?"

If it were happening to someone else, he was thinking. Which it must be, because surely it wasn't happening to them. But her face convinced him that maybe it was. He was still groping for the right way to ask whether she planned to keep it when she answered his question.

"We'll stay," she said. "We'll raise the baby here."

"What do you think of the costume?" Just asked in the morning over bagels and cream cheese, gesturing to his clothes. Miriam had already left for work. Just was wearing slip-on brown shoes, khakis, and a red polo shirt. "Do I look right?"

Costume? That implied Harry knew what Just dressed like normally, which he didn't. "Honestly?" Harry said. "You look like you work at Target."

Just looked down at himself, then got up from the table without a word. Poor kid, Harry thought, alone with his mom out there in the desert, has barely seen a Target. Maybe he isn't allowed to shop there, at the big-box stores. Maybe it's all thrift shops and farmers' markets. Just returned in a forest-green polo. "Is this the uniform for anything?"

"Dick's Sporting Goods? Bennigan's, maybe? But I don't think there are any more Bennigan's. I think they all went out of business."

"So the shirt's safe?"

"I'd say so."

Compared with the other prospective students' outfits in the MIT admissions office, Just's costume turned out to be marginal. He wasn't painfully underdressed, but most of the others wore button-downs. There were almost no backpacks, and none were as ratty as Just's. He'd unpacked since the airport, and the deflated bag sagged off his shoulder.

"Do you want me to take that?" Harry asked. "Leave it in the car?"

Just declined the offer, clutching the strap like a security blanket.

One poor child had a sweater-vest and a puffy insulated lunch bag. Harry felt a flutter of relief—he was doing better than that kid's father, at least. There were more girls than Harry had expected, wearing shorter skirts than he'd expected, and he felt creepy watching all the teenage legs.

"I'm doing the shadow-a-student program after the info session," Just reminded him. "You can still meet me after lunch?"

"I've got a showing scheduled nearby, but I'll be back in time."

"Great. I've got your number in my phone," Just said. "I should go get a seat."

Harry could tell he was being dismissed. The reception area was emptying as students filed into a nearby room. But it wasn't just students. "There are parents going too," Harry said. He'd meant it to come out as a disinterested observation, but he could hear his own neediness.

From the look on Just's face, his son heard it too. "Sorry. I didn't realize other people could come. And now you've got that showing scheduled."

Other people. That's how far Just was from calling him

Dad; he wouldn't even put Harry in the category of *parents*.

The possibility of living year-round in Arcosanti had dogged the workshoppers all session as both promise and threat. Workshoppers had to be officially invited to become residents, but none of them knew who made the decision or by what criteria. At first, Harry had thought perhaps Soleri took notes during the weekly classes, peering into their souls. By the end of the summer, he suspected one of the beady-eyed foundation reps was looking through their financial declarations to see whose families might donate the most. By then, most of the acolytes were tired of the labor, of the food, of one another. They wanted to go home and feel, from a safe distance, like they'd contributed something, like they'd watered a pale green shoot so tender that it was nobody's fault if it failed to thrive. Soleri was just too far ahead of his time. The foundation couldn't build Arcosanti any faster without big donors, and big donors did not line up to support revolution. Actually taking up residence in Arcosanti seemed to Harry like believing in something that had already been lost, like pledging oneself to the Temple of Apollo while knowing the Christians were coming to raze it.

"I didn't realize you could just turn it on and off like that," Willow said. "Belief." She'd grown up in the Pacific Northwest on a succession of live-off-the-land efforts that all went sour: goats, organic tomatoes, mushrooms cultivated with a secondhand marijuana-grow setup. Then her parents gave up on the mushrooms and started growing marijuana—the kind of thing no one gets in real trouble for, they assured her, until they did, and she lived with a grandfather in Olympia until her mother got paroled. By the time Willow came to Arcosanti, her parents were living in a clothing-optional eco-village outside Bellingham.

"They're in it for the long haul," Willow told him once. He hadn't been quite sure what she meant, but he'd liked that she thought he was the kind of person who would know. He was flattered and in love. Maybe he loved her in the way only a nineteen-year-old loves somebody, but most nineteen-year-olds don't know there are other ways to love. And he still wanted to love their city. He wanted to look at Arcosanti and see what she saw, not the ruin of something, but its beginning.

At the residential interview the foundation rep asked about the tenets of arcology, then whether Harry and Willow understood that they would be classified as volunteers and paid only a modest stipend beyond room and board.

"We're in this," Harry said, "for the long haul."

Miriam called to check in. Harry answered his phone in his car, waiting in front of a property he could already tell the buyer wasn't going to want. He knew before he shared it that a description of the morning would rile Miriam, but as soon as she started in—"Does he know the difference between MIT and ITT Tech? Did he see the TV ads and get confused?"—he felt disloyal for having said anything. "Lay off him," he told Miriam. "Please."

"Okay, sorry. But I had an idea this morning: What if it's all a pretext? Maybe he knows perfectly well that he won't get into these schools, but he needed an excuse to come see you."

"He didn't need an excuse for that."

"But maybe he felt like he did. To tell Willow, maybe."

"She would have let him come."

"Would she?"

No, not when Just was younger. She would have been too worried that Harry wouldn't send him back. And neither of them had had the money for travel. But more recently? Just could simply have asked. He didn't need to playact an entire college trip. It was both flattering and ugly — that Just might have invented a pretext to see him; that Just thought he needed one. It inflated Harry's heart and cracked it all at once. Like having children, Harry thought. This was what it felt like from the moment they were born. He'd forgotten how it was, the light and the shadow. Still there, after all these years, his capacity to be destroyed.

"I thought you were named Justin, officially," he told his son at a café in Kendall Square. Turkey sandwich and a Coke for Harry, coffee for Just, since he'd already eaten in the MIT dining hall. "For almost three years I believed that. Your mother and I had agreed on Justin. She never told me she changed her mind."

They'd invented a last name, a combination of their family names. They'd agreed to pair it with Justin, and Harry didn't mind Willow calling the boy Just, though it could be confusing: *Just, go to sleep. Just go to sleep.* But later, on the birth certificate, he saw that she'd actually named their son Justice. No middle name at all, although that was the place, he'd suggested, that you were supposed to put the risky, potentially embarrassing part of the name. "You think it's okay for a child's name to be embarrassing?" she'd said when he'd tried to explain this, about middle names. "*You* named him Justice," Harry retorted. "Without telling me." But Willow said she thought Justice was beautiful, not embarrassing. She had a way of making every argument into one he couldn't win.

"How'd you find out?" Just asked.

Harry told him he'd finally seen his birth certificate. What he didn't tell Just was that his parents, who were encouraging him to file suit for sole custody, had told him to make a copy. Harry hadn't filed the suit after he and his parents were counseled by lawyers that the Arizona courts were never going to side against the mother.

Just asked him if he'd been mad, and Harry said that he had, but not about the name. "Justice is fine," he said. "I just thought we'd settled on something different."

"I like them both," Just said diplomatically. "I would have been fine with either."

He'd taken his coffee black, and Harry couldn't tell from the way he was drinking it if he actually liked it or if he thought it was what he ought to want. Harry was tempted to offer something different. Root beer? Hot chocolate? Kid drinks.

"The info session," Just said. "It would have made me nervous, having you there. That's all."

"You don't have to explain."

"I didn't want it to be, like, something hurtful."

"You didn't hurt me," Harry lied. "I mean, I wish I didn't

make you nervous, but I get that we don't know each other that well."

"It's not that," Just said, then opened his mouth like he was going to add that they knew each other fine. Then he shut it.

An honest boy, Harry thought. He might not get into MIT, but he was honest.

The long haul—two years in, Harry thought he'd figured out what it meant. The only diapers they could afford were old dish towels from the cafeteria, which had given Just an intractable rash. The foundation refused to advance Harry the money he needed to take his son to a doctor. Harry was supposed to be grateful that they'd been moved out of the plywood dorm into a family apartment with leaky windows. The long haul—a lifetime of pretending you didn't want or need the things other people wanted, not just TVs or fancy shoes but shampoo and diaper cream, a lifetime spent paying the price of pushing back against what your life was supposed to look like. Maybe Willow's parents had moved to the nudist colony because after decades of the long haul, they didn't have the money to buy clothes.

Willow kept the faith, kept it years beyond his ability to understand her. Did he understand how rare Arcosanti was, she asked, a place that really *meant* something? And he could hear how long she'd watched her parents look for such a place, how miserable they'd made her, trying. Arcosanti was supposed to be the city of the future, but he could see every single day of his future there and they all looked the same, dusty and exhausted and poor. The only other child living in

Arcosanti was a four-year-old so grubby that tourists stuck money into the chest pocket of her overalls. Not Justin, Harry was determined. That would not be his son's life.

Just had scheduled visits to Emerson College and Tufts the next day, nearly back to back. If he had more time that week, Harry offered, they could visit Northeastern. Or UMass Boston. Or even Roxbury, which, Miriam said, was a really solid community college. "You know, if you wanted to get some Gen Eds out of the way before trans-ferring to a four-year school." Harry kept his eyes on the road, but he was aware of his son turning to give him an inscrutable look.

Last night Harry had been unable to sleep, imagining Just receiving an endless stream of rejection letters, growing frustrated and angry at the whole Northeast, at his father. What if he didn't return for another fifteen years? Harry had ended up insomniacly reading online message boards full of panicky teenagers posting their grades, test scores, desired schools, asking other anxious teens to estimate their odds of acceptance. All the subject lines read *Chance me?*

Chance me for Harvard? Chance me for MIT? I got a B+ once and I think I'm doomed.

This morning he'd followed Miriam into the bathroom, asking her to strategize where else Just could apply, how he might be lured back to Boston, where Harry could start to learn things like what his son liked to eat or drink, what he liked to study, what he wanted his life to be.

"Of course you can use our address for the in-state tuition," Harry rattled on now. "I mean, more than that—you know you're welcome to stay with us for as long as you like."

"Is Miriam okay with that?"

Miriam had not been asked about that. Harry imagined she wouldn't be okay with it. Not for an entire semester or year. But she would understand why he'd had to offer. She would understand that this was Harry's last, best chance. "Emerson is mostly an arts school," Harry finally said.

"I know," Just said and, after a long silence, added, "It costs, like, thirty-six thousand per year. That's not even including room and board. That's, like, another fifteen thousand."

"Well, it's in downtown Boston," Harry said, as if he thought those numbers were reasonable, which he didn't.

"If I used your address, I'd have to list your income," Just said patiently. "For the financial-aid forms."

Willow had been vehemently refusing Harry's money for the past fifteen years. Harry hadn't realized that the federal government wouldn't care—he'd be automatically expected to contribute.

"We're keeping you out of the picture," Just assured him. "If I apply to any of the really expensive ones, Mom and I are going to say my father's unknown. Or that he died. You'll be protected either way."

"They're going to declare me dead," Harry told Miriam that night in bed, but he'd made the tactical mistake of mentioning the cost of every school's tuition first, so she expressed more relief than shared indignation. "It'll be like I never existed."

"Just on a financial-aid form. Not in real life."

"You still think he's here to see me?"

Miriam had no response. She put her hand on his head in sympathy, but it felt awkward, like he was a little kid she was checking for fever. He reached up and pushed her hand onto the pillow.

"I'm sorry," she said.

"Any of this making you reconsider your no-children stance? You too could have a teenager planning to pretend you never existed."

"Ha," Miriam said. "No. Holding firm on that one."

But as she spoke Harry felt something crumple inside of him, heard a small voice protest. If he could do it again, he thought, surely it would all go better? Where was his second chance to get this right?

He wasn't sure what he was waiting for, by the end. His parents had twice set up elaborate itineraries with paid-for taxis and plane tickets. The nearest scheduled bus service was thirty miles away. Twice he'd crouched at the edge of the Arcosanti parking lot in the predawn dark until he heard the cab crunching down the dirt road. Then he'd grabbed his backpack and run in the opposite direction, back to his and Willow's room. His parents had called Arcosanti's main office both times in a panic after he failed to get off the plane in Newark. They were sure he was being held against his will. No one had taken his ID, he told them, and no one was holding him prisoner. "I just couldn't do it. I couldn't leave them." His parents sent cash then, paper-clipped to a phone number for a company in Phoenix that had agreed to send a car up, "for whenever you're ready to leave."

But when he finally left, he didn't call the number or take the cash. He put it in an envelope on his pillow with a letter for Willow and a series of flip-book drawings for Just. Harry couldn't really draw, but there was a big stick figure and a little stick figure and if you flipped through quickly enough, they hugged. He hadn't wanted to sneak away in the dark, hadn't wanted to feel like he was doing something that required sneaking, but he knew he'd never make it in daylight. He wouldn't survive the goodbyes, would cave again, convince himself that maybe the next day, or the next, Willow would either agree to leave with him or let him take Just or, conceivably, his belief in arcology might reawaken strongly enough for him to make it through another year or five or ten. In the dark, though, he knew none of this would happen.

That night he pressed his cheek against Just's and inhaled. His boy's face was impossibly soft and smelled like the silt beds in the foundry. Harry left on foot, the road shining white under a full moon, and hiked out to Cordes Junction. The town wasn't more than a truck stop huddled against I-17, but he found a trucker willing to take him south to Phoenix. He called his parents collect from the airport, and they arranged a ticket for a flight home. During takeoff he watched the desert drop away beneath him and felt no relief, just a gutting pain. They were at cruising altitude, Arizona gone already, when he had two thoughts: that he'd stayed so long because he'd wanted his son to at least remember him and that he hadn't stayed long enough for that to be true.

*   *   *

At Harvard's Agassiz House, Just didn't even want him in the foyer and still refused to surrender the ugly backpack. Harry said he'd find a café to answer some e-mails and sift through new listings. He walked back toward Harvard Square, peering in all the independent cafés for an available table, and paused outside a Panera Bread on Mass. Ave. Panera; he imagined Willow shaking her head, his own younger self wincing. He kept walking. Maybe he could work under a tree. Or at a library, at least until a security guard chased him out. Could he pass for a graduate student? Probably not at Harvard, where he imagined they all finished their PhDs by twenty-seven.

He crossed the street and went back through the brick and iron gates. The campus was shamelessly beautiful, a stately parody of itself. He wondered if Just was falling in love right this moment with something he was never going to have.

Harry's last year in Arizona, he'd thought a lot about college. Not just the parties—late-night pizza and red plastic cups—but those darkened rooms full of ideas. Every idea Arcosanti ever contained felt bleached and flattened by the desert sun. Harry had been in his early twenties. He could sit in a classroom and look just like everybody else. No one would ever know he had a son. They would never even know he'd left college. He'd wanted to believe that Arcosanti was like Narnia, that you could step out of the wardrobe and back into the very afternoon you'd found it. But of course you couldn't.

Students started to stream out of the buildings, changing classes. They wore nice sweaters and had clean backpacks. Harry tried to picture Just among them. He couldn't. Until he could, because there was Just, walking straight by him, holding a video camera in front of his face. He was walking alone, without a tour guide or admissions host. He hadn't made it twenty feet past Harry before a campus security guard stopped him. They were close enough for Harry to hear when the security guard said, "No filming." Just was trying and failing to convince the guard he had a video permit from Public Affairs when Harry walked up behind them.

"I'm sorry, Officer," he said. "My son's a prospective student. He didn't know about the filming rules." *My son.* Harry could taste the words in his mouth long after he'd said them.

"Can I see some ID?"

"I don't have one," Just said too quickly, and the guard bristled.

There was so much, Harry thought, that his son needed to learn about the world. "Here's mine," he said, pulling out his wallet, and he watched the guard write down the name.

After being escorted to the nearest campus entrance, they were left courteously enough on the sidewalk outside.

"Different last names," Harry said. "This won't hurt you if you decide to apply." Just was raising the video camera to film the guard's retreating back. Harry swatted it down. "What are you doing? What *were* you doing?"

"We're on city property," Just said. "They can't stop you filming from here."

"You researched this?"

"Sure. But someone from Tufts had tipped Harvard off. They asked me to leave admissions before I got much of anything."

"What did you do at Tufts?"

"It's for a documentary. I'm not just screwing around. Mom's been dating this Italian video artist. He gave me this," Just said, holding up the camera. "I've been recording audio from the info sessions on my phone, but he said I should try for some quality footage too. He's going to help me edit everything together. You know college in Italy is, like, completely free? Harvard costs sixty thousand a year. It's so fucked up."

"You're making some kind of exposé?"

"Mom said not to tell you. She said she wasn't sure you'd be cool with it."

"What else did your mom say about me?" It was a huge question, ridiculous, too big for the rest of their lives, let alone for a sidewalk outside of Harvard Yard with students pushing past them.

Harry led them across the street to the nearest café's outdoor tables. They sat, and Just returned the camera to the backpack, wrapping it carefully in the red polo shirt. It took him a long time to answer.

"Honestly?" he said. "Not a ton. You two were on a summer workshop together, and then you went back to school."

"Four years. I was there four years." Harry tried to meet Just's eyes, but his son was staring at the perforated black metal tabletop. "I didn't want to leave you."

He just hadn't seen how they could love the boy as much as they did and still raise him in Arcosanti. Willow hadn't seen how he could love the boy as much as he said he did and still threaten to leave. There'd been no possible compromise, not one Harry had been able to see then and not one he was able to see even now. Which meant that in the great forking of his youth, he had ended up with nothing but bad choices. The painless road must have split off earlier, before he'd fallen in love with Willow, before he'd fallen in love with arcology. But that meant Just would never have existed.

"If you finish the movie—what do you do with a film like this? Submit it to festivals?"

"Put it on YouTube, probably. Higher education in this country is out of control."

It sounded so rehearsed that Harry wondered who Just was imitating. Willow? The Italian filmmaker? Or maybe the words were really Just's. Maybe this was what his son sounded like. At sixty thousand a year for tuition, he wasn't wrong. Harry wondered what he'd sounded like as a teenager, parroting Paolo Soleri. Soleri had died last year, ninety-three years old. There'd been a memorial celebration at Arcosanti, a reunion of past residents and workshoppers. Harry hadn't attended, but he'd been invited. He still got all the mailings, the pleas for donations. He still read them before he put them in the recycling bin.

"You should have told me," Harry said. "What you were doing."

"Mom said—"

"Whatever she said. You were lying to me, and you were using me and Miriam. That wasn't fair."

Just took a moment to think about it, and when he said, "I'm sorry," even though he said it to the sidewalk, it sounded sincere.

"Do you still want to visit Boston College this afternoon?"

Just's head jerked up, his expression hopeful but suspicious.

"For footage," Harry said. "I'm assuming you don't actually plan to apply."

"You'd do that?"

Was this a desperate ploy for his son's affection? And did he believe this documentary would ever get made or that if it did, it would say anything that hadn't already been said better by somebody else? Probably not. But maybe. This was his son, would always be his son. Didn't you have to hope, totally and shamelessly, for "maybe"?

"I would. Although, for the record, I really liked college. I learned a lot. You should go. It doesn't have to cost sixty thousand dollars."

Harry thought of himself scribbling notes in a dark room, desperate for someone to show him a picture of the future. That there wasn't one was perhaps the best fatherly advice he had. Every possible arcology, they were all shipwrecked and insufficient. There was no city of the future, only the lecture slide before it, blank except for a question mark. But uncertainty could be a superpower. It could even be a love story, if you looked at it from a certain angle.

AND LOOKED DOWN ONE
AS FAR AS I COULD

Winter clings to the porch, a sheen of ice across wet boards, a hard white crust on the railings. From a recliner in her living room, Gloria watches birds flutter around a feeder hanging from the porch gutter. Seed hulls scatter dark across the sinking snow, punctuation marks without words. There is no urgency to this weather, just its slow dripping from one moment into the next. There is no urgency left in Gloria, just the slow settle of her body into her chair in the mornings, into the bedsheets when night falls.

Inside the house, the priest comes, the church ladies. It is a small town, and her neighbors watch the mailbox, salt the walk while checking for footprints. No one wants to find her days after the fact. They're not that kind of neighborhood, that kind of congregation, to lose track of someone in her final days. But this kindness feels macabre to Gloria, as if they're trying to arrive as close as possible to the event, to be there when it happens. When she was a girl her mother told her that a window should be raised in anticipation, to let the soul escape. Her mother died, decades ago, in an eighth-floor hospital room whose windows did not open. She tells the church ladies this, about raising the sash.

"Oh, let's not talk about sad things," they say.

Not one of them will open a window for her, Gloria thinks.

They bring soups and casseroles and lasagna, microwavable single portions. They sit on the couch and watch her eat while they chatter: errands, recipes, children, work. Gloria wonders what stories she is supposed to be offering them in return. She gives away objects instead: a set of coasters, a glass bell, a porcelain parakeet. She props beside her chair the framed poem the principal gave her when she retired from the high school. It is the poem she was asked to read every commencement for forty-five years—two roads diverging in a wood, one path slightly grassier than the other. She has always hated this poem.

She holds on to the family pictures of siblings gone, husband gone, children gone in a different way, voices on the phone, the grandchildren bigger at every holiday than it had occurred to her to imagine them. She keeps her Audubon prints, her Minnesota bird guide, the pair of binoculars on a side table in the bay window. Most of the birds that come to the feeder are ordinary. There is a colony of sparrows in the juniper bush in the yard. Chickadees, finches, wrens. Sometimes a blue jay or cardinal. A bluebird. The bluebird of happiness. She doesn't know where the phrase comes from, but there it is, in her head.

"A bluebird?" the church ladies ask.

"It m-must have just flown away," Gloria stammers. But having erased the bluebird, what has she done to the happiness?

Her husband used to call her "chickadee," sang *chick-a-dee-dee-dee* as he poured the morning coffee. There were moments so sweet she felt like she needed to wash her own mouth out. They'd been married five years when, drunk at a dinner party, he threw his arms around her and squeezed. "Plain but lovely. My plump little birdie." He dropped his weight back in his seat, made himself small and round and twitched his head as if looking for seed. It was a good impression. It was meant to be an impression of her. She laughed so the party guests could do the same, gave them permission by tucking her hands under her arms and flapping little wings. The laughter egged her husband on, and he bent his head to her plate, plucked a green bean up with his lips extended in a beak. The worm dangled until he flung his head back, and it disappeared down his throat.

He said that night that she was round in the ways that counted, not the ones that didn't, but what she heard in her head after the light was off, after he put a hand on her belly and she rolled away, was *Plain but lovely. Plainbutlovely. Plain and plump. Fat little chickadee.*

She might have asked him, *Boreal or black-capped? Carolina or blackpoll? Be specific with your words.*

"Boreal?" The church ladies flutter.

She commanded specificity from her students, more times than she can count, more weeks, more semesters, more years. Students felt they could talk to her; she was young, and then when she wasn't anymore, she still had carrot-orange hair and earrings in the shape of little books. She was ages and ages hence, and way had led on to way, and that alone seemed like a promise of wisdom. Students sneaked to her classroom during lunch period or stood in her doorway with their arms wrapped around themselves like blankets. To the neediest ones she'd give her phone number, scrawled on torn-out grade-book pages. They still send her invitations years later—weddings, college graduations, baby showers—so she knows that at least some of her words must have been the right ones, though it's impossible to know which. Every choice is a forking, she told them, every phrase, and no one can stand still in that ugly yellow wood forever.

The church ladies leave. The priest comes the next day, or is it the day after? The conversation lags, too little news to report, and when he trails off midsentence, staring out the window, she feels his exhaustion. How endless, the secrets of others. How endless, the reassurance they need. She sees his distaste at the porch, where the harsh winter has brought the birds in flocks. They gorge at the feeder and then shit copiously over the peeling rail.

"You must keep your strength up," the priest says, and then he is handing her a cup of soup. She sniffs and recognizes the cream of mushroom the church ladies brought. She does not recall him rising, going to the kitchen. Sometimes she does not recall eating. She is thin now, but still plain. Her swollen knuckles are beads on a string. Kebabs on a skewer, she thinks, and laughs.

"What?" the priest says, because her hand is in front of her face, and the soup rattles dangerously on her lap.

She asks him if he'd like some soup, holding out the bowl, but he shakes his head. What she would have given in another decade to be thin. God gives us all different gifts, her mother used to tell her. *Chick-a-dee-dee-dee.*

A great horned owl came to the porch once, night bird in broad daylight, sitting on the railing, big as a football. She held still, watched until her muscles ached, and then tapped on the window glass to say hello. It rotated its head toward her. Its stare was baleful, but only because of the shape and set of its yellow eyes. Owls always looked solemn, the way panting dogs always seemed to be smiling. More photographs to be dealt with—the parade of departed Labradors in the upstairs hallway, the same dumb unburdened expression on all their faces. Really, she thinks, we have no idea what they're feeling. We never know what anyone is feeling.

"There's no owl there, Gloria."

She nods her head. Yes, there is no owl. There was a day with an owl, and today is a day with no owl, and two roads once diverged in a yellow wood, birds watching from the branches.

"I have something for you," she tells the priest and tries to give him the framed poem.

"You don't need to do that, Gloria," he says, because people are always using her name now, as comfort or perhaps reminder.

The passing had worn them really about the same, and there she was in this house with a baby in her arms. She had said she would have no babies. She had said she would be an actress. A radio actress. She was never a complete dreamer.

And when the leaves were trodden black underfoot, she took her daughter shopping and said of a sleeveless pink dress with a narrow red sash, "It's really not the most flattering, is it?" And then the blousy white frock that swallowed her daughter up, a tiny blond head atop a gull's wing. She regrets that dress. She regrets that it made her feel better to see her daughter a frump. Two plump drab sparrows, she is telling this with a sigh, ages and ages hence.

"Take the poem," she says. "Please." She thinks he will. Unlike the church ladies, he won't pretend that she is not dying.

The priest slips away from her and the house is dark and she remembers to reach behind her and turn on the light. The curtains are still open, so there she is, her reflection in the dark window, another bird beyond the glass. She does not recognize this specimen, hunched and flightless. This traveler. Fly, she thinks, fly.

She rises for bed and stumbles into the framed poem. He has not taken it like she thought he would, or did she only imagine offering it to him? She is a long time going up the stairs. They are grassy and want for wear. Her bedroom is too warm. She opens a window to let in some cool air. A traveler, she thinks, I wish I had traveled. A migratory tern, a swallow, a swift. I wish I had asked to read a different poem. I could have called him a grackle. I wish I had bought her the pink dress she liked. That has been all the difference, and no difference, and oh that hopeless wood.

MURDER GAMES

Ella's backpack sagged with flashlight and string, fruit snacks and masking tape and two forks and a bike helmet. The best part of adventures was always the planning. "Goggles," FootFoot the Kangaroo suggested. "A compass," said Duncan Hines, a bear the chocolate color of the frosting. Ella considered the one in her mother's phone; she played with it while they waited for allergy shots. The allergies were why Ella didn't have pets, the flesh-blood-drool-noise kind. Her animals were real in different ways.

At the allergist Ella looked for north, true north, and then her mother pointed seven thousand miles southeast. This was where Ella's father was. It was hot and dry and her father wore only clothes the color of the dryness. He slept in a long building where the sand sneaked in, and he blew this sound into the telephone for Ella, the fizz of dirt against metal. It was a different hour in this country, sometimes a whole different day, and Ella often asked her mother what her father was doing at particular times. "Sleeping," she'd say, or "Eating," or "Working." Ella's father was a mechanic, and these past months it had been easy enough for Ella to picture him underneath trucks instead of cars, brown beasts instead of their red minivan. "He's thinking of you," her mother would say, even when she'd already said, "Sleeping." "He's safe," she added, although it had not occurred to Ella to worry, and then Ella did.

"No compass," Ella said to Duncan Hines, because her mother needed to be avoided. Her anger was palpable, rising off her like cartoon stink lines, filling the rooms downstairs. All Ella had done was ask her where Blanket was, and *boom*. A thousand-pointed star of Angry. Blanket was missing, but Ella would have to find him herself. This was the mission.

Missy the Kitten begged to be on the expeditionary force, but Ella didn't like girl toys. She didn't like the pink thread dividing Missy's paws into toes or the curled lashes painted on her plastic eyes. Missy gave warnings like "Be careful!" and "Not so high!" and "Don't get caught!" This was what being a girl meant to Ella, because this was what Ella herself was like. She was afraid and tired of being afraid.

Once she overheard her mother say, "Well, they're very resilient at this age. It's hard to know how much they're really picking up on."

Everything, Ella thought. *I am paying attention to everything.*

She listened and collected the items she didn't understand, held them like the lobed pieces of a puzzle that might yet be completed. So far there was no image, only holes, but she was trying. Blanket's disappearance, her mother's mood—perhaps this afternoon some key piece was at hand, a corner or edge.

All her best animals were big-souled, fearless, and adventuresome. They were all boys: FootFoot and Duncan Hines and Dinomite the Dinosaur and Bonk the Bear, whose butt was a rubber ball that was supposed to bounce. But he was named after the sound he made when Ella threw him, the way he thudded against the floor and slumped over. He wanted to be on the expeditionary force anyway. Boys were brave. Brave but stupid. They smashed themselves against objects that had no give. Last week Ella's brother, Josh, leaped off their backyard swing set and an exposed screw ripped across his upper arm. The skin split and even before the blood, something yellow bulged out. Fat, she supposed, it must be fat, but who knew their swing set could unleash it, could expose the body's secrets?

Blanket was splitting too, ragged around his edges. Every night in bed she walked this territory with her lips, ran the unraveling hem across her mouth until she knew each thread. She held him the way her mother held rosary beads, the way she knew God with her fingers. Blanket could read the inside of Ella's head without words, without judgment. He would never be angry with her. He was like God in this way, but better. As his hem unraveled, the old river of him ran out, the white fabric stiff against her lips. She thought of how small she had been, back when Blanket was this white, and how perfectly he knew her even then.

Her mother had been insisting that Blanket needed to be re-hemmed, his edges turned under before he unraveled

141

completely. This was murder to Ella, mutilation. She would sooner sew her own edges shut, her fingers to her palms, arms to her sides, toes agonizingly to her ankles.

"We have to re-hem it before it falls to bits," her mother said.

"You *can't*. You just can't."

Her mother sighed. "Why are you being like this?" she said, and Ella could hear that she meant more than the current situation with Blanket. As if Ella had a choice to be other than the way she was.

"It'll hurt him."

"Even if it does, honey, the hemming has to happen," her mother said, exasperated but steely.

When the topic of the blanket comes up, years afterward, her mother means it to be funny. Ella is a sophomore in high school. Josh spent a year in college, dropped out, and joined the army. He's stationed down in Texas. He says it's hot. He says he's happy.

Ella's first boyfriend's mother has driven the couple home from the movies and waits while the boy walks Ella to the door. Ella's mother invites them inside. The boy gestures at the idling minivan—he shouldn't keep his mother waiting. The minivan is nice, but not too nice. The boy's family has more money than Ella's, but not so much more. The women wave at each other, a little salute. This is a milestone for everybody, the children old enough to be shepherded home in the dark, monitored with concentration: *Is that lip gloss rubbed off on the boy's mouth? Are those blue marks on the girl's neck?* A satisfaction along with the worry: *We have all made it this far, all of us grown up tonight, or nearly. No one has been lost along the way.*

"How was the movie?" Ella's mother asks, and both teenagers shrug. They bought tickets for a PG film so they could sneak into an R-rated one, and neither can think quickly enough to form an opinion of a movie other than the one they weren't supposed to see, flying body parts, a sinister serial killer. A teen died in a swimming-pool drain. Another in a blender, bit by bit. Ella will have nightmares tonight, but she won't admit it. Not to her mother, not to Liam. Things have always been too real to her. They take on life when she isn't looking, the world filled with inadvertent spirits. Her mother has told her this is melodramatic, the way molehills become haunted mountains in her mind. She's tried, but she can't blunt her own imagination the way this boy apparently can, the way he laughed out loud during the scene with the industrial dough kneader.

Something sailed into her bedroom and hit Ella in the back of the head. A Nerf ball, she was relieved to realize, without needing to look. She turned. Josh still had a bandage around his upper arm. When their father was on a video call, Josh wore long sleeves. Their father told him to take care of the house, take care of his sister, and sometimes for an hour Josh and Ella tried to play catch in the backyard. "You're afraid of the ball," he complained, and Ella thought, *Duh.* Josh had lost half his baby teeth to balls. The Tooth Fairy left him a note saying, *Be more careful or no more quarters.* Their father was at home then, and the Tooth Fairy's handwriting looked suspiciously like his. Everybody wanted Ella to be tough until they wanted her to be some-thing else. They wanted her to stand in front of the ball until it hit her in the face and then they wondered why she didn't move away. They wanted her to be strong and not miss her daddy too much, and then when she didn't come to the phone because she was in the tree outside with Blanket and it had been a lot of work to climb that high, her mother yelled at her.

"*What,*" Ella had said then. "What did I *do?*"

"If I went away, would you stop caring about me?" her mother had asked.

Of course not, Ella thought, but everyone was telling her all the time that her father was safe, so why did it matter if she spoke to him now or tomorrow or next week?

"You're a little monster sometimes," her mother had told her.

"Look out," FootFoot whispered now, and Ella felt the animals crowd closer to her. Josh picked Banana out of the heap and threw him into the air and this was supposed to annoy her but the joke was on Josh because Banana was already a bird, and Ella didn't even like him. Banana was from the Goodwill. When her mother gave him to Ella, camouflaged as new in a toy-store box, for her birthday, she could tell he was already dead. He had empty black eyes and the weird scent of the secondhand store, the damp, gray smell like...dirty? Poor? Poorness? Poor people? To Ella, poor people were the ones on television with no food but round stomachs, something she didn't understand but refused to ask about. She did not know what poor people in America might look like. She did not know why their

144

things smelled so weird. And she did not know why they had owned Banana before she did and why this smell had come to infect her house.

Josh bounced Banana off the ceiling a few times. The fan was off, and the bird flew neatly between the still blades. Ella kicked the backpack with the expeditionary force's supplies under her bed. She took a pink Barbie hairbrush from her nightstand to groom Bonk's fur.

"I'm having people over tonight," Josh said. "So you have to stay out of the way."

The black paint on Bonk's eyes was scratched. His gaze drifted leftward.

"Mom said we're ordering pizza but once we eat, you should play up here."

"Okay," Ella said. She didn't even want to play with her brother's friends. All their games were boy games, all with *murder* in the name: Murder Ball and Murder Jump and Murder Swing, and when it was dark and their mom was in bed, there was Murder, plain Murder, the boys wandering through the house tagged out one by one by the Murderer. Once, they invited Ella to play and left her alive on purpose, stumbling in the dark by herself while the boys played video games in the basement. She cried when she found them and she couldn't tell, as Josh took her hand to lead her back to her bedroom, whether he was sorry or just embarrassed.

"Don't get in the way."

"*Okay.*"

If Blanket were here there would be preparations. He would be folded, hidden under her pillow. She knew how

145

he looked to anyone besides her, how limp, how gray, how ragged. She didn't want Josh's friends to laugh at him, at her. But Blanket could be anywhere, could be found and tossed up into the ceiling fan tonight. The mission was more urgent than she'd realized.

"Do you have Blanket?" she asked her brother.

"I *told* you. No. I don't know where it is." Josh stopped tossing Banana. "You know Mom needed to hem it. You know it was falling apart."

"He's fine."

Josh shrugged, looked at her with a dangerous pity. He changed the subject: "You can borrow my reading book tonight, if you want."

Now Ella shrugged. This was a privilege, but she didn't want Josh to know. Her own reading textbook was dull, with stories about things like crossing the road and eating vegetables. Josh's book had adventures. The best story was about a thief caught in the act. The owner of the house promised not to call the police, and the thief laughed. "You think I'm naive?" he asked, and there was an asterisk after *naive* and a definition at the bottom of the page: "child-like." This offended Ella. What was childlike about the thief—the hushed confrontation, his doomed leap from a window, or the way he appeared on the next page with a bandage around his head? She sensed that the word really meant something else but she couldn't tell what. "Foolish"? "Stupid"? But why would there be a book for kids that insulted kids?

Josh brought the book from his room and she turned to her favorite page. Someone had drawn two black fangs in the thief's mouth, erased the eyes to two white spots. "It wasn't me," Josh said automatically.

Maybe *naive* meant "trusting," in which case how adult a definition, how trusting *they* were to think kids so trusting. Ella tried to imagine the way her mother imagined her, a bright rubber ball whizzing through the world. *Naive,* she thought toward her mother. *You are so naive.*

Nine years later, when Ella stands on the porch with her boyfriend, she knows he would rather die than kiss her in front of her mother. They would both rather die. In a blender. But he wants to be manly. He takes her hand and then lets go, brief as a kiss. It feels ridiculous. Ella looks down at her surrendered hand, dangling fingers, green nail polish. She does not love this boy, not even close. They started sitting next to each other in mythology class, their language arts elective, so he could copy her answers about the Moirai and Parcae. He is hard to joke with because he takes everything literally. *He's pretty naive,* Ella thinks, but she doesn't mind. They both know—even if they don't acknowledge it to each other, or themselves—that they are only marking time. They are learning things they will need later on for other moments, other people, other kisses.

Ella's mother thanks the boy for getting Ella home safely. Ella goes inside and watches out the window while Liam switches places with his mother so he can practice driving. Ella is one month younger, still waiting on her learner's permit. She holds her breath while the boy backs out slowly, but he doesn't hit anything. Then he is gone, out of sight up the road. In the kitchen Ella takes a soda from the fridge.

Her mother follows her, a conspiratorial smile lurking, as if there are details Ella will now divulge, girl talk they are about to have. Her mother even braces her hands behind her on the kitchen counter, pulls herself up, and thonks the cabinets with her heels. She begins joking about the embarrassing things she could have done, wanting credit for not doing them: showing Liam naked baby pictures of Ella, clumsy old drawings, Ella's animals. "Duncan Hines!" her mother says. "Or Bonk. Remember when your Blankie—"

"Yeah," Ella says flatly, because she remembers, and this story is not funny to her. She can grow up and get old, but it will still not be funny. Her animals are stashed now in her bedroom closet, tied in plastic bags she once would have been terrified would suffocate them. They are not alive to her anymore, but they are not quite dead. An aura clings to them, even if it's only the memory of what it felt like to be certain they breathed and spoke and loved her. To be certain there was a set of rules, a code that governed who lived and who stopped living.

With Duncan Hines in her backpack, Ella surveyed the up-stairs: her room—already torn apart from searching—the bathroom, the linen closet. There was Josh's room and her parents' room, but she wasn't supposed to go into either, and she was still hoping to find Blanket on undisputed ground. Downstairs, in the living room, she imagined her-self the thief in Josh's reading book, poking through the couch cushions and behind the forest of photographs lined up on a bookshelf—individual portraits, family portraits, her father, over and over again. It was disconcerting, this forest of faces. When her father first deployed, her mother suggested that Ella stand at this shelf and talk to his pictures about her day at school. Ella had talked about how Bonk the Bear hid in her backpack without her permission, and Gus Stepansky saw him and made fun of her.

"Your father says you shouldn't take your toys to school," her mother said. "He says to tell you you can't be bullied if you don't give them reasons to bully you."

Gradually Ella stopped telling stories in the living room. She still talked to her father, but at night, in her bed. She talked about how Gus Stepansky's father was married to a stepmother, and Ella wondered if the stepmother thought of Gus the way that Ella thought of Banana: *You smell funny. Someone else has already loved furrows in your hair. There have been other lips on your skin. Scratches across your eyes.* Or maybe it wasn't that way. Maybe it was too different. Gus would grow, he would change, he would get bigger, but animals only got grimier, looser, until eventually they fell apart. Ella understood this better than she did the death of the bird Josh found one day on the sidewalk, in a way more real than the death of Bambi's mother or her own grandfather. More real than what she knew her mother feared, her father leaving and being gone so long he never came back. She understood things through her animals, and this was not a small or stupid way of understanding, just different.

149

"I need to find Blanket," Ella told her father's picture. "Have you seen him?"

Her father's bright smile never changed. Ella imagined her mother choosing another man to bring into the house, a new father who might nuzzle her head and find her smelly.

Out the side door and into the yard. Plastic table, plastic sandbox in the shape of a turtle, two plastic chairs blown over. An empty bird feeder. Ella had no idea why Blanket would be out here but she had to check everywhere. In her backpack the string was unused, the flashlight unlit. She took the fork out and shook it at the swing set still marked with Josh's blood. *"En garde,"* she said.

Her mother rapped on the kitchen window. She held up the phone and gestured Ella inside. "Your dad," she said as Josh finished his turn and handed the phone over.

"How was school?" her father asked.

"Fine," Ella said. They'd done math worksheets where correct answers gave the colors for a picture, and her bee ended up purple. But with her father gone, she could leave things out. He'd never see the purple bee. Josh could wear a long-sleeved shirt. Later, when she was a teenager, she would think that maybe this year had been the beginning of a new way of being a daughter, the beginning of—not deception, exactly, but editing, perhaps. The silences that exist inside all stories.

He asked her what she was going to do tomorrow, which was an impossible question to answer. She wondered if he had any idea what her life was like. She went where people told her, took the brown paper bags they pressed into her hands, and at the appointed hour, she ate what she found there. In the afternoon her mother's car pulled up, and they usually went home, but sometimes they went to the grocery store or the dentist or the Goodwill. "Maybe tomorrow we'll go to the dentist," she told her father.

"You have a dentist appointment?"

"I don't think so."

"Then why...never mind," he said. "You keep doing good at school, okay?"

The doorbell rang. "Pizza's here," Ella said.

"What kind did you get?"

"*I* don't know."

"Well, have a piece for me, okay? Pepperoni."

"What if there's no pepperoni? Josh likes sausage and Mom likes mushrooms."

Ella hated both these things and hoped perhaps her dad would remember and comment on the injustice. But he said, "Have a piece for me of whatever it is."

Ella nodded, which her father couldn't see. Her mother paid for the pizza and, after putting it on the counter, reached for the phone. "Be careful," Ella said to her father. "Don't be naive or anything."

He laughed. "Okay, sweetie. Back atcha. Don't be naive."

There was sausage and mushroom but also plain cheese, which wasn't as good as pepperoni, but it was something. Josh's friends began to arrive. Ella stood with her back to the wall so no one could make fun of Duncan Hines poking out of her backpack. "Take your pizza upstairs," her mother said, handing her a grape soda, a paper plate, paper napkins. Ella was never allowed to take food upstairs.

She carefully set the pizza on her bedroom floor next to the pile of animals. "There's something I have to do," she told them. "I'll be back soon." Downstairs, she could hear her mother chatting with the women dropping their sons off.

Her mother's laughter, or perhaps just the thudding of her mother's heels on the cupboard, conjures Ella's father up from the basement into the kitchen. They hear his footsteps starting at the bottom of the wooden stairs and wait for them to rise. His presence has long since ceased to be special. Ella is grateful only when she remembers to be. In church sometimes. At Thanksgiving dinner. He has left the Reserves and with the extra weekends he builds furniture. He has a workshop in the basement, loud saws that allow him to stay hidden and oblivious, that give him an excuse to say he never heard any boy at the door. Ella's mother says he spends too much on tools, but he owns his own shop now, auto body and detailing, and there is enough money even for the saws.

"How was the movie, sweetie?" he says, and Ella shrugs.

"I finally met Liam," her mother says.

"Finally?" In Ella's mind they've barely been together.

"He's perfectly nice. He was very gentlemanly."

The dough kneader, Ella thinks. *His laughter.* She looks balefully at the blender on the counter behind her mother, the cord coiled around it.

"I was saying I could have brought out the baby pictures," her mother says. "The Blanket."

"What blanket?" her father says. There were so many of

these moments when he first came back, reminders of gaps that could be dodged or backfilled but never completely erased.

"I thought you got rid of him," Ella says. "That's what you said, that he was making me too upset."

"Of course," her mother says. "I forgot."

In the kitchen there is a long, awkward silence. Ella wishes Josh were here to throw something at somebody, to rip himself open accidentally. "So what did happen to him?" Ella asks. "*Could* you have brought him out?" Nine years and this is the first time she's asked this question.

"No," her mother says. "No, I couldn't. I didn't think about it. It's been a long time."

Ella's father steals the soda out of her hand, trying to break the tension. He takes a long swig, asks what she's doing having caffeine so close to bedtime. She looks at him, his effortful smile, pale dust on his jeans, wood shavings caught in his bootlaces. She remembers to be thankful. There was a time she could have lost him and she didn't. Her story is not that kind of story. She can forget the way he hides downstairs, the way he sits inside of silences. She could throw her arms around him but doesn't. She is not the little girl anymore who would do that, dance unselfconsciously on top of her father's shoes. She is wearing flip-flops, and she kicks one off. She presses her right foot on top of her father's boot, brief and light as a kiss, and hopes he understands.

Ella turned the doorknob of her mother's room and there, folded neatly beside the sewing machine on top of the dresser, was Blanket's body. She screamed, and her mother came running to find her unfolding Blanket and pressing the hemmed, amputated edges to her lips. There was nothing familiar left. Blanket spilled limply in her arms. "He's dead," Ella said. "He's dead."

"He can't die," her mother said. "He's a blanket."

Of course he could die. He'd been dying already, unraveling into threads and dust and laundry detergent. But now he was like an old house burning to the ground before it could be allowed to collapse. Ella had failed to protect him. The mission had come too late. Her mother was a murderer, but so was she. Her mother took Blanket's corpse from her, like maybe if she hid him, Ella would calm down, but Ella kept wailing, barely able to breathe, and her mother rubbed exasperated, angry circles on her back until Ella imagined the skin over her shoulder blades splitting like Josh's arm.

She woke up later in bed, in her nightgown, her throat aching and her eyelids gummy. Her mother sat on the floor in a cone of light from the bedside lamp. She was peering into her lap and did not look up to notice Ella had woken. Her mother looked warmer, softer, in the light from the pink lampshade. A small piece of metal with a sharp, curved point glinted in her hand. The house was quiet so it must have been very late, Josh and his friends exhausted and silent downstairs, the murder games concluded. Ella's mother held Blanket up farther into the light, trying to undo the new stitches. But Blanket's flesh was too fragile. Where she pulled, the old fabric gave way before the new thread. A hole opened up and another and another and her mother swore softly, pressed her hands together, crumpled the corpse. Ella said nothing, did not reach to touch her mother's hands or head, so unusually low, at Ella's eye-level. She looked at the part in her mother's hair, the pale scalp and the tiny holes where the hair began. *You're naive,* she thought. *You're very naive.*

This night would come back to her for years, feeling more and more like a dream. It came to her when her father returned, at the ceremony in a local gymnasium, balloons and confetti. It came to her when she talked to her brother before he left for basic training about that year their father was gone, and they realized they had completely different memories of that time. "I cut my arm on a BMX bike," Josh said. "Not on the swing set." Neither she nor Josh could recall how the story with the thief had ended. Growing up had been so far a great un-knowing, an erosion of the facts that had once seemed very clear and precious to her. Ella forgot, eventually, whether she really saw her mother crying on the floor trying to undo what was already done or whether she'd only wanted to see her mother crying. She forgot the rage and grief she felt, the satisfaction at her mother's unhappiness. It was childlike but incandescent, furious, alight in a way she worries sometimes she'll never be again. She wants to know if her parents have ever felt that way, but she doesn't want to ask. All the possible answers are bad ones: That they never have, and she's a little monster after all; or that they did once, but age leached it from them; or that adulthood holds such pain and rage that Ella knows nothing yet. That so much worse is still to come.

That night in the kitchen, Ella decides she does not want to press the issue. She does not want to know one way or another if Blanket is still in a box somewhere in the house, if he ended up at the Goodwill or in the trash. After all, he's been dead for years. She once thought that when she grew up she would be able to choose what she felt, one single, practical, voluntary feeling at a time. *Naive,* she thinks now. *That was naive.* She says good night to her parents, hugs them both, leans into her mother's softness and her father's sawdust and flannel, embarrassed by how eagerly they hold her. That night she dreams the memory, her mother white-draped and ancient, herself the child she'll never be again. It no longer feels like a puzzle piece, a sharp corner or edge. It is a scalloped question that could fit anywhere. There is a chorus of whispers, ancient weaver women whose names were on that week's mythology midterm: Penelope, Arachne, the three Fates—spindle, rod, knife. *There is no blade that mends,* they sing. *Only the thread going forward. Only our readiness for the cut.*

ON THE OREGON TRAIL

My husband, Elias, was a banker, so we left with more than most. A total of sixteen hundred dollars to spend at the outfitters—three yoke of oxen, two thousand pounds of food, boxes of bullets and spare parts: tongue, axle, wheel. Two sets of clothes for each of us.

"What kind of clothes?" the children asked.

"Who knows?" I said. "The store sold only 'clothes.' In sets, though. That's something." They asked what we would eat. "Food," I said. "Just 'food.' Make your peace with it."

We left Independence in April and saw the first tombstone before we reached the Kansas River. Timmy, Susan, and Edgar, our children, ran to read it. *Here Lies Stinky*, it read. *He Stinks*.

"That's not very nice," I said.

"I bet Stinky does," the children said. "Stink. Now he does, anyway."

The graves were endless: *Toot, JoJo, Boogerface. Here Lies a Dork*. The children had no sense of solemnity. They read them all, howling: *Farty McButt Farts Oxen. Turd Is Dead HAHAHA*. Only one bothered them, fifty miles east of Fort Kearney. *TaraRoxx Died of Pooping*, they read, then asked, "How do you die of pooping?"

"It's called dysentery," I explained. This terrified the children, that too much poo could be deadly. *Dysentery*, they whispered to one another, the way they might once have said *Werewolf* back in Illinois, or *Skunk-ape*, or the way they said *Indians* those first nights on the trail. They tapped one another on the shoulders as we tried to sleep and hissed: *Dysentery.*

The journey would take four months or five, people had told us. Leave too late and we wouldn't make it over the mountains before winter. So we left too early and watched the snows turn to heavy rain. The Big Blue was running high but there was a ferry, fifty dollars to cross. We paid it. Caution was one thing our money could provide.

Timmy went down with the typhoid three weeks in. We tried everything: moved slower, ate better. We rested for days and when he didn't improve raced to Chimney Rock to rest there. We tried to trade, but there was no medicine to buy. There was never any medicine. Outside of Chimney Rock, the trail began to climb, the beginning of the Rocky Mountains. Timmy died outside Fort Laramie and we had to bury him next to someone named ChezyPizza.

Elias started to hunt more after that, like he'd given up on ever reaching Oregon. It had been hare and buffalo on the plains, now squirrel and deer in the forest, bear if he got lucky. He shot wildly for days on end and the carnage was immense: Too much meat to carry back to the wagon. Too much meat that went sour in the heat days later. An embarrassment of flesh. For some reason Elias always left the skins, the fur and leather, the things we could have traded. "We can't take them," he said. "I don't know why. We're just not allowed."

August was boiling, even up in the mountains. The meat clotted in our mouths and I imagined my children turning into bears on this strange diet, sharp teeth and rank breath. They would growl and lumber and stink. But they would not be afraid, I thought. They would no longer whisper *Dysentery* and *Typhoid* in the shadows when the campfire went out. They'd begun to ask if we could just turn around, or build a house where we stood. "We can't," I told them. "Are you familiar with Manifest Destiny?" If the journey had been educational, all they'd learned were the harms that could befall them: the storms, the diseases, the drownings, the wagon wrecks, the broken limbs.

The Green River, drained by the heat, was running low. Wagon after wagon forded it easily before us, and we were nearly across when one of the oxen slipped. Two hundred fifty pounds of food, three sets of clothing, a wheel and an axle, eight boxes of bullets, and Edgar. We didn't leave a headstone; we'd lost the heart for it. We needed to trade for an axle but days passed until someone asked for something we owned. "Are you sure there's nothing else you want?" we begged them all. "Can we just show you what we have? Can we pay you in cash?"

"Your money's no good," they said. "Just isn't. Only works at general stores and rivers."

At Fort Hall, the new axle broke, and broke again, and we paid someone a hundred and fifty bullets and three sets of clothing for another. We would have been left traveling naked were there not fewer of us now to clothe. We paid the Indians at the Snake River to guide us across; what was our money worth now? Nothing, if we never made it to our destination. Even if we did, some clerk would total our account in Oregon City and say, *Not too impressive, considering what you left with. Did you know there are farmers who do it with eight hundred dollars?*

The trail was an evil joke in the miles to Fort Boise. Susan, our last, ate berries she'd found and made herself sick. When we let her ride in the wagon, she fell off and broke her ankle. She got the measles next. We rested for days, as if rest could heal her. It was all we could do. Wagon after wagon passed us. "You'd best get on," they said. "Winter's coming." We stayed where we were and Susan died anyway.

Now childless, we traveled as fast as we could, trying to make up lost ground. One ox died from the pace. Another died in the first blizzard of the year. A third died for lack of forage after the snow fell. *In another life,* I thought, *this might be funny.* We crawled to Oregon City with fifteen pounds of food, two sets of clothing, and a dying ox. There was a last stretch of river we had to travel, the wagon a caulked rectangle.

We capsized. Elias hit his head on a rock and drowned. The ox made it across along with exactly twelve of our bullets and three pounds of food. I traded them all for clothes enough to cover me. The bystanders who fished me out of the river told me not to feel sorry for myself. "You made it," they said. "You've won."

I thought then of the general store in Fort Laramie months ago when we had money still, but Elias had wanted to barter. "Why did you kill so much?" the trader asked, wrinkling his nose at the nearly spoiled meat.

"I don't know," Elias said. "I am driven. I am forced. I am spurred to do these things that make no sense."

"I'm sorry about your little ones," the trader said.

"'As flies to wanton boys are we to the gods,'" Elias said. "'They kill us for their sport.'"

"What the hell does that mean?" the trader asked.

"Don't mind my husband," I said. "He was a banker. He's had more education than's been good for him. Who ever knows what he's on about?"

It was a disloyal thing to say, I feel now. I knew exactly what Elias meant, and I loved that he knew lines of Shakespeare. He had recited me love sonnets once, back in Illinois, when we were young and green. Greener than grass, greener than the treetops in the damp Willamette. The valley spread beneath me when I finally made Oregon. *Greener than this, God,* I thought. *What were we thinking, and why did You make us? What business did a banker have shooting bears?*

ALL OVER WITH FIRE

Thereza told him to call her Jenny, her English name, the name she once chose from a list in a school textbook.

"Can I call you Theresa?" George bargained. "Tess?"

Thereza shook her head. "I'm just—Jenny, in English. Jenny, when I'm with you." She smiled and squeezed his leg under the table. The Hostinec U Kocoura had wide wooden tables, and her hand did not reach farther than his knee.

George wondered if this meant that Thereza was really someone else entirely, someone she did not wish him to know or speak with or touch. "Who were you in Russian class?"

She'd never taken Russian, she said. It wasn't required anymore by the time she was old enough to enroll.

"And you didn't choose to take it?"

"Why would I? Losers language."

George tried to hear where an apostrophe might be, whether there was a single *loser* or many. Was Thereza making a sweeping statement of national superiority or did she consider speaking Russian a more personal failure, like picking one's nose in public?

"What if I asked you to call me Jiří? That's the Czech version of George, right? My landlord told me."

"You can't even pronounce it properly. You are not allowed to have a name you can't pronounce."

George wanted to volley the serve, but her pronunciation of Jenny was aggressively correct, the English *J* bouncing like a hard rubber ball each time she said it. "Then who is this Jenny person?"

"She drinks tea," Thereza said, wrapping her fingers around her glass of beer as if to conceal the contents. "She eats biscuits and says, 'How do you do?' just like she learned in her lessons."

"And who is George?" George asked her.

"I think he has a big American house, with a yard for the children to play in, and a car he drives every day to work. He has a dog that is yellow and happy. So American! I think he has a wife too—but maybe she is not so happy."

"The kids are both away at college, and the dogs are brown. Two mutts."

"And the wife?"

"Oh, she's happy sometimes. Just not with me."

Thereza finished her beer and returned the glass to the table with a hard thunk. "Would you like if I took you sightseeing tomorrow? I am a good guide. When I was a student I worked at the castle, giving tours."

"I'd like that very much," he said. As they parted ways at her tram stop, she leaned in and kissed George on the tip of his nose. He wondered if she'd simply mis-aimed or whether she'd meant to confuse him. After all, he'd thought he was going on a dinner date with Thereza Lenhártova and she'd turned out to be a Jenny. Bait and switch.

They'd met the night before at one of the bars George's landlord had suggested. He'd pulled a pile of pamphlets and maps out of a drawer in the apartment kitchenette and penned little red Xs on popular expat clubs, *hospodas*, and *restauraces*. The landlord was Austrian, friendly but businesslike; he knew how extortionate his weekly rates for the studio apartment in the Malá Strana were. He assumed George was a tourist vacationing in style. George didn't know what he was, what he was doing, or how long he might stay. It was mid-November, and the landlord attempted some commiseration about how the American election still didn't have a clear winner.

"Still? I've been trying to avoid the news, honestly." The landlord looked at him with disapproval, and George felt the need to explain. "I don't see it making much difference, really, whichever way things go."

It was the same thing he'd said to his wife, Maria, about the absentee ballot he told her he'd cast for Bush II. He hadn't actually voted for Bush. He'd forgotten that he'd be out of the country for the election—he'd never been out of the country—so he hadn't remembered to vote at all. He'd thought of how annoyed the fact that he hadn't voted would make her, and then he'd seized the opportunity to annoy her even more by saying he'd voted for Bush. Except she hadn't been annoyed; she'd been furious, and when he'd said it didn't matter—they lived in Texas, for Christ's sake, land of foregone conclusions—she was scornful.

"I guess you're the kind of guy who gets to think that," she said. "I guess you're the kind of person who can pretend that's true."

What kind of person is that? he'd almost asked her but held his tongue. Their couples counselor had recommended they try to save "charged discussions" for their weekly appointments.

The bar had been packed, the music painful, and George had felt a decade too old for the place until Thereza asked him to dance, at which point he'd felt even older. George didn't like to dance, had never been able to dance, but was unsure how to explain that to this woman half his age, fully his height, half again more attractive than anyone who'd ever stood this close to him at a bar. Her hair was long and black and her eyes deliberately sleepy, outlined in dark makeup. He tried to extricate himself from the dancing but still get her number. He had to explain that he didn't have a Czech phone yet—*yet*, he emphasized.

She asked if he was American and when he said yes she said, "I thought so." George asked if it was a good thing or a bad thing and Thereza said it was just a thing.

"I didn't vote for the idiot. I voted for the other guy," George lied.

She didn't look up from her purse, from which she fished out a business card.

He held it right in front of his face but still couldn't read it in the dim light. "Can I take you to dinner? Drinks?"

They were shouting over the music, and George felt like a caveman, his courtship reduced to its most basic elements: *You pretty. I provide food.*

"Sure. Call me. We don't have to dance."

Any further attempts at conversation would have just left them hoarse, so she eased her way back into the crowd, her fingertips touching his arm and then sliding away in a whisper he imagined he could feel the rest of the night. When he staggered out of the bar into the chilly air of the Staré Město, he found a streetlight bright enough to read the card. *Thereza Lenhártova*, he read, *Feasibility Analyst*. The breathy *T* and *Z* slid down his tongue like Thereza's fingers on his arm, but the job title was so opaque it prompted him to wonder suddenly if Thereza was an escort, this whole exchange part of some well-heeled come-on. Walking back to his apartment, he found an internet café still open, nobody but tourists inside, and bought ten minutes. He searched the firm listed on the business card and found a staff page with thumbnail pictures. There she was, Thereza Lenhártova in slightly pixelated glory, her business degree and contact information listed below. Along with relief, George allowed a breath of excitement to enter into him, a sweaty-palmed, quick-hearted thrill for his first date in almost thirty years. Thereza Lenhártova was not a prostitute. She was a feasibility analyst with Novak/Hrbac and Associates, and she had for some as yet unidentified reason found George feasible.

*   *   *

The morning of the sightseeing plans, the morning after the dinner and the nose-kiss, George stood shaving in front of his bathroom mirror and thought, *You're making a fool of yourself.* But it wasn't an organic thought, a judgment he would pass on himself. He heard some other voice saying it, his mother's, his wife's. He squared his shoulders, there in his apartment where no one could see him, and tightened the muscles of his runner's body, the legs he knew were lean and strong. On the weekends he ran 15Ks with graying men whose wiriness had stretched to gristle, bodies gone stringy or soft; that was not George, not yet, anyway, and he was proud that he could say so.

George's rental was wall-to-wall Ikea, new and pale and clean-lined. The front windows looked out on Kampa Island, the wooden waterwheel on the Čertovka canal, trees with autumn's last leaves clinging dead to their branches. A rank of brocaded town houses stretched to the north and south of George's building. The air was fresh and very cold and George opened the windows and pretended to be an exiled nobleman. He turned on the satellite television and pretended to be rich. He picked up the secondhand phone he'd bought and told himself, *You are a rich exiled nobleman. You are George of Nosticova Street. A beautiful girl met you for dinner and she is going to show you her city.*

Jenny-Thereza was indeed a good guide; she paid attention to what interested him most, cutting short the intricacies of baroque architecture and pointing out instead the twenty-seven tiled crosses in the Old Town Square

that commemorated the beheadings of twenty-seven Prot-
estant noblemen; she took him to the church where the
paratroopers who'd assassinated Heydrich took sanctuary
until they were all shot to death by Nazis. They looked
down at the black cross bubbling out of the cobblestones
at the foot of the National Museum, the spot where a
young man had set himself on fire to protest the Soviet
invasion.

"So this is where he died," George whispered, inching
his toes closer. He fought the urge to kneel.

"This is where he put himself on fire. He died later, in
hospital. His friends, they were supposed to suicide too,
and he told them no, please don't, the pain is so much, we
did not think it will be so much pain."

George was already looking at the charred cross through
the lens of his camera when Thereza said this and then he
couldn't decide whether to take the picture.

They finished the day at the statue of the martyr John
of Nepomuk, thrown off the Charles Bridge, where tourists
closed their eyes and made wishes.

"Put your hand here and face north," Thereza told him.
"And it is sure that you will return to Prague someday."

George had already laid his hand on the brass cross
thinking he got his choice of wishes; he didn't know how
he felt about returning to Prague. He had been here eleven
days and some mornings he woke up and never wanted to
leave. Other mornings he was convinced that this city had
destroyed his life. He had to make a deliberate effort not to
pull his hand away.

"Another day we can see pretty things," Thereza said. "I

would like to show you some. But you seem to like better political things. Dead things."

George didn't know what to say. He felt embarrassed now, exposed as a historical voyeur. But she took the tram home with him anyway.

"Very posh," she said as he held the door for her. "How much are you paying?"

George told her, and she looked both amused and horrified. George took her to his bedroom and she began to undress. She was so pale he could see everywhere the webbing of her veins, trellised up her legs, down her arms, converging on the bottoms of her wrists, the backs of her hands. George closed his eyes and pressed down on her skin with his palms, relieved that the feel of her was unmarred, smooth and anonymous and youthful. He felt awkward but couldn't tell if he was actually being clumsy or whether, after so many years of only Maria, he might be utterly suave and still feel strange. If Thereza perceived his self-consciousness, she didn't let on. She seemed eager and assured, and George could barely breathe under a wave of what he told himself was pleasure but recognized as gratitude.

George bought a guidebook and researched field trips to take while Thereza wrote feasibility reports for German retailers considering expansion into the Czech Republic. He took the bus to Lidice, where little bronze statues of long-dead schoolchildren huddled in the foundations of their ruined schoolhouse, and to the Terezín concentration camp, where he watched vacationing couples try to decide whether they should smile in their photographs. He wasn't sure where his new interest in martyrdom had come from. Thereza asked him in front of the penguin exhibit at the zoo the next weekend what he had done all week and he was ashamed to answer, although he did. She seemed visibly disconcerted that George was a man of such insatiable appetites, that the corpses she'd offered last weekend had been insufficient.

He had no idea how to explain it to her, didn't think she'd understand. He kept asking her about what life was like before, under the Communists, and she always told him that she had been a child, that she remembered little, that life after the revolution was very nearly the only life she knew.

"There was one kind of yogurt in the shops," she said, "and then there were eight. It was hard to choose."

She was impatient with the topic but he kept asking. It was important to him to feel like he was making her life better, like he was an *after* rescuing her from an inclement *before*. In truth, he knew she didn't need him. She wore clothes bought on Národní Třída and owned the slimmest cell phone he'd ever seen. George was unsure what he had to offer, and this seemed like a test, a quiz he could ace only if he had all the relevant information.

"But what else?" he said. "What else is different now?"

"I don't *know*. The shoes are better. What do you want me to say?"

What George really wanted were answers to questions he didn't have the nerve to ask, either because Thereza would be angry or, worse, because she might just shrug, shake her head no. *Do you know anyone who was tortured?* he wanted to ask. *Imprisoned? Informed on? Do you know anyone touched by fire?*

After the zoo they took a tram to the Nové Mĕsto so Thereza could do some shopping. George paid for a blouse, a pair of shoes. She didn't ask him to and he didn't offer; he simply took her selections out of her arms and carried them to the register. At the Metro station they held hands in the middle of the platform, waiting for trains traveling in opposite directions.

"I'd like to see you again," George said. "Soon." And it was only after Thereza said yes, after her train shouted out of the tunnel and opened its doors, that he handed her the shopping bags.

The evenings that Thereza was busy with work or with a life she did not care to tell George much about, he did not live in his apartment like a nobleman. He sat at his kitchen table with stacks of receipts, a calculator, his best guesses at the previous balance of his checking account, savings, the limits on his credit cards. He estimated the date SoluMed would have officially stopped paying him and added in Maria's November pay as an accounts receivable manager. He tried to remember if there was another tuition payment to Texas A&M due this semester or not until January. He tracked the shifting exchange rate between dollars and crowns. It was slipping constantly, in favor of the crown. He looked around at his nobleman's apartment and no longer felt rich. He left the windows cracked open for the sharp air and the sounds of the river and turned off the game on satellite television, Sparta Praha versus Tottenham

Hotspurs. He'd thought maybe, if he stayed in Europe for a while, he should try to get into soccer. He'd gathered from half hearing the news that his country still didn't have a clear future president. He realized he didn't know who the current president of the Czech Republic was either, though he could list all the Communist ones in order.

So maybe he wasn't a nobleman, George thought. Maybe he was an oppressed citizen of a Communist regime. Maybe he spent an entire winter eating cauliflower and boiled potatoes. George had bought several memoirs from the Museum of Communism and read them carefully. He went to the local market and bought a wedge of rye bread, white cheese, harsh coffee. He ate and read that night about traveling to East Germany to buy oranges for Christmas. He thought about asking Thereza to take the train to Dresden with him. They would go to the German department stores and he would take an escalator to the basement supermarket while she shopped upstairs. He would lift a single orange from the stacks of hundreds and try to feel what had once made it special.

Maria's most recent e-mail to him had been about the holidays. *Both boys are planning to come home for Thanksgiving,* she'd written. *What do you want me to tell them? And what about Christmas break?*

He hadn't replied, because he had no idea.

It had been two and a half weeks since George let British Airways Flight 807 leave Prague-Ruzyně without him, just let it plow up into the air and sail westward while he sat nursing a beer at the Holiday Inn Congress Center hotel bar, his suitcase between his feet. When he finished the beer, he asked to check back in to his room. "I'd like to buy another night," he said, and another and another, until the desk clerk had observed that that might not be the best idea, that after all the frantic calls—from his wife, from his boss, from the Houston Police Department, from their couples counselor, Dr. Valenzuela—George had become something of a burden on the front-desk staff. "Perhaps you should make other arrangements," the concierge had suggested, and George had combed the *Prague Post* for listings, called the Austrian, counted his money, and packed his suitcase. He had sent an e-mail to his wife from an internet café on a square named after the boy who'd set himself on fire. *I'm fine,* he wrote. *Please stop calling the hotel. I'm not staying there anymore. No phone at present. Love, George.*

In his previous life, the one he'd spent as a medical-equipment sales representative in Houston, George had found himself vibrating. He would take a paper out of the fax machine and watch it tremble. His coffee shivered in his mug and he wedged his knees under his desk as if he might otherwise float into the air. His elbows quivered like dragonfly wings; his fingers twitched like antennae. He drafted catalog copy for the direct-consumer mailing, gently describing devices that could help caregivers perform what a loved one's body no longer could. George did this so well that SoluMed had signed him up months ago to present at an industry conference in Prague. He had counted the days until the trip. He was a bird, a mosquito, a balloon, a zeppelin. He was rising.

It would be his first time in Europe. He and Maria had

met young, married young, had the boys before they were thirty. He'd been working flat out since graduating college, mostly jobs that bored him, though neither he nor Maria had grown up with the idea that work should be interesting. Work was work, and there'd been enough of it to cover the bills, but by the time there was enough left to travel, the versions of themselves that would have known what to do on a romantic trip with each other were long gone. The prospect of a long-haul flight beside her was a terror; what would they talk about, those nine hours in the air to Heathrow? He was relieved when she expressed no interest in coming with him, even when Dr. Valenzuela suggested that it might be a good opportunity to reconnect. He was less relieved when he started to piece together that she was almost definitely having an affair. They hadn't talked about it because he hadn't wanted to know for sure, because then he would have needed to have some reaction, some idea of whether what they had was worth fighting for, which meant having some idea of what they still had. Instead, he'd done things like fail to take out the garbage or bait her about his vote, feeble little rebellions. Refusing to come home—he didn't know quite what he was doing or why, but the *scale* of it, at least, felt right.

One Sunday morning George went for his run, down cobblestoned Nosticova Street and through the park on Kampa Island. Thereza was still in bed when he returned, sleepy but waking, and he showered and crawled back under the covers with her. He wished he had coffee, a doughnut, the paper, in English. He settled for tracing the veins at

Thereza's temples, the way they spread like fingers from the edge of her eyebrows into her hair.

"Why?" he asked her. "Why are you with me?"

"I like you?" she said, the question mark palpable.

"I'm too old."

"You're not too old."

"I'm ugly."

"You're not ugly."

"I'm out of shape."

"Ha. You want compliments. You are as bad as a woman. Shall I tell you your legs—no, thighs, they are nice and slim?"

"Seriously. Why?"

"Men your age, you are always so polite."

"That's an explanation?"

"You like nice things. Good wine and food. Not always *pivo* and a *smažený sýr* at two in the morning."

"I like fried cheese as much as the next guy."

"No, you don't. You like your clean apartment and your nice food. It's a good life, the things you like."

George made lists in his head of things his life no longer contained: a job, a house, two dogs. He missed his dogs, their uncomplicated, eager love, their excitement over their unexciting lives. In Texas right now, his mother-in-law was saying, "You were always too good for him." The neighbors were saying, "I haven't seen George lately, have you?" His sons probably weren't saying anything at all, being loving but oblivious boys who let weeks pass between phone calls or e-mails. He didn't know what Maria might be saying.

★   ★   ★

Thereza had tried to talk him out of Letenská, but he'd insisted on visiting; the world's largest statue of Stalin had once stood there on a concrete platform the size of a football field high above the city. Now it was simply a concrete platform the size of a football field, covered in graffiti and teenagers smoking weed. Thereza was visibly annoyed to be there, and George tried to conceal his disappointment, staving off any *I told you so*s. They sat with their feet swinging off the end of the platform that overlooked the river, and he confided in her about the affair.

"I don't believe in monogamy," she announced. "I don't think it is possible. Twenty-eight years, and you really expect to have only the one person forever?"

Monogamy; he was impressed again at how good her English was. He couldn't pretend that she didn't know what she was saying, dismissing his heartache. Except it wasn't even heartache. It was more diffuse, this life-sick uncertainty. He asked Thereza if there was a Czech word for the feeling, or a German one. Possibly one existed in Russian, but neither of them would know it. Instead of offering a word, she asked him to describe the feeling.

He thought of the bubbling cross, the sorry suicide. It was an obscene comparison, and he made it anyway: "Like being set on fire."

"And this is what you do when you are on fire? Instead of finding a bucket of water, you run around the world in your little orange jog shorts. You stay all over with fire."

"Did I do something to make you angry?"

Thereza kicked her heels against the concrete like a child. "No. But you are a type of person, you understand—the man in middle life, unhappy with his wife, unhappy in his country, so he comes to Czech and thinks everything will be better."

I guess you're the kind of guy who gets to think that, he heard Maria saying. "Look, I'm not a type of person, I'm a person."

"You are both. Me too. I'm the pretty girl who makes things better." She blinked at him like a cartoon ingenue.

He did not feel, in this moment, like she was making anything better, but he understood that he had told her about the affair because he had expected her to.

"I'm not trying to be mean," she said. "Only that I know this story already, and it is a boring story."

"Then you can tell me how it ends," George said, but Thereza declined.

Five weeks after George arrived in Prague his ATM card stopped working. The machine whirred and beeped and ate it. He went to an internet café to confirm the balance of his checking account, the limit on his Visa. The pages refused to load, the bank claiming he had a defunct user ID. He gave up and checked his e-mail, found a message from his wife. She had closed the joint checking account, reopened one in her name only; she had emptied the savings account into a twelve-month CD under her name. *Come home and we'll talk,* she had written. *I'm sorry for a lot of things. But I'm not financing your midlife crisis.*

Riding the tram back to his apartment, George was

terrified of pickpockets. He pressed his wallet against his thigh, forgetting that almost everything inside it was now useless. At the apartment, he returned a call from the Austrian. "I'm not sure I need a whole week. Would that be possible, to just buy a couple of days?"

"You've been a good tenant. Two days, we will say."

George asked if he could pay by credit card this time, gave him the number of the one card he'd always held in his name only, asked if the Austrian might be able to process a larger amount, let George have the difference: "So many of the places around here only take cash."

The answer was a polite no: transaction fees, exchange rates. "Congratulations, though," the Austrian said with more than a hint of sarcasm, and George froze.

"On what?" The absolute mess he'd somehow made of his entire life? Had the Austrian guessed why George needed the money? How many tourists had flailed in and flamed out of this apartment? All the birch-colored, clean-lined furniture suddenly looked sinister.

"Your new president," his landlord elaborated, though George had watched so little news he didn't know who had been declared the victor. "You finally have a winner."

"I guess that's good?"

"I wouldn't have said so myself. But of course, there is value in knowing the outcome."

The only hobby Thereza had ever talked about was beach volleyball, of all things; she met people once a week at BeachKlubPraha, a few sandy courts and a plywood cabana wedged into the yard of a junior high school near Pankrác

Prison. George waited for her evening practice to end; he'd counted the money left in his wallet and didn't eat that day. It took him half an hour of walking from the Pankrác Metro station to find the BeachKlub, and his stomach growled audibly as he watched Thereza play. He'd been hungry for a single day and it was all he could think about. He would have made a terrible dissident, he knew.

It was much too cold to be standing still outside but the players were jumping and diving and Thereza was sweating in leggings and a T-shirt. He handed her the water bottle beside her gym bag as she came off the court, and she began to shiver almost immediately, gooseflesh flaring across her arms and legs.

She seemed both surprised and unsurprised to see him there. "What are you doing this weekend?" she asked him. George didn't respond, keeping his face carefully blank in the hope that Thereza might suggest an escape plan. "If you are free, I thought we might go to Dresden, maybe Berlin. Lots of sightseeing for you. Maybe some shopping?"

"Jenny. Thereza. I'm not a rich man," George said.

"I know, you are not made of money. Or you don't grow on trees, or something."

"It's not a joke. It's a—confession," he said, searching for the right word and feeling a bit surprised that he'd found it: he had a secret to confess. "I'm broke."

"Really?"

Shame kept him silent, but the answer was clear enough.

"Then I suppose we shouldn't go to Germany."

"I really can't afford it. I'm sorry."

"Will you go home now?"

"I don't know."

"Then where will you go?"

"I don't know."

"You need cheap places, Bratislava is very fine. Romania, Ukraine, the life there is very hard, so the prices very low. Go to the villages. My parents, they have a weekend house in Mokri. The restaurant there serves soup for eight crowns."

"I'm really broke, Thereza. I don't have the money to go anywhere else."

Thereza stared at him. "You need money."

"I'll pay it back."

"You have no job."

"I'll get one."

"*Do prdele*. You are asking *me* for money."

"If there were anyone else—"

"How about your *wife?* She can wire you money. Buy you a plane ticket online. You are not in Siberia."

"A plane ticket?"

"You have some other plan?"

It was only then that George realized how badly he wanted Thereza to say, *Stay in Prague. Stay with me. Stay in my apartment that you have never seen, and call me by my name, which I have never let you use.* He understood at the same time how impossible it was for her to say it. It wasn't even that he thought they could live well together. He couldn't picture himself looking for a job here, couldn't picture what he would be qualified for. Couldn't picture making pork and dumplings for Sunday dinners at home. He just wanted to hear her say, *Stay,* and to feel as if there were still a choice to be made.

"The very earliest she could get me money would be tomorrow."

"So?"

"I haven't eaten all day."

"This is not my problem. You are not my problem."

"Thereza—"

"I told you to call me Jenny."

The other players were pulling on coats and sweatpants, carefully looking away but standing close enough to hear. George wondered how much English they understood. Thereza grabbed her bag and pulled him around a corner of the school until they were standing by themselves under a rusted basketball hoop. She pulled her wallet from her gym bag and took out the cash. She counted it, handed it all to him. Three hundred crowns. Twelve dollars.

"You can see," she said. "All the cash I have this moment. You will need to call your wife soon. You will be so hungry, the plane ride will be happier. You will be going back to America, but they will feed you. You will see her in Texas and you will say, *Wife! My stomach is full now of frozen chicken, thank you! Cruel Czech girl, she gives only sandwich and bus fare to airport.*"

That much was true, George thought. That as he got on BA Flight 807 two days from now with a ticket his wife had paid for, the same flight he refused to board five weeks earlier, he would be thankful. He would soar toward London and then Houston and when they brought him a plastic-wrapped sandwich, a thin foil tray, a tiny cup of soda, he would be agonizingly grateful.

THE UNTRANSLATABLES

He was a collector. He put the words in notebooks, on the backs of envelopes, and on index cards, like recipes. He typed them up in computer files without any attempt at alphabetization, *hyggelig* following *ilunga* following *Scheissenbedauern,* the last of which meant "being disappointed when something turns out better than expected," a feeling he could not remember ever experiencing.

He believed that one day he would put all the untranslatables in a scrapbook dictionary. It would be large and heavy with startlingly sharp corners, and he would place it on a shelf and wait for the woman who would notice it. Leaving her in his living room, he would go to the kitchen to make coffee or pour wine. Lingering, he'd listen for the sound of the book being pulled off the shelf, the slight grunt as she realized how heavy it was, then returned to the couch with it. He would wait for the woman who loved his untranslatables, who would say, *The word* gökotta *means "to picnic at dawn on Ascension Day and listen for the cuckoo's song."* This, he promised himself, was the woman he would marry—the only woman he could marry—but his book was not yet done. There was no purpose even in inviting a woman to his home before then, because he would not be able to learn the one thing about her he needed most to know.

Many of the untranslatables were German, but not all. *Luoma,* Finnish, verb: to give up something, but peacefully and wholeheartedly, as after a long illness or a deep suffering, and to step, however wistfully, into the next part of your life. *Mamihlapinatapei,* from Yaghan, an indigenous language of Tierra del Fuego: a wordless glance between two people, lingering and meaningful. They can be lovers or strangers but they are both hoping very much for something to happen. Neither risks initiating.

There was a temp at the insurance agency where he worked with whom he once shared such a glance. She had pale orange hair and eyes so green he thought she might be wearing colored contacts. He was delivering papers to her to be alphabetized and filed. She took the papers and their eyes met and *mamihlapinatapei* passed between them and then her phone rang. She apologized and answered. He never saw her again. He was both grieved and pleased that he had experienced the true meaning of this Yaghan word, and he felt closer to those faraway people who had invented it. He understood them, he thought, and they him, even if he didn't understand the temp.

He treasured even the words he could not pronounce,

could write only by tracing: Ιστορίες με αρκούδες, "stories with bears," meaning anecdotes so improbable that the listener doubts their veracity even as he hopes ardently for them to be true. Over the years his house had filled with thousands of words. They burst out of desk drawers and underwear drawers and cutlery drawers. English, although his native tongue, looked poorer and more enfeebled by the day. He was desperate to tell someone about all these words. He wondered what the temp might have said, if she would have believed him or if she would have dismissed him for telling stories with bears. He wondered if her eyes had really been so green and what the word for that shade might be.

He surrendered himself to *toska,* about which Nabokov had once bragged: "No single word in English renders all the shades of *toska*. At its deepest and most painful, it is a sensation of great spiritual anguish, often without any specific cause. At less morbid levels it is a dull ache of the soul, a longing with nothing to long for."

And in the throes of *toska* the collector acquired *Kummerspeck,* "grief bacon," which was extra weight gained through emotional overeating. And when he wanted so much to *cafuné,* to gently run his fingers through someone's hair in Brazilian Portuguese, that he could barely breathe, he calmed himself by reciting more playful words like *tingo,* which on Easter Island meant to slowly remove all the objects from a neighbor's house by borrowing and not returning them.

One day, however, even his untranslatables could not console him, and he began to write descriptions with no words. He knew he could just make up a string of syllables, but he didn't feel like he would be good at it. He would need an ear for it, and that went on an index card as well: *A feel for the sounds of spoken language, an instinct for what noises will best suit a particular meaning.* He chanted nonsense syllables to himself in the shower, knowing that they might be incantations in some language he had never heard or that had long since died or that had yet to be created.

He realized that he might be a *Korinthenkacker,* a "raisin pooper," someone so taken with trivial details that he spent all day crapping raisins, someone like his office manager, who left trails of obsessive Post-it notes across everyone's desk. But his untranslatables didn't feel like raisins or like Post-its. They felt immense, so immense they couldn't be contained in a house, much less a scrapbook, and the man began to build a shed in his backyard. The untranslatables filled the outbuilding before the roof was finished, and in a rainstorm the sheaves of paper grew soft and damp and then mildewed, and he could find no word for what he felt when he looked at them, at the work of so many years rotting in his hands.

But such a word must exist or else the collector was feeling some emotion that no human, in all the ages of the earth, had ever felt, and that was such a lonely thought that he thrust it immediately from him. He redoubled his research, searching for this word, and then began to worry that perhaps it was already in him, hidden in plain sight, and mistakenly assigned to a utilitarian object. *Toast,* perhaps, was meant to mean something grander than warm, crispy bread. *Milk,* or *eat,* or *check the mail,* or *check,* or *mail.* He sat at his office desk and whispered aloud the names of all his office supplies, waiting for one to bloom. These recitations he tried to make sound like the patter of a radio, to avoid drawing his coworkers' concern. But eventually he stopped talking altogether; ordinary words had become potentially deceptive, and he couldn't even be sure what he meant, much less what others meant.

Poor communication skills, the office manager wrote in his dismissal letter.

He asked if she could recommend a temp agency that might sign him. Where had the insurance company hired its temps from?

That was confidential, she said. No, she couldn't refer him. She couldn't even give him the name.

Aceldama, a place where much blood has been shed. *Orenda,* a single human's will set against the encroaching forces of destiny. That was a Huron word, which, given the near decimation of the tribe, took on extra resonance. He wondered about a new category of untranslatables: Words that in their historical context became ironic or inefficacious. Words that did not even mean themselves once history was done with them.

His house softened and rotted like paper while grass grew tall and fierce, and the city came and posted new words on his doors and windows until he left. He felt *Torschlusspanik,* which was the gate-closing panic caused by one's life narrowing to a tunnel. And finally he felt as if he were living with *yoko meshi,* "boiled rice eaten sideways," the stress of trying to communicate in a foreign language.

His whole life, he had been eating and eating, all of it sideways.

That was the last of his definitions without words: the loneliness, the tension of the tongue, the torque of a jaw that has held as many words as it can, and a heart that is still empty. He did not believe he could be the only person who had wanted for this word. He knew it must be out there somewhere. And so he kept a chewed pencil nub beside a single sheet of paper, blank and expectant. He waited along with the paper, desperate to hear the word in someone's mouth, to recognize it. To recognize her, looking up at him with green eyes and a mouth full of names. *Luoma,* he sometimes tried to tell himself. *Luoma.* But he could not accomplish it. Instead, he swallowed the word and crouched, listening, until his whole body was an ear.

PARADISE LODGE

The plane from Cuzco arrives only a little late; the mini-bus gets only a little stuck on the muddy road; the long motorized canoe scrapes threateningly at the river bottom but does not run aground. This group of tourists is not as fat as the last one, Victor notices cheerily. They are easily charmed too—by the sticky rice wrapped in banana leaves that Victor serves from a cooler for lunch; by the cartoon jaguar that the park security checkpoint stamps in their passports. Victor does not tell them that this is the only jaguar they will see all week. He does not tell them that the animal is so endangered in the Tambopata that they're as likely to see a *chullachaqui* or a unicorn.

From the dock, the guests clamber up the muddy slope to the main building, a giant A-frame of dark logs, thatched roof. A manager assigns room numbers and guides. A single mother with two kids and a bickering young couple

189

are entrusted to Victor's care. It's a bad draw, and some of the other guides nod sympathetically. But no one offers to trade. Victor asks the children where they're from, making conversation while the luggage is brought up from the boat. Bogotá? Yes, Colombia, despite their North American accents and corn-silk hair, heads and arms and legs catching the sunlight, flashing like traffic reflectors in the clearing beside the lodge. They do not ask him where he is from, so he does not have to lie, pretend he's jungle-born.

Their mother notices her children glistening. It should be beautiful, and it is, her long-limbed, fuzzy children, but the emotion that lingers longest is sympathy at how many hours of life her daughter is destined to spend shaving or waxing. Aileen would never force her, plans to sit her down when she asks for a razor and say, "You know you're beautiful just the way you are, honey." Then she'll hand over the shaving gel. The world is the way the world is, and there's no point wishing otherwise.

The guide—Victor, he said his name was—escorts the family to adjoining rooms, a porter following with the luggage. All the rooms in the lodge are doubles, and of course Aileen reserved two when her husband was scheduled to come. Then he couldn't get away from work, or, more properly, he didn't want to. There was no one in the Bogotá office who would brave telling Julian what he should or shouldn't do.

Might it be possible to move one of the beds into her children's room, she asks Victor, and make one triple room? There'd been a last-minute illness, no time to change the booking. Her son's face furrows. His father is ill? "It's not about the money," Aileen says. "I can pay for the original reservation." She suspects this is the wrong thing to say—the guide seemed to understand the request when he assumed it was about money. But she doesn't want to try to explain how lonely she'll feel listening to her children giggle together on the other side of the wall.

"It is not possible," Victor says and shows her how the twin beds are built into the walls, how the individual mosquito nets are rigged from the towering ceiling, a cathedral of dark wood and thatch. Anchored to the beams are miles of fishing line, crisscrossing under the eaves. "To keep birds from nesting?" Aileen asks.

"Bats," Victor says in a tone that suggests the lodge would prefer guests not notice this particular feature. Better they notice the in-room hammocks, the neat rows of bio-degradable soaps and shampoos in the low-flow bathroom. This is a serious lodge, management insists: educational, conservation-minded. No steamy jungle idylls or boozy colonial fantasies.

If there *were* jaguars, Victor would be forbidden to take guests anywhere near them. This season the Mammal Walk trail has been rerouted to avoid disturbing a rare nesting pair of harpy eagles. Against orders, Victor sneaks off alone sometimes to see them. Week after week the eaglet is no more than a fuzzy gray lump, a moldy potato, even through his most powerful binoculars. He's not sure why he keeps visiting. Maybe he is waiting to see something change, although he doesn't know what.

Victor leaves Aileen to check on the young couple. The porter has already dumped their luggage, barely inside their bedroom doorway, probably assuming, based on the scruffy backpacks, that they won't tip. Victor looks at their cheap T-shirts and flip-flops and worries the porter is correct. The girl is already sunburned; she's red-haired and so pale Victor wonders why she hasn't learned to be more careful. Her boyfriend is brown-skinned, with lank, shaggy black hair. Their children will look weird, Victor thinks, if these two stay together.

He takes the young couple on an orientation tour that finishes in the dining room, where there are eggs and fruit salad every morning. Bananas are available all day, suspended in a special cage to keep insects off. Guests usually joke that it looks like the bananas are in jail: "What are they in for? How much time are they serving?"

"Ha-ha," Victor always says. "Good one."

The young couple say nothing about the bananas, and the porter's assumption turns out to have been wrong, because as soon as Victor points them back toward their bedroom, the boy tries to give him money. It's all change, pressed hard into Victor's palm with a nervous pressure.

"You don't have to give this now," Victor says carefully. "You'll see a lot more of me over the next few days."

"Take it, please."

"Shall I give it to the porter?" Victor asks. "For taking your bags to your room?"

"Uh, sure. Okay?" The boy looks at his girlfriend, who shrugs.

Victor likes that she is not going to bother pretending to know things she doesn't. He explains the usual tipping protocol. He doesn't even inflate the numbers. He is a professional. The guestbook is full of compliments about him personally, as if he were an amenity like the all-day bananas. *Impressive vegetarian options. Victor spoke perfect English!* And *Very homey decor. Victor is like a Wikipedia of the jungle!* The less popular guides make fun of him, call him Wiki. At night, in the staff dorm, they tease him about the eagle nest, how he spends his rare free hours in the jungle or studying on his bunk, poring over wildlife guides borrowed from the lodge library. Between guest changeovers in Puerto Maldonado, his girlfriend, Ana, tries to replace the books in his backpack with guides to Incan terracing or the Nazca lines, the corners of their country they've never had the chance to see. The lodge's parent company owns other properties—mountain aeries near Machu Picchu, seaside resorts near Lima. On his one weekly night in town, they whisper in the bedroom she shares with her sister in her parents' apartment. Victor always feels tense and hurried, anxious about her parents knocking or her sister coming home early from her late shift at the family store downstairs. But before they undress, Ana insists on quizzing him: the dates of the last Incan emperor's reign or what to do in case of altitude sickness or angry llamas. She quizzes him on when, exactly, he'll demand a transfer. He asks her what is so very awful about the place they live.

"You don't even live here," she says. "You live in the jungle six days a week. You live like an animal."

Maybe, Victor thinks, he admires the eagles' silence. They sleep and hunt and vomit food into their baby's mouth. If that were all that was required of him, he could be a good husband. A good father to the baby Ana has told him is coming.

After he left her apartment last night, he stopped at the family store and pulled an Inca Kola from the cooler. Ana's sister usually charged him full price, but that night she pushed both the bottle and his money back across the counter toward him. "She finally told you?" she said.

"Finally?" Victor said, and he wondered how long Ana's sister had known.

She added a Cua Cua bar from the display near the register, then a lotto ticket.

"Because I'm on such a good run tonight," Victor tried to joke. "Lucky me."

"You *are* lucky. You know you are."

This was true, although she didn't mean the baby. She didn't mean Ana either, although her sister was one of the prettiest girls in Puerto Maldonado. The sister meant that Victor was himself a winning lotto ticket, albeit for one of the cheap games—El Reventón, not La Tinka. No millionaire, but he's got his English, his memory for facts, his bright, reassuring smile, even the way the indignities of tourist work slide right off him. Being angry at the wealth of strangers was like being angry at the rain, his first supervisor told him. It came whether you liked it or not, and it made things grow. It grew the jungle, grew the lodge, grew the jobs. Better it flow than stop.

Ana's sister broke the chocolate bar in half, took a bite, and spoke with her mouth full. "If the lodge were as good as you could do, fine. But it's not."

"It's not that easy."

"Don't settle. That's all she wants for the two of you. The three of you."

"Why am I having this conversation with you instead of her?" Victor still held his half of the candy bar, the waxy coating already melting onto his fingers.

"Because she's scared to push you any harder. She's scared you'll meet some rich gringa and fuck your way to a green card."

"That's not going to happen." He stuffed the Cua Cua bar in his mouth and scratched at the lotto card with his short nails, grubby with chocolate. "See? Nothing. Not as lucky as you think."

In their room before dinner, Lizzie tests the hammock. She insists there's space for Walt, but he doesn't see how, not without the fabric pushing them together like two rocks at the bottom of a bag.

"Do you think he means ten per person per day," Lizzie asks, "or ten for the two of us?"

Walt has no idea, but since it's the difference between a hundred dollars he doesn't have and fifty he still doesn't have, he supposes they should try to find out. But he doesn't know how to ask. He never has the right words. He didn't know how to convince Lizzie not to come on this trip in the first place or what to tell her father when he steamrolled Walt's original itinerary, insisting on hotels with private rooms over co-ed hostel dorms. He canceled their bus tickets to Puerto Maldonado and booked flights, replaced their chosen lodge with this one. He wanted to feel like Lizzie was safe, he told her—as if all the airplanes in the world could ensure that. He put some money toward the trip, even wanted to be thanked for his largesse, but it didn't cover all the charges he'd cowed them into accepting.

Walt's original plan had been several weeks of scrappy solo adventures before his study-abroad program started in Lima. He'd wanted a chance to test his courage, his Spanish, to see whether and how well he could convince people that he truly belonged. There weren't many international adoptions out of Peru even today, much less when he'd been adopted; someone at his parents' church had gone to college with someone who managed an NGO in Lima, and somehow he'd ended up in western Michigan. The picture books his parents read to him—*God Found Us You; I Don't Have Your Eyes; I Like Myself!*—always claimed happy endings all around. But even as a child, he'd felt the displacement, the misdirection of an author urging his attention toward the grassy lawn and the fridge full of milk and Coca-Cola, away from wherever he'd come from, whoever had once cared for him. Like a magician performing a card trick, his parents waved their love in front of him, trying to make it all he could see. It was a sincere love, fierce and depthless as any parents'. But it didn't make him look any more like the other kids in town, the strapping blond descendants of Dutch immigrants. The high-school marching band, where Walt and Lizzie had trooped beside each other in the clarinet section, performed in wooden shoes.

In Cuzco, Walt kept staring at the faces on the street, daydreams pouring out of him. He stared too much, which made him more likely to get mugged than discover a long-lost sibling, but he couldn't stop. He'd never been anywhere with so many faces looking something, anything, like his own. And then there was Lizzie, trotting along beside him, her frizzy red hair waving like a flag, like a fistful of money.

"You want me to wear a hat the whole trip?" she said, after his unease became obvious. "How about a burka?"

"Wrong country," Walt said. "Wrong continent."

"I was making a joke."

"Were you?"

"Why are you being so mean to me? You've been mean since the airport."

She'd written off the entire semester at Grand Rapids Community College to take this trip, which she spoke of as if it were an act of God rather than tickets she'd purchased in full possession of a calendar. Lizzie and Walt had started at Grand Valley State University together; Walt was still on track to graduate next year, but Lizzie had dropped out after one semester. There was an assortment of colleges within an hour's drive of their hometown, and Lizzie had sampled several, driving back to Walt's dorm or apartment on the weekends and collecting transcripts that were an expensive bouquet of Fs and Ds. Whether she fails on purpose or because she can't do any better, Walt isn't sure. Is she that lazy or that stupid, or both, or neither? Walt doesn't consider himself an ambitious person, but he's got more ambition than Lizzie. A rock has more ambition than Lizzie.

After dinner, Aileen's son conks out immediately, exhausted from the long travel day, but her daughter insists she wants to read, charmed by the novelty of the bedside candle. Aileen waits ten minutes, then creeps back in to blow out the candle, slide the book out from under her daughter's slack hand.

In her own room, she finishes unpacking by lantern light, trying not to creak the floorboards. Her children wake easily. They've always lived in compounds, houses with walled gardens, in luxury apartments so far above the street they contain a plush, impervious silence, whatever language spoken in that year's city dissipating in the air below before it could reach them. It was often unclear when Julian announced a new move whether it was forced or requested, lateral or vertical, good professional strategy or restlessness. But as Julian pointed out—sometimes subtly, sometimes not—the money kept coming. A creek, a river, a flood.

In her suitcase Aileen finds a folded piece of notebook paper with his handwriting. She assumes it will be a love note or an apology note or at least a thinking-of-you-and-the-kids-sorry-I'm-not-coming note. Instead it's a barely legible sentence about socks and being prepared for anything. It makes no sense until she unpacks her socks and feels how crackling and heavy they are, how Julian has stuffed them with an insane, anxiety-producing amount of cash. She knows he's trying to be helpful, probably trying to apologize, but she's always been a cautious packer, overprepared with currencies and cards. Now she's a walking jungle ATM. A piñata. She stuffs folded bills around the room, hoping that the hiding places that seem convincing in the dark won't look ridiculous by daylight.

*   *   *

The first day of wildlife excursions involves very little wild-life. The lodge front-loads more dependable attractions like the ethnobotany trail, the decommissioned Brazil-nut farm, the farmer across the river, toothless and tobacco-stained. As the guides usher their small groups into motorized canoes, Victor rings a bell on the lodge dock, a signal to the old man to rouse himself, put out his cigarette, and creep from under his rusted metal roof. The farm tour is purely horticultural, but the Q&A gets personal. "He lives here alone?" the guests want to know. Yes; his wife ran off after the last of the twelve children left the jungle. "Twelve!" the guests invariably exclaim. The old man grins, gestures to the scraggly fruit trees and the slow brown river, says, "Not much else to do." Some of the guests have enough Spanish to understand this without Victor's translation, and the laughter comes in two waves. Victor feels like he and the farmer have a comedy act together, an over-rehearsed skit that's bound to go stale. He realizes that no one, him-self included, has ever inquired where exactly the children went, so he asks.

"To the city," the farmer says, clearly startled by Victor's change in routine.

"To Puerto Maldonado? Or farther?"

"Both," the farmer says, an expression flickering across his weathered face that Victor's never seen before or hasn't wanted to notice. "Looking for jobs."

"Did they find them?"

Now the other guides are uncomfortable, and so are

a few of the guests. The Wikipedia of the jungle is off his game.

"Not here," the farmer says, forcing a laugh, gesturing at the endless brown and green around them. The horizon is broken only by a small smudge of smoke, a distant logging operation. "The younger ones said they might come back when the road is finished." He means the Interoceánico Highway, which is supposed to skim across South America like a pizza cutter, bringing trucks in from Brazil. People have been waiting for it since Victor was a boy. It's projected to cross the Madre de Dios River at Puerto Maldonado. The bridge site is currently nothing more than a pile of dirt, concrete, and orange plastic construction mesh.

Victor gives him cigarettes at the end of every visit. Usually the farmer palms them so gracefully the guests never even notice. Today he grabs Victor's wrist and twists his hand open. "You want to ask so many questions, you bring a second pack."

Walt and Lizzie notice and ask on the way back to the canoes if they should tip the farmer. Victor tells them no.

Aileen's heart breaks a little for the crusty old man. She thinks of her bedroom full of money. Should she try to give it to him? How would she even offer? *I'm sorry about your children,* she might say. *I worry about mine leaving. I worry about my life being too small without them.* Maudlin—she shakes herself; she's being maudlin. What is the farmer supposed to say to her pity, her desire to pretend their lives are anything alike?

★   ★   ★

Dinner is a hill of purple potatoes served with steaks brought in from who knows how far away or, maybe worse, how near. Which acres of rain forest were torched for pasture? Lizzie pays attention—see? She does!—to the environmental articles Walt posts online. At dinner she can feel his anger at the white-haired retirees in khaki vests, at the families with binoculars and wildlife guides, at the posh, pretty mother and children they're sharing every meal with. She feels as out of place as he does, but that's no reason to stew about money, about her father, about the stupid twin beds when he won't even get in the same hammock with her. At least his anger is better than his endless, pointless, self-lacerating guilt. He thinks he hides it from Lizzie and his parents, but she sees it in every link he posts online, in the way he pretends he picked Peru purely for the course offerings.

"Maybe you should go with him," his parents suggested, having contacted her without telling their son. "He won't talk to us, and he certainly won't want us to come, but we worry about him going there alone." *He doesn't talk to me either,* Lizzie tried to tell them. *Not anymore.* Dropping hints about accompanying him hadn't worked. She had to elbow her way into this trip, and she's pretty sure now it was a mistake.

"This is not the real Peru," Walt said as they were heading toward the dining room along the romantically lantern-lit elevated wooden walkway. But how would he know what was the real Peru and what wasn't? This was the problem, the whole reason for his trip, and to say it straight out seemed cruel.

Lizzie tries hard never to say anything cruel. Flow like water, her yoga teacher tells her, and after every class Lizzie contemplates asking the sinewy instructor how she should respond to her boyfriend who says she's flowed all the way to corpse pose. Maybe she should ask the instructor what it means that yoga is the only class she's attended in three years that interests her in any way. The first few weeks of every semester, she wrestles herself into the little chairs with attached desks, pinches herself awake, scrawls some notes. Then she can't bear it anymore, feels like she's earned a few days off, stays home and gets high and binge-watches an entire TV series, and by the time she returns to class, the professor says she's burned through her allowable absences. This is so obviously unreasonable to Lizzie that she finds it infuriating. How can she predict the future? How can she promise to be in the exact same place at the exact same time for weeks, vow that Early Modern Europe 1450–1789 will be her absolute highest priority? She can't tell if the professors are presenting her with a challenge she is supposed to rise to meet or if they're trying to get rid of her.

Her parents have asked if she's depressed, but she doesn't think so. It's not that she's sad, it's just that all of the things she's supposed to be doing with her life make her unhappy when she does them. She wants someone to fix this, tell her what she should be doing instead. College supposedly helps you find your purpose, but so far all college has helped her find is that she hates college, and she can't figure out what the alternatives are because there she is, stuck in college. She has a dim sense that girls who hate school are supposed to go to a cosmetology academy, do hair or nails. But she doesn't care about hair, and every woman who's ever done her nails was Vietnamese. They have a lock on nail salons as far as Lizzie can tell, and why would they hire a white girl who couldn't gossip with them?

"Those chemicals cause health problems," Walt told her. "You don't want to do nails. You don't want to be Vietnamese."

"Why not?" she said, feeling contrary.

"You have a lot of privilege," he said, which wasn't really an answer. "As a white woman. You're very privileged."

"I guess," she said, thinking that she had too much privilege if privilege meant all the childhood bullshit about how you could become an astronaut or an actress or an explorer. What were you supposed to become once you realized that you wouldn't be any of those things, couldn't be, that you weren't even capable of staying awake for fifty minutes of Early Modern Europe?

Aileen seems to have things figured out, Lizzie thinks, sneaking looks here at the dinner table whenever Aileen is occupied with her kids. She's got money, nice jewelry, manners—for instance, she returns Lizzie's compliment on her ring with one for Lizzie's bracelets of woven neon thread.

"Oh," Lizzie says, laughing, "these are from some kids I babysit. I always feel bad cutting them off."

"I used to babysit," Aileen confides. "I was an au pair. It's how I met my husband." After several moments she quickly adds, "He wasn't the father. Of the children I was caring for. It wasn't like that. He couldn't get away," she adds, stumbling forward. "My husband. From work. He wanted to come with us." She spins her ring on her finger, or tries to, but the humidity has made her hand swell, and the ring gets stuck with the biggest diamond facing inward, jabbing into her palm.

Lizzie is disappointed in these revelations, not for the facts, ordinary enough, but because the woman still cares what Lizzie thinks. Lizzie wants to believe there is an age and level of success beyond which a woman won't give a shit whether some scruffy backpacker suspects she slept with her boss. *Please don't care what I think,* Lizzie mentally urges. *No one else ever does.*

Aileen cares, but she cares more that she forgot to say her husband was ill rather than busy at work. Now the guide has heard two conflicting stories. Victor eats his potatoes studiously, betrays nothing. He and Walt converse in halting Spanish: *How is the food, where are you from, how old are you?* Victor and Walt turn out to be the exact same age, twenty-one, and both seem surprised, a little embarrassed. During dessert, Aileen's daughter sings a song in French about bananas. Aileen can't tell if she's trying to defuse the awkwardness or if she's simply hungry for attention. The moment she's done, the younger boy starts a song he learned during their year in Singapore, some kind of school-yard rhyme, although Aileen doesn't understand the lyrics. Her daughter must; her eyes widen, and the boy's body jerks, the song stopping. She's kicked him, hard, under the table, and he turns and punches her in the arm.

"That's enough," Aileen says, and she hustles them out of the dining room, leaving her coffee unfinished. She supposes she should ask one of them what the song was about, but she isn't sure which one to ask. And she hates to admit she didn't understand a word of it, although both children must have realized this; it's why the boy chose it and why the girl took it upon herself to stop him.

After dinner, Victor helps some coworkers rearrange the games lounge. He goes back and forth in front of the lodge bar carrying bedraggled, unpleasantly moist boxes of Monopoly and Scrabble. Cardboard doesn't last long in the jungle. Every single pass, Walt nods at him in what Victor can tell is an invitation to have a drink together now that Lizzie's disappeared to bed. Finally Victor stops in the door and calls out, "We should have a drink another night. Tonight, I have these boxes." He holds up a stack as proof.

"Yeah. My treat," Walt says, and Victor nods, glad that's established. The drink prices are extortionate, and there's no employee pricing because the employees aren't supposed to be drinking. Not even to keep the guests happy by making them think they've made a local friend.

The highlight of the day-two itinerary is a massive clay lick adorned by scarlet macaws, gathered across the gray cliff dense as tapestry. They're Victor's favorite, the bright, riotous birds, their hunger that looks like delight. The afternoon features a charismatic tarantula, hairy legs waving, and an agouti snuffling along the forest trail. Then a nocturnal caiman-spotting expedition, their eyes orange in the glow of flashlights and headlamps. Their teeth flicker white, and Victor expects the children to be frightened, but they just squeal and dangle over the side of the canoe.

"This isn't a zoo, kids," he says. "Hands in the boat."

Aileen apologizes, but Victor waves her off. "They don't know any better. No caimans in the United States, I guess. I don't know about Colombia."

"We're Canadian, actually," Aileen says. "At least I am. Not that it matters. Who knows what the kids are at this point. Citizens of the world."

"It matters," Victor says, surprised and pleased. Canadians have been his private jaguars, rare enough in the Tambopata that he's never guided one.

"I'm from Saskatchewan," Aileen says, encouraged. "One of the provinces in the middle. Big and empty." She grew up restless, deferred her college scholarship for a gap year au-pairing in Switzerland. Julian worked at the same company as her host father. A wunderkind, the host father said, with ambition to match. She didn't return to Canada. Instead she took the plunge with Julian, which became one plunge after another, between countries and continents, places she didn't speak the language, didn't have legal permission to work. She has been in so many expatriate wives' book groups. She has read *The Kite Runner* three times and three different Paulo Coelho novels. She hopes that out there somewhere is a book club that hates Paulo Coelho as much as she does, a group where she'll find the earthy, cynical friends she's been waiting for.

Sometimes she feels she ought to be filling her empty hours with an affair. It isn't a physical or romantic hunger. Sex with Julian is still good—in fact, in bed together is

the time they're kindest to each other, when they understand each other best. The prospect of sex with anyone
else makes her feel more anxious than aroused. When she
fantasizes, she skips over the assignations to the part where
Julian finds out; he always does, and he never leaves her.
I didn't realize you were so unhappy, he says earnestly. *Tell me
how I can make this right.* Then the fantasy dissolves to static
because she has no idea. What alternate life does she worry
she's been cheated of? It's like she shut a door behind her so
long ago she no longer remembers what was on the other
side. Being with another man—maybe it would be a way
of knocking. Maybe something in the next room of her life
would finally answer back.

The third morning threatens rain. At breakfast Victor holds
a vote on whether they want to set out anyway. The result
is a unanimous yes; guests are always willing, even eager,
to walk in rain, as if it proves their mettle. Victor warns
them that they may not see anything, that the animals go
to ground when it rains, not wanting to get wet any more
than people do. The guests nod as if this is some great
revelation, and to them apparently it is. Maybe that's why
they pay so much to come here, Victor thinks—they're
trying to visit a world where animals and humans get wet
together.

The group walks single file away from the river toward
a system of interconnected lakes, individually small and un-
assuming as farm ponds. Directly above the trail, a ribbon
of gray sky threads through the dark green canopy. At the
water they pile into a dented metal rowboat. Victor never

rowed anything before this job, and the lake is his least favorite part of the itinerary. He delivers the safety briefing (life jackets), animal briefing (what to look for; how to silently signal a sighting), piranha briefing (keep all limbs inside). They row close along the shore. The only sound is the slap of oars, rustle of leaves, howler monkeys in the distance. The hoatzins are perched where they always are, but Victor lets the children spot them first, blue faces crowned with a rowdy crest of feathers. Walt makes an unkind comparison to Lizzie's hair. The hoatzins croak and grunt and rattle their wings. "They aren't upset," Victor assures everyone, "just talkative." He keeps the boat still while everyone snaps photos. He's skilled at knowing when people have looked long enough to be sated. Eventually he rows on, all six of them peering into the tangle of roots and branches lining the shore, a possible freshwater-otter habitat.

Victor feels excitement out of proportion to the dismal odds of actually spotting a highly endangered otter. This is his job, and he takes it seriously—he would like to show these people an otter—but he would also like to see one for himself. He's genuinely excited by every wild creature lumbering or flitting or scurrying into view, envoys from a nonhuman world, their magic so durable he always feels it. He can't imagine giving it up for good, trading it for mountain bus tours, speaking into a crackly microphone about Incan wall-building techniques while guests sleep or stare out the windows. Besides, he'd still be gone for days, maybe weeks, at a time. He tries to imagine what Ana wants their life to be so he can decide whether he can give it to her, whether he can make himself want it as much as she does. He wants *her;* he does. He thinks he wants their baby. But everything else about their future feels lurching and blurry.

In his distraction Victor steers over a tangle of branches under the water's surface. The hull grinds, the boat jerks to a stop. Victor almost swears but catches himself, tries to give the guests a smile one-quarter sheepish, three-quarters confident reassurance. He braces an oar against the branch and pushes backward. The rowboat barely budges. He lowers an oar straight down, testing the depth and consistency of the bottom. Chest-height, he guesses.

Then Lizzie shouts, "Otter!" In her excitement she forgets the silent hand signals, just yells and leans forward, flinging her arm over the water to point, and Aileen, imagining leaping piranhas, tries to stuff Lizzie back into the boat. Lizzie, grabbed from behind, struggles reflexively. The boat seesaws over the fulcrum of the branch. There's a splash in the direction of the otter sighting, but in the racket of an entire flock of hoatzins taking flight, it's impossible to tell what, if anything, Lizzie saw. "An otter. It was just over there. I saw it." She bends over the gunnel.

"Get back in the boat," Walt barks, but she leans out farther, scanning the water to either side. The boat tilts sharply, and Aileen's daughter shrieks. "Are you trying to kill us? You dumb bitch," Walt says, yanking her back onto the thwart beside him.

They've already made so much noise that everything around them has fled; even the breeze has stopped, and there's nothing left to drown out Walt's words. Victor shifts his weight, and water laps audibly against the side of the boat. Finally a branch falls somewhere deep in the jungle. The clouds thin and sunlight dazzles the water. Aileen's golden children flash.

Great, Victor thinks; now the day's weather forecast is something else he's screwed up. "I'm going to get out and push," he says. They all look at him like he's crazy. "There are almost definitely no piranhas. It's just something we're told to say." This is true, but Victor's stomach twists. What if Lizzie did see an otter? What if the realms of the possible and improbable are colliding, and there are piranhas after all? *Not like this,* Victor thinks. *I do not want to die like this, with these people.* He unlaces his boots, takes them off, and slides out into the water barefoot; he's relieved when his feet hit bottom and the bottom holds. He walks around to the bow of the boat, grips the painter, and pulls. At first nothing happens, but then there's a splash on the other side of the boat and it lurches forward. Walt's hopped out too and has joined him at the rope. Victor is annoyed and grateful. Mostly annoyed. It will be hard enough to explain why he's sopping when he walks into the lodge, harder still to explain why a guest is wet and filthy.

Victor assumes that this is Walt's apology for yelling at Lizzie, but then Walt gives him a needy, eager look, meant for Victor alone. Braving the lake is to impress Victor, not Lizzie. If there's an apology, it's for having paid money to let someone else row him around a pond, risk piranhas to free him. Once the boat is liberated from the snag, Victor holds it steady while Walt climbs in, then heaves himself ungracefully over the gunnel, more like a caught fish than a wilderness expert.

"See?" Victor says. "No piranhas." The kids look both relieved and disappointed.

The group walks slowly back to the lodge, spreading farther and farther apart along the trail, like beads coming unstrung. Victor, then Walt, then the kids, then Aileen and Lizzie, falling so far behind they aren't in earshot of anyone else.

"It isn't my business," Aileen says, and she waits for Lizzie to bristle and tell her that she's right, it isn't, but Lizzie looks up at her expectantly. Such pretty eyes, but not so pretty they will solve her other problems, Aileen thinks. Lizzie is not beautiful in any way that could be a life plan. *I was so pretty,* Aileen could tell her. *I suppose I still am, and it doesn't make that much difference in the long run.* Instead she says, "You shouldn't be with him. It's none of my business, but the two of you, you're not going to make it. I'm sorry if that sounds awful, but you aren't. You should end it now, while you're both so young."

Sometimes Lizzie feels very young; sometimes she feels very old. What she feels in this moment is gratitude—finally, someone willing to tell her what to do.

"I've been fighting with my girlfriend too," Victor says to Walt farther up the trail, not entirely sure why he's saying it. Guilt, maybe, that he didn't even offer Walt a thank-you at the lake. Especially since he hopes Walt will keep quiet about the rowing mishap, invent some other story for his soggy clothes.

"I just got nervous back there," Walt says. "I didn't want her to do anything to hurt the kids."

"Sure."

"What are you and your girlfriend fighting about?"

Even though Victor can tell Walt tried to say it casually, he can hear Walt's hunger for revelation, for some connection Victor doesn't understand. It's too much, this neediness. Tourists are all the time so hungry. For food, for conversation, for friendship, for magical glimpses of endangered animals over which Victor has no control. For some reassurance that their ability to pay for all this doesn't make them assholes. Victor doesn't actually think Walt's an asshole, but the prospect of trying to convince Walt of this feels exhausting.

"Stupid things," Victor lies and picks up his pace. He draws his lodge-issue machete, although the current trail is wide and clear. He attacks the foliage on either side, forcing Walt to walk well behind him, out of the blade's range.

On the trail, between the two pairs of adults, the kids quietly experiment with the phrase *dumb bitch*. Lizzie doesn't seem like one, not to them, but they try it out for their gym teacher and whoever designed their school uniforms.

The rain Victor predicted that morning finally comes, so torrential that the west end of the open-air dining room is soaked, and the guests squeeze uncomfortably around the remaining tables. The banana cage swings and creaks. Victor keeps bumping elbows with Walt. The children complain that fruit salad does not count as dessert, and if that's all there is, can they be excused to the games lounge?

"You can wait a little longer," Aileen says, showing her full cup of coffee.

"I'll take them," Lizzie says. "I'm qualified. And I can see them back to their room after." She holds up her kid-made neon friendship bracelets as proof. "Are you staying or going?" she asks Walt.

"I don't know. What do you want?"

Lizzie shrugs, and Walt gets up to follow. The new games lounge turns out to be only a small annex to an upstairs play area, huddled under the pitched roof. There are a few shelves of plastic toys holding up better in the humidity than a pile of damp picture books. All the available furniture is child-size. The kids pull out a copy of Trouble, the dice protected under a plastic dome. Lizzie chooses Scrabble, unfolds the board on a tiny table, and arranges two racks for tiles. Walt sits down on one of the kid-size chairs. Lizzie's so small she fits almost normally, but his knees are up by his armpits.

It's a Spanish Scrabble board, and he gets the *LL* and the *RR* and the *Ñ* and doesn't know what to do with any of them since they're playing in English. He loses a turn cashing in his letters for new ones, ends up with *H-E-T-H-E-R* and hopes for both a *W* to make a bingo and a spot on the board to put it. Then he remembers that Spanish Scrabble won't have any *W*s. He can't spell his own name in the Spanish tiles. He doesn't need Lizzie to look out of place. All those faces he was peering into, they all knew him for a foreigner even without her. He is carrying a neon sign, a disco ball of unbelonging, and he's never going to be able to put it down. He can't concentrate—he knows his turns are taking forever—so he tries to make a joke about the absent *W,* about his name, to explain the delay.

"No proper nouns allowed, though, right?" Lizzie asks, missing the point.

"I didn't know you knew what a proper noun was."

She stops shuffling her tiles, one hand poised with a single letter pinched between thumb and forefinger. Her hand is shaking when she puts it back on the rack. "What you said to me today—"

"I was afraid," he says, cutting her off. "You scared me. You were scaring everybody."

She shakes her head, then keeps shaking it, shaking it, like what's inside needs to be knocked free before it can be said aloud. "I know you think I'm dumb."

"I don't think you're dumb."

"I embarrass you."

Walt is silent, because protesting won't turn them around, won't whisk them back the way they came. It will only forestall what's coming, and maybe she's finally taking them somewhere they both need to go. He can tell he is going to remember his silence at this moment for the rest of his life, how awful it felt to hurt someone he'd once loved but didn't anymore and the relief that what was left between them was ending.

"We shouldn't be together," Lizzie says.

Slowly, because it should look like he still needs to consider this, he says, "I think you're right."

Lizzie stays curled in her chair, a hunched little eaglet, until all of a sudden she's standing, lifting the game board, and pouring the letters into the box.

"Do you want me to sleep somewhere else tonight?" Walt asks. He's never had a breakup before, and this seems like the kind of question you ask.

"Where?"

"There are those couches in the lobby."

"No mosquito netting. You should sleep in the room."

"Are you sure?"

"I don't want you to get *malaria*," she says, as if she'd be fine with him contracting something slightly less severe.

"What happens tomorrow?" Walt asks.

"How should I know? I'm just a dumb bitch." She snaps the lid over the box.

"I'm sorry." *Not just about that,* he wants her to hear. *About everything.*

"I'll call my dad when we're back in civilization. He'll move my flight up."

"You don't have to. I mean, you came all this way. I know there's probably stuff you wanted to see."

"I came to be with you. Which was pretty fucking stupid," she adds before Walt can say anything in response. "But I got to see an otter. I'm glad I got to be here and see that."

"I'm glad for the last four years," Walt says. "I am." He's grateful; he regrets nothing, certainly not the sex or how he had no sisters and had never exchanged more than a few sentences with a girl in his whole life until he learned to talk with Lizzie. She was nice about his crappy gifts, the last-minute grocery-store flowers, and he'd never let her pick the movies they watched, and that was wrong, and he'd do better with the next girl, he would, he'd be different, because of Lizzie.

"What you're looking for here? I don't think you're going to find it," she says.

Walt's gratitude churns immediately back into anger. "You don't know anything about it."

"I know you better than you think I do."

This could conceivably be true, since he feels like no one understands him at all, and he doesn't dispute it.

"You should go have that drink with Victor," she says. "You were looking forward to it."

"I don't think he wants to have a drink with me. He's probably ready to be off the clock." Walt wants her to tell him he's wrong about this and realizes that yesterday she would have and now she won't, and maybe that's part of what made her look so dumb, all those lies that she knew were lies and told him anyway.

This is the first loss of Walt's first breakup from his first girlfriend: that all Lizzie says now is "True."

Just as well, because Victor is having a drink with Aileen. He's actually having a third drink with Aileen. Only Cusqueñas, but since he rarely drinks at all, he's feeling the beer. Fueled by pisco sours, Aileen gets more and more flirtatious, but it's a performance, not a lowering of inhibitions. She is becoming not more herself but someone else altogether. When the bartender catches Victor's eye, he doesn't offer a congratulatory wink but an inquiring eyebrow. Aileen orders another round and patches together a conversation covering Saskatchewan, llamas, soccer, what candy bars are popular in different countries.

Victor has not been to any other countries, and eventually

he is ready to be done with whatever it is they're doing. "It's getting late," he says, and then Aileen puts her hand on his leg. "No," he says. "We can't"—he surprises himself by finishing the sentence with—"be obvious."

Aileen tilts her body to better conceal her hand but doesn't remove it.

"It's against company policy," Victor says.

"So we'll leave separately. Meet in my room. You remember the number?"

Victor nods, which is good because Aileen doesn't remember it. She knows it's the fourth doorway after the giant carved parrot on the walkway. When she passes her children's room, they're disputing the winner of Trouble and complaining about a set of Uno too limp to shuffle. She hears water running, toothbrushing. Her lovelies, brushing their teeth without reminding. They will enter the adult world with clean, white teeth. There are things she has done correctly. She knocks softly on the door frame—there are no actual doors in the lodge, only curtains. "Good night," she calls out. "I'm going to bed. Don't stay up too late talking." She wants to go in and kiss them, see them safely under the mosquito netting, but she forces herself to keep walking. She is practicing, she thinks, for the next part of her life. They will leave her someday, like the farmer's twelve children—she must be ready.

In her room she lights the candles and sees that the rain has soaked the side of the room open to the jungle. Her bed and suitcase are dry, close to the inside wall, but the hammock is drenched. So is Julian's money, she realizes, crawling on hands and knees to extract wads of bills from where she hid them in fissures in the rough-hewn floor. She smooths out the bills, shakes them, although the air itself is so moist she doesn't imagine she can flap them dry. She fans the stack, puts it on the nightstand of the unused bed. Brushes her teeth, changes into her pajamas. They aren't sexy—drawstring pants, a tank top—but better for an assignation than her hiking boots and khakis. Once her arms are exposed, she retreats under the mosquito netting. To her it looks romantic, like a lace canopy, but maybe to someone who lives here it's like wallpaper or medical equipment. She thinks he'll come but she can't be sure, and the minutes tick by excruciatingly.

Footsteps echo along the walkway outside—an employee turning down the kerosene lamps. Finally, a soft knock on the door frame. No doors. What is she doing, in this room without doors, only curtains, open to the jungle? Her children on the other side of the wall.

Still, she says, "Come in," and he does.

He hasn't changed clothes, she notices, then wonders if he has any other clothes to change into. She hasn't seen any of the lodge employees out of uniform. He's abandoned his binoculars and machete somewhere, but otherwise he's dressed for an expedition. *This* is *an expedition,* she thinks, and tries to smile. If she were meeting him anywhere else there'd at least be a bottle of wine. Maybe a minibar. A bucket of ice. She is desperate for something to do with her hands. When he comes close enough to reach, she pushes his safari vest off his shoulders, and it slides to the floor with a thud, surprisingly loud. She tries to remember what's in there. Compass, knife, first-aid supplies. A professional Boy

Scout. She's been assuming he's done this before, that the lodge's supply of eager, foreign strangers offers a steady stream of action for the guides. But Victor stands very still, looking uncertain, almost unhappy. Aileen's worried he'll back out, and she'll have to wonder what's wrong with her. She goes for his belt and pulls him close to the unused bed, the sheets still fresh, until she can reach up with her other hand and flick the mosquito netting around them both. Finally he starts to move, stripping his clothes off with brisk efficiency, pulling her tank top over her head. He looks at her appreciatively, but he isn't hard, and she realizes that in all her fantasies, her shadow lover has always been ready to go, ready to take care of everything.

She presses her palm to his side, goes in for a kiss. He's brushed his teeth. His body is compact, sturdy. Everywhere she touches, she can't help comparing to Julian. She wonders if this is normal or her own inexperience. She wonders who Victor is comparing her to. They've slipped their hands beneath each other's underwear when he says, "I don't have a condom." Aileen can hear that there's something else he doesn't say, but she can't tell what, whether it's a story about not finding another guide to give him one or not asking another guide because of the gossip or about how he didn't have one himself because he was faithful, he had a pregnant girlfriend he was going to marry.

I am going to marry her, Victor thinks, with Aileen's hand wrapped around him, working.

"We can do other things," Aileen says, trying to sound encouraging rather than disappointed. And they try, but none of the other things go very well. With the kids next

219

door, everything happens in vigilant silence. She can't relax enough to come, although Victor does his best. They trade places, and she needs such frequent direction he might as well be jacking himself off. In her mouth, finally, he's close to coming but gives her so much warning that it slips away when she moves, and he finishes himself off with an urgency Aileen can tell is anticipation of being done more than anticipation of pleasure.

Afterward, they lie together under the netting. Something rustles above them, risking the maze of filament to shelter from the rain. Aileen cringes, expecting to be strafed by damp feathers or clicking talons. The room, soggy and bare, with vermin in the rafters, feels sinister, the bed the only safe space. The jungle in time will lick all this to nothing, she thinks, the wood and thatch collapsing like soft cheese, the only remnants clouds of fishing line glinting in the mud, the white bones of whatever has entangled itself above them.

"I have a girlfriend," Victor says, and Aileen doesn't know if this is a confidence or confession or explanation. He's going to marry her, he says, and keeps talking—the baby, Ana's hounding, how badly she wants out of Puerto Maldonado, how he doesn't know what to do.

Aileen wonders how lonely he must be if he's confiding all this to her. She wonders what she's supposed to say. She has just two kinds of advice, she thinks: cut and run, which she already gave to Lizzie, and stay and follow, which is the only way she's known how to live her own life. "You should try," Aileen tells him, "leaving. You can always come back here if it doesn't work out."

But she doesn't know if that's true. If Victor gives up this job, can he be guaranteed another? She grew up without money, had little enough to understand its weight and value now. It is plush and silky, like the otter-fur coat Julian bought her though they hadn't lived anywhere cold in years. The coat stayed in her parents' storage closet, deployed on rare winter visits home. She knew it had cost more money than every coat her mother had owned through every winter of her life. She'd urged her mother to wear it when she wasn't home, to get some good out of it, but it stayed in the closet. That was the weight of money, the glossy heft you might feel guilty over but couldn't help being grateful for when you stepped off the plane in Regina and there it was to keep you from the cold. Her kids didn't understand what this felt like because they'd never been without it. They never would be, unless Aileen tried to inflict on them lessons she had no heart for, no stomach. She thinks of Julian's money in the abstract, and then she thinks about it in the specific, in the here and now, in the pile of wet bills on the table.

"I want to give you something," she says and rises naked from the bed. "A wedding present." The bills are still wet as she hands them to Victor; she starts to rummage for an envelope or Ziploc.

"I can't accept this."

"Of course you can." She removes sunscreen and Tylenol from a sandwich bag, creeps back under the netting to find his face hard and angry. The money sits on the mattress.

"Do you know how much this is?" he asks.

"Of course I know." Did he think she was too rich to bother counting or too helpless? "I want you to have it."

He reaches for his clothes, starts to dress. "Why?"

Aileen blushes. "Not for—this. I'm not—paying. You." She gestures helplessly at the bed. It enters her mind to say that this is his tip, but that would make everything worse. "It really is just a gift. I want to give it to you. For the baby."

"It's too much."

"Not for me." She says it flatly, a plain fact like the weather. "It's just money. Only money."

"Money is not just money."

"It can be," Aileen says, though she knows this isn't true. She puts the cash into the bag, holds it out until he takes it.

The schedule includes one last morning nature walk before the canoes depart. The guests' luggage is already piled in the hallways. Victor sits with his charges at breakfast, and the kids, picking up on the stony silence between Walt and Lizzie and the awkwardness between Victor and their mother, make caps for everybody out of orange peels. Victor wears his until he feels it slide off the back of his hair. The money's in his vest, too precious to trust to the staff dorm, and he's not sure whether he's hearing the plastic swish as he moves or if he's only imagining it. He feels the bag's strange buoyancy in his legs, its heaviness on his chest.

With his thoughts snagged on the money, he accidentally leads the group down the old mammal path, toward the harpy eagle nest, instead of along the new route. He stops suddenly when he realizes where he is, and the group accordions, the children squashed between Walt and their mother. The boy howls, and Victor turns quickly to shush them.

"You are going to see something very special," he says, deciding to play off his mistake as part of the tour. "Not everyone gets to see this, so please don't tell the other guests."

So much of his job is storytelling, and he begins this one with the harpy eagle's size, its rarity. Harpy eagles are the national bird of Panama, though they are driven almost to extinction there. The Amazonian population is healthier, but the birds are still endangered. Pairs mate for life and raise only one chick every two or three years. Like humans, Victor says. The female lays two eggs, but whichever hatches first receives all the care and attention; the second is left to die. Not like humans, he says. At least he hopes not. The girl whispers something to her little brother that makes him elbow her.

"We have to be quiet," Victor says, "so the parents don't scare. Or they'll fly away and leave the baby to die."

"Really?" Lizzie asks, as if alarmed that after the lake, Victor trusts them with any information whatsoever.

"It's true," Victor confirms. "That is completely true. Not like the piranhas." The mother has a seven-foot wingspan, he adds. She can carry away a full-grown howler monkey squirming in her talons. He gets caught up in his own facts, in the anticipation of seeing the eaglet. This is what Aileen was paying him for, he thinks, even if she didn't know it. He is a very good guide. He has earned every sol he's ever been given. He doesn't need a lotto ticket. This is what he'll tell Ana about the money. A Canadian gave it to him for showing her a secret, magical bird.

The stick nest is huge, probably five feet across, but it's also nearly a hundred feet up in a tree, and for people unaccustomed to looking through binoculars, the scale isn't clear. Only the eaglet sits in the nest, the parents out hunting or possibly perched somewhere nearby. Victor scans the trees but can't find them. The eaglet humped in the middle of the nest looks dingy and distant. The five guests nod solemnly without removing the binoculars held to their faces. Every chin tilts upward at the exact same angle. They look like shabby robots—part man, part machine—attention fixed on this clot of sticks they want to appreciate, knowing it's the last and only time they'll see anything like this. Victor can tell the magic isn't working and passes around his own binoculars, higher-powered than the guests'.

They are all trying very hard to feel the right thing, to see whatever Victor sees, but they just can't do it. Victor's binoculars, his guide knowledge, aren't enough. Finally he takes his binoculars back. He raises them to the nest. But after the guests' polite indifference, he can't see it either. He sees the bird clearly enough. Slightly larger than the last time he came here alone but otherwise no different. What had been so special about it? Fuzzy gray beastlet. Fat little idiot. *Chump,* he thinks. *Enjoy your jungle life, bird. Enjoy your breakfast vomit. Enjoy growing up and being shot by a logger or a construction worker.*

Goodbye, he thinks toward the eagle and the caimans and the invisible otters, testing it out in his mind. *Goodbye to the friendly tarantula and the imaginary piranhas.* He feels nothing. He wants to cheer and he wants to cry. None of these love him back the way he's tried to love them. It's not that kind of place. As the group returns to the lodge, he creates a story about the Interoceánico Highway slicing its way through the eagles' habitat. He exaggerates their peril, or maybe it's not an exaggeration. Maybe the highway will finally bring the transformation that everyone has been talking about his entire life, wiping all of this away. The group is wary; are they being lectured? Is the highway something they're supposed to feel guilty about?

"I don't want to be here to see that," Victor says, and he means both that he does not want it to happen and that he hopes not to be here if it does. The guests nod politely, their minds on departure: the canoes, the security checkpoint, the bus, the plane. The girl asks if she'll get another jaguar stamp in her passport. He never did see a real jaguar, Victor thinks, and he won't now, wherever he's going next. But he feels no regret. Like the jaguars, he's already gone.

LIFE AMONG THE
TERRANAUTS

We all have our favorite places: Campbell lies on the beach while Esparza takes the dinghy out on the ocean; Park's in the lab; Bhatnagar's in the savanna. No one hangs out in the swamp, because that's the bioremediation site. Wastewater treatment. I can appreciate the science, but I don't want to hike there. Igor and I, we're belowdecks. We roam the tunnels because they're something real, real pipes, real intake and outflow and monitoring stations. We trade the bleached light aboveground, the desert sun pouring in past white-painted steel girders and triple-layered glass, for the concrete comfort of mechanism. We don't need the labels—DESERT BASEMENT, UPPER RAIN FOREST, OCEAN FILTRATION—to know where we are. We have been in NovaTerra for 542 days and when I stand in the blast of air below the habitat-cooling system, I think I can last for the 188 that remain. At night Igor and I go to the North

Lung and listen to our voices reverberate in the dark. It feels like a church, peaceful and echoing. A giant temple of nothing but air.

At dinnertime we meet in the habitat pod and take turns cooking meals. Bhatnagar makes beet soup and sorghum porridge. Campbell makes beet salad and sorghum patties. Park doesn't even try; she slices raw beets and mashes raw sorghum and slops six tiny portions on six little plates. I hate beets. When I found out we were growing beets, I thought, *Okay,* because we were growing corn and sweet potatoes and rice and blueberries and we had mango trees in the rain forest and chickens and goats and pigs on the farm. But then the corn failed and the rice died and the potatoes got blight and bugs ate the blueberries. The fruit trees thrived until they pressed against the rain-forest ceiling and Mission Command ordered us to cut them down before they shattered the glass. Without the corn we couldn't feed the animals, so we slaughtered and ate them as quickly as we could. We don't have any freezers. I tried to dry meat in the ventilation system, but I just made NovaTerra smell like rotting pork for six weeks. Now I say, "I'm going to die if I eat one more beet."

"I can make that happen," Campbell says.

But I don't really want to die. I just really, really, really want to leave.

Before dinner we put our heads down and take turns describing what we wish we were eating: sushi, spaghetti and meatballs, pad thai. It's a ritual of terrible little prayers that never get answered, but we can't seem to stop. Not even me, and I swore five years ago I'd never pray again for anything. Tonight, I ask for cheeseburgers.

During dinner we discuss what will happen if we run out of food completely. We talk about inputting our emergency exit codes, stumbling out into the Arizona air.

"We wouldn't have to leave," Igor says.

"What's the other option?" Park asks. "Starve?"

"We'd eat each other," Igor says, like this is obvious, and Park laughs. Then Esparza laughs and Bhatnagar and Campbell, and I realize that I'm the only one who knows that Igor isn't joking. Then the four of them look at me so I laugh too, but it's a stiff laugh. I'm trying to tell them, *Oh, that crazy Igor,* and I'm trying to tell Igor, *I know you're serious and I don't approve.* But I guess the laugh's too good because Igor glares at me and runs his tongue over his chapped lips like he's thinking, *You first.*

That night I lie in my dorm pod and wonder what I'd taste like. I hear Igor's footsteps, then his fingernail scratching the door, our old code. I ignore him and he scratches harder until I let him in. "I'm really tired," I whisper. Park's next door; the others are just down the hall. NovaTerra wasn't built for privacy.

"Do you think everyone thinks I'm going to eat them?" Igor asks, concerned. He sits on my bed, starlight behind him. The dorm pods have single round windows, like ship portholes. They look out over the swamp.

"I'm sure no one thinks you're any weirder than usual," I say. I stand while he hugs me and I feel his skull against my ribs, bone pressing bone. His hair's gone limp and uneven—too many kitchen-shears haircuts, not enough soap or vitamins. My stomach growls loudly and I'm embarrassed, even though I shouldn't be.

"Hungry?" he asks.

I roll my eyes. "If you're going to keep me up, tell me a food story. Tell me what your family ate for dinner tonight."

"I don't know. Veal. Foie gras. The blood of the innocent. I don't want to talk about them."

"They're family. Don't be that way."

"What do you think your parents ate?"

"Beets and sorghum, for all I know. We stopped eating meat when I was in high school. *Illumination* requires the body to be cleansed of animal protein."

"So saith the Apostle," Igor declaims, like he's going to break out into a gospel solo.

"It's not funny."

"You said it wasn't that bad, growing up."

"It wasn't," I say, because I know Igor wouldn't believe me if I tried to change my story now. But I've had a lot of time to think, and the more I think about the New World Apostles, the more I realize that it *was* that bad, all-day Sunday services becoming evening study and night prayers and weekend retreats and the way I'd grown up so afraid, thinking we were alone in the world, counting the handful of people in folding chairs who would survive the coming fire. Or the year I lobbied to attend regular school and spent the seventh grade staring at everyone who tried to speak to me, thinking, *You're going to hell, and you, and you, and you.* Or the way suspicion crept in slowly, tentatively, that maybe not everyone would burn after all. And when doubt crept in, some of God crept out, and there was an empty space in my stomach that grew no matter what I filled it with. When I came to NovaTerra, I'd already been hungry for a long time.

"You should leave," I tell Igor. "Really."

"I just want things to work out. You and me. This whole place."

"I know you do," I say. "But you need to go now."

If Igor eats me, I hope I taste like beets.

At the morning staff meeting, Bhatnagar's in a mood. For the first six months I thought he was always in a mood, and then he got really pissy and I realized that the first six months he'd been on his best behavior. Bhatnagar was a navy doctor; he used to deploy on submarines for months at a time and figured this wouldn't be that different. But on the ships they had vending machines, movie nights. Here he's taken to looking out at the desert through the giant greenhouse grid of steel and glass and announcing, "All shore and no leave."

He delivers the task list, which has Daily Maintenance ("harvest beets") and Specials ("seasonal monsoon"). While he talks, Campbell cuts her fingernails with scissors. She's our only agronomist and has been on Farm Daily Maintenance each of the last 543 days. Park heads to the lab, and Igor and I are stuck with the Special because Esparza's taken off for his weekly boat ride.

Esparza's the only local. His wife and dog live nearby and visit every Friday afternoon; Esparza's mooniness afterward is how we remember what day it is. The clearest private approach, up to the wall but away from the visitor window and media lot, is to the ocean, so Esparza rows the dinghy into the little waves and bobs near the glass. His wife comes through the sage, their golden retriever bounding alongside. The animal sits and pants while his owners pretend they can read lips. Esparza used to hold up notes until we ran out of paper. Now there are smudges on the glass from their thwarted kisses, trails of drool from the dog.

"God, can you at least wipe off all the lip prints?" Campbell always complains on Friday evenings.

"With what?" Esparza asks, and this is a fair question. Our towels have been depleted by the Great Kitchen Fire and the Regrettable Fertilizer Spill. Our jumpsuits aren't lasting as long as projected and the last thing anyone wants is to have to look at one another naked. Campbell's most prized possession is an oversize beach towel with electric-blue stripes. She dries off after the monthly shower, lies on it on the beach, says she will make a wrap dress out of it if and when the day comes. She keeps it locked in her dormitory safe, and yes, I know this because Igor and I broke into her pod once to look for it.

Igor, Bhatnagar, and I start dragging the fog machines cross-country, out of the rain forest and into the desert. It's a long way, nearly the length of NovaTerra, and Bhatnagar curses when Igor disappears down the Swamp West stairwell. When we finally get both machines down the chaparral ridge, Igor's there waiting, jumpsuit unzipped to his waist and palm fronds tied to his head. It's time for the rain ceremony, he tells us.

"Are you serious?" Bhatnagar asks.

"You remember last year. We learned the dance by heart."

Bhatnagar looks uncomfortable. We all did a lot of things last year when we were a few hundred days younger and more enthusiastic. Igor is still very big on ceremonies. We are a new people, he says, a new society of Terranauts. We need our own ways.

"We're scientists," Bhatnagar argues, but Igor isn't one, and this has been the general problem with him. He's a philosopher, but, more important, he's Mr. Karpov's nephew. This is why we don't call Igor by his last name—because *Karpov* already means the man who paid two hundred million dollars to build NovaTerra and is paying us one million dollars each to live here.

I spent the one-year celebration (beets and sorghum and bananas, with party hats made of rolled ferns) thinking, *Half a million down,* but of course it doesn't work like that. If we come out early we don't get anything. Karpov claimed he had hundreds of people desperate to do this for free, and there'd been so much media attention that I'm sure he wasn't lying. The problem was that those people were mostly like Igor—or less sincere, more exhibitionistic versions of Igor—and Karpov needed people like Campbell the agronomist, Esparza the chemist, and Bhatnagar the navy doctor. He needed people like me, systems engineers trained to maintain oxygen levels in sealed environments.

The Karpov family fortune came from gold, from open-pit mines and slag heaps soaked in the diluted cyanide that separates metal from rock. A few years ago a Karpov mine reservoir collapsed in Romania and leaked a plume of cyanide sixteen hundred miles long into the Danube. It happened again in Guyana, and then twenty-six hundred people gathered in Guatemala to protest the opening of a new mine. Karpov told them that gold and cyanide were as natural as anything else on Earth, that even damaged habitats were self-regulating. That ecosystems were alive and could achieve and re-achieve homeostasis no matter what people like the Karpovs did to them. The Gaia hypothesis, Igor has always called it, and he believed in it like a religion, like someone in possession of pure revelation. I've seen that kind of faith before, and it probably should have made me run screaming. But instead he felt familiar. In the first months he even felt kind of true. *Why should the Apostles be people of the past?* I heard my parents whisper in my head. *Why is it so impossible that one would appear to us now?*

We all assumed that Karpov shared Igor's sincerity, but as the months went by it occurred first to Campbell, then to Bhatnagar, then to Esparza and Park, and finally to me that all Karpov had done was promise us money and promise the Guatemalans proof that environmental equilibrium was not only possible but inevitable. He'd built a new world, but he didn't seem interested in how well it worked as long as it could be endured.

We'd been chosen for fortitude, for pigheaded faith, as much as for skill. There was in all of us a streak of what ran so strongly through Igor. We had upset the equilibrium of our own lives on Old Earth, and we needed NovaTerra to put things right. Bhatnagar had gambling debts. Park had six-figure student loans. Esparza planned to buy a piece of local land, build the dream house that would convince his wife she could be happy in the desert. After he'd spent 543 days looking out at it like a hamster in a ball, we thought he might have changed his mind, but we didn't ask. We were forbidden to mention the money to the media, and as time went by we even stopped mentioning it to one another. Every plan felt more and more distant, daydreams as unreachable as our food recitations. The more we talked about money, the hungrier we got. So we stopped.

Igor hops from foot to foot for a while, invoking the ability of the Gaia entity to inspire peaceful coexistence. Igor's assigned role is to bring a spiritual dimension to life on NovaTerra, and his philosophy has been evolving in response to all the unanticipated events. Life on NovaTerra was never meant to contain mangoes, he said when we were asked to chop the trees down. Ditto meat and dairy. On day 104 of the beet-and-sorghum regime, Esparza and Park went down wrestling over the last papaya.

"On NovaTerra," Igor proclaimed, "wanting the old life will only cause us pain." Four failed crops in, this had become manifestly true, and we let him go on. "Old Earth cannot provide infinitely, and neither can the New. The usefulness of our project to the world lies not only in a new equilibrium, but in the redefining of our relationship to the Terra." He climbed up on the dinner table and announced, "We must embrace our new identities as Terranauts."

In the moment, this felt so true that Esparza and Park hugged. We were unhappy because we were old-fashioned humans, insatiable and needy; Terranauts would make peace with their surroundings, would create useful knowledge from predicament. This held us for a long time. This is what got Bhatnagar to dance a rain dance twelve months ago. Twelve days ago someone wrote *Fuck Terranauts!* on the bathroom wall.

Bhatnagar and I watch Igor chant and then plug the fog machines in. Some of the fiberglass boulders have outlets. The machines thunk to life and start choking out musty clouds. Igor stands with his arms outstretched, hitting the high note to his rain song; it's a shrill, wild noise that carries under the glass, and the lemurs in the rain forest call out in response. He holds the note impossibly long and then lets it go with a gasp. A coyote howl answers from the desert, the real one, beyond the glass. Even Bhatnagar is still, watching Igor in the mist. There's so much mold in the machines that the fog isn't healthy to inhale, and Bhatnagar takes Igor by the elbow to lead him to higher ground. But Igor misunderstands and thinks he's got a dance partner. He whirls him around so fast that Bhatnagar goes down hard on one knee, right on top of a cholla. Igor has the sense to run, palm fronds bobbing, even before Bhatnagar starts cursing him out.

I help Bhatnagar up, offer to walk him to the infirmary, but he shrugs me off. His knee is a porcupine of cactus needles, blood already seeping through his jumpsuit. "I'm fine," he says. "Stay and monitor the monsoon." Since he's the only doctor we have, I let him limp away alone. I monitor the foul-smelling fog until the desert has received precipitation equivalent to a normal January monsoon in the Sonora. Then I unplug the machines and look for someone to help move them back before the rain forest dries out.

I can't find Campbell, and Esparza is still in his boat,

although no one's making kissy faces. I pull Park out of the lab, which she isn't happy about. NovaTerra was supposed to be her postdoc; she showed up with a zillion research projects, samples to collect and data sets to mine and articles to write. Then the crops started failing and Campbell yanked her off-task to work twelve-hour days on the farm. The crops died anyway and Park hasn't been able to finish an article since she got here.

"Two years without a publication?" she says. "I'm toast. I'll get out of this loony bin and never get hired."

We pass a ventilation shaft disguised as an armadillo burrow and hear Bhatnagar shouting at Igor belowdecks. Park's looking gray, gulping for air. There are hollows at her cheeks and neck.

"Maybe we should take a break," I say.

"So you can rescue your boyfriend? What'd he do to piss Bhatnagar off so bad?" She grimaces and I can see blood on her gums and teeth. We take vitamin supplements, but they only do so much.

"He's not my boyfriend."

"Whatever."

"Bhatnagar fell on a cholla. That's all he's yelling about."

Park shrugs, wipes the sweat off her face with the sleeve of her blue jumpsuit.

"Igor's never been my boyfriend."

"He's all yours whether you want him or not." It takes her two tries to get the full sentence out, her head thrown back like that'll make more room in her lungs. Her hair is in a sweaty, slack ponytail and I want to reach over and yank it as hard as I can.

"You don't know anything about me," I say.

"You don't know anything about me either."

We stand there and think about how this is mostly true. I wonder who her family is, what they're like, where they are. I think about telling her that if she wants Igor she can have him, because as crazy as she thinks he is, he's worse. But we just keep pulling the machines. In the rain forest the leaves are already yellowed.

I was taking classes at the local community college when my parents announced they were quitting their jobs and selling the house to live full time with the Community. I said that I liked college, that getting an education was important to me. I thought we'd have a discussion. But they smiled calmly—with *illumination,* the Apostles called that look of peace—and I knew they'd already chosen.

There wasn't a phone out in the Community, and after a year they stopped writing letters. After two years I tried to visit but they weren't there. A girl I'd known from the New World Apostolic Youth stopped me halfway up the forest two-track and said that they'd moved and that unless I was there on God's business rather than family business, I had no business there at all. That was five years ago, and the only rumor I've heard was that they're somewhere up in Idaho on a piece of land the Community bought cheap because the soil's full of silver-mine tailings. They had to promise not to farm it and they were farming it anyway, killing themselves slowly. I don't know if this is true. My old seventh-grade teacher looked me up because he thought I might know where his daughter had gone, but he'd heard more than I had. He dreamed aloud to me about hiring private investigators and lawyers, which was really dreaming about money neither of us had.

That night Igor and I sneak off to the North Lung, even though I promised myself I'd stop. The air in NovaTerra expands and contracts with the temperature, and the lungs give the air an escape route; they keep us from exploding into a supernova of glass and metal over the desert. The lungs themselves are the only part of NovaTerra not made of glass; they're concrete, two gray domes rising out of the scrub. The boobs of the desert, Campbell says, although since the biomes and the habitat pod sit right between them, from the air, NovaTerra wouldn't look like a woman, or like anything else. Just a straight line with a circle on either end and a bunch of glinting squares in the middle, a blacktop parking lot to one side.

Igor's brought a flashlight and we shine shadow pictures on the dome walls. When we first came, we made elephants, giraffes, the easiest things. Now we make lemurs, scorpions—the creatures of our current world. Igor makes an armadillo, lumpy knuckles and his thumb a winking eye. "I saw one today," he says, "after the monsoon."

"An armadillo? We don't have any. They weren't on the list."

"I know. But I saw one."

"It wasn't, like—" I try to think of things in NovaTerra that can look like other things. We have a limited stable of objects. "A potato?"

"We don't even have potatoes anymore."

"I know. But we don't have armadillos either."

Igor and I made sense together the first year not because we were ever perfect, but because we were the youngest, because we were about the same level of attractive in our jumpsuits, and because there are only so many combinations six people can make. Because he didn't like beets either, and we passed funny notes to each other in staff meetings before the paper shortage, and because he told me that he saw in me, even though I was really just NovaTerra's mechanic, a seriousness of belief. "This place means something to you," he once told me. I don't know if it's still true.

It's been a long time since we came to the lung, and I forgot to bring a blanket. We lie down and I can feel every vertebra pressing against the concrete. Igor pulls my head onto his shoulder. The flashlight is on the floor, still lit; from my angle it looks like light breaking over a horizon, the beginning of a sunrise across Igor's bony chest.

"Eve," he says.

"That's not my name."

"Eve of the Terranauts."

"I'm not going to say what you want me to say." I sit up and push my hand into his chest. I can feel his heart beat against his sternum, his lungs fill.

"Eve."

The longing of it echoes, and I'm sad not only because Igor wants me to be something I'm not but because even if I tried, I wouldn't be able to be her, this person he imagines. He wants me to call him Adam. He's wanted this for the last 394 days, and I won't.

"E—"

"Gor." I zip my jumpsuit back up, stand over him in the cold. We still have nothing decent to eat, we still have 187 days to go, I haven't used toilet paper in eighteen months, and I don't have any friends here except him. I don't think I have the energy to try and fit all over again with anyone else. I don't think there's anyone else to fit with. So I lie back down and put my hand over his mouth. "Just lie here with me," I say, and he switches off the flashlight.

I interviewed for this job with Karpov himself. He had slicked-back hair and white French cuffs fastened with little planet Earth cuff links, blue and green enamel with gold backings. He twisted them open and shut, slowly and deliberately, while I talked; he was a man too sure of everything in his life to fidget. "I'm a better match for this project than you can possibly guess," I told him. When we shook hands my fingers disappeared into his grip, his fingers so soft and large they felt swollen.

I know all about new worlds and I know what it is to be one of something, part of a small and righteous tribe, and I know what it is to have a door crack open in front of you and be able to walk through and become something else. At the time Karpov was worried about reentry, thought that NovaTerra might be so successful we'd have trouble leaving. We've all laughed at that since, everyone except Igor.

"You'd never eat me, right?" I whisper, my hand still over his mouth. But if there's an answer on his face, I can't see it in the dark.

★   ★   ★

On day 550, Park radios us to the lab and makes us sit to hear the news. There are only three chairs, but she stands with her arms crossed until Igor and I sit on the floor. "Ants," she says, and then waits until we realize she wants us to say "Ants?" or "Ants!" or maybe "Ants!?"

"What about them?" Campbell says, and this is as good a response as Park's going to get.

She's discovered an infestation, some native desert ant that isn't supposed to be here. It's replaced the NovaTerra ants and is crowding out all the other insect life. We can't grow crops in overrun dirt. "There's no way we'll make it six more months," Park concludes.

"This is not the end of the Terranauts," Igor pronounces.

"Fuck Terranauts," Park says, and I think of the bathroom wall. I wonder how long she's known about the ants.

Campbell dismisses us, says she wants to go over the lab reports with Park privately. Igor stomps off by himself, then comes back to tell Esparza that his wife's outside the ocean, trying to flag someone down.

"What do you think?" I ask Igor as we stand on the chaparral ridge and watch Esparza untie the boat. It's like one of us is already leaving.

"About what?"

"About going home."

"I think we are home," Igor says. "Terranauts don't need beets. Terranauts don't need any of this bullshit."

I stare at him, trying to think of the right thing to say,

trying so hard that when my mouth finally opens all that spills out is "I really want a cheeseburger."

Igor gives me a look of disgust and disappears down a ladder shaft.

I decide to work through the day's task list, even if we may be leaving. I lift a scythe to cut the savanna grass and think, *This is the last time I'll ever do this,* but I can't get nostalgic. In truth I feel only relief. For the first time in a long time the labor feels good. I feel lean and strong. When I'm out of here, I'll find my parents and they'll be proud of my strength, of this body stripped to its essentials.

I drop the scythe when I hear strange sloshing noises coming from the ocean. Esparza's waving his arms wildly, rocking the dinghy. *Two years,* his wife is mouthing, *two years,* enunciating so powerfully I can read her from the savanna. *I'm sorry!* she shouts. *I'm sorry.* She holds a letter to the glass and a picture of her with another man. Esparza points at his wrist, holds his thumb and index finger together: *A little more time, maybe?* Just a little and he might be out. *No,* she mouths, her eyebrows sideways tilts of apology. Esparza kneels in the boat. Finally he points at the dog. His wife shakes her head. He won't get the dog either when he returns to Old Earth. Esparza howls and his wife walks away through the desert.

That night we have to fish Esparza out of the ocean, untie the fiberglass rocks from his ankles, and wrap him in what blankets we have. We put him to sleep on the dining-room table so we can take turns watching him. His skin is the flat pale brown of a cardboard box and his hair smells like the mildew in the ocean-filtration system. There are cameras in the infirmary, and we know Karpov still cares about appearances.

Day 551: At the morning staff meeting we talk about Esparza. We talk about the ants. Campbell confirms Park's report. We talk about the lack of food and how life in NovaTerra is one long lack of everything that made our lives on Old Earth worthwhile.

"I want to leave," Park finally says, and it feels like my voice, like I'm saying it alongside her.

Esparza curls into a ball. Campbell has laid her blue-striped beach towel over him; it's the tenderest thing we've ever seen her do. "And he needs to," she says. "That's two. Anyone else?"

I raise my hand. I can't speak, not with Igor looking at me. Bhatnagar raises his. Campbell announces a majority and tells us to pack up; she'll prepare a press release and we'll input the codes for the air lock.

"You didn't ask for my vote," Igor says. "The decision to leave needs to be unanimous."

"We can't do this anymore. It's not worth it," Park says.

"All new societies demand sacrifice."

"It's not easy, giving up the money," Bhatnagar offers, trying to commiserate.

"The money?" Igor asks.

"A million is a lot," Bhatnagar says. "But we don't have much choice."

"You're being *paid?*" Igor asks, shocked.

"You aren't?" Park asks, but the answer's already on Igor's face.

He looks at me and I shake my head but I don't know what I'm really saying: *Yes, I was being paid too. No, I would not have been sorry to take the money. No, I didn't know you weren't being paid, but also Yes, if I'd thought about it, I could have guessed.* And finally: *No, I'm not on your side, whatever that side is.*

Igor stands with his fists clenched. He steps onto a chair like this is the papaya fight all over again, like there's something he can still say to rally us. *A betrayal of faith is a betrayal of the self,* my parents whisper. *The motives of the faithful are pure, and light fills the righteous.* Igor is silent, looking at us one by one with disgust. I feel like a child again at service with my parents. The Apostle looks down at me and I am convinced that whatever he sees he does not like.

"You're traitors," Igor says. "You're all traitors."

"To what?" Campbell asks.

But I know. I understood and I betrayed it anyway. Igor looks at me with rage and disappointment. *The truly Illuminated cannot contain their own righteousness. Their light spills forth.* I imagine myself in the North Lung, standing in a blast of flashlight. I am my own shadow picture, small and frail and guilty.

Igor spits on the ground, jumps off the chair, and walks out the door. Bhatnagar stands to limp after him, but Campbell grabs his elbow. "Mission Command can come and pull Igor out their own damn selves," she says.

But they won't.

Day 552: "Did you even *read* your contracts?" Karpov asks on the command center's screens. He's so close to his webcam, his face is warped like an image in a fun-house mirror, giant nose and piglet eyes. "Six people, six codes," he booms. "You all agreed."

"There has to be a way," Park insists. "You can't just leave us in here." She's written *Freedom Now* on a bunch of giant philodendron leaves and stuck them to the visitor windows, facing out. She used piñon pitch from the desert for glue and white chalk from the lab for the writing, and now there's no more chalk.

"We need to brainstorm," Campbell says. "How are we supposed to brainstorm when there's no chalk?"

Park makes another sign, *No Work Without Dry-Erase Markers,* and when Karpov logs off in frustration, she props the leaf up in front of the webcam streaming live. We watch the media lot slowly fill with more vans than we've seen since the sealing-in ceremony. It doesn't do any good. Six people, six codes, or no air-lock release.

At first we consider striking, but our work is the only thing keeping us alive. I go swimming for a day instead of monitoring oxygen levels, fall asleep on the beach, and wake up with a buzzing feeling in my ears. I reel through the sea cave down into the ocean basement. There's a glass wall onto the dead coral reef. The water is cloudy. The scrubber below the swamp is quiet, shut down completely. A few standby lights glow yellow in the dark; I trip over something and fall full-length on what it takes me a moment to realize is Igor. I'm worried something's happened to him until he speaks.

"What were you going to spend yours on?"

I sit beside him cross-legged, my knee just touching his

shoulder. He doesn't move away. "My parents," I say. "They don't belong there, with those people."

"Just because you don't feel what they feel doesn't mean they don't get to choose. It doesn't mean they're wrong. It doesn't mean they're going to drink the Kool-Aid or put bags over their heads."

"You don't know that."

"Neither do you. Maybe you don't get to be the hero. Maybe you don't get to rescue them."

"Because they don't need rescuing, I know. I know how you feel about it. But I just want to go home."

"Where is that?" he says, and he knows I don't have an answer. The Gaia hypothesis, he explains. The ants, Esparza's wife; they don't end the experiment, they just change it. We are a self-balancing system. "Maybe NovaTerra was never meant to support so many people. Maybe there should only ever have been two. Two of us, to start things over."

"I don't want to start a new world with you, Igor. I just want to get back out into the one everybody else already lives in."

"You've never lived there. You can eat the food and speak the language but you've never even been."

I climb over him and turn the lights and CO_2 scrubber back on. I take deep breaths as the scrubber wheezes back to life, as if it could already be making a difference, as if there's pure air to be had.

"We're already home," he says. "I can make you see that."

I expect him to try to stop me from leaving the room, but he just watches me go.

*   *   *

We suspend farmwork and eat all our seeds. We set a trap for the lemurs and grill one on an open fire. Smoke blackens the roof of the habitat pod. We don't see a trace of Igor, and no one knows what he's eating. Bhatnagar gets the diving equipment out and nets endangered reef fish. Our plates shimmer with blue and yellow scales. One night it's my turn to cook, but there's a pot already simmering on the stove. It smells good, some kind of soup, bits of tangled white noodles burbling in a clear broth. I think Park's trying to be nice to me for once, or Campbell found something left in the provisions room, but when we sit at the table it turns out none of us cooked the soup.

"Igor?" Bhatnagar asks me.

I shrug. It has to be, but I don't know if the soup is for my benefit or everyone else's. "This might be poisoned or something," I caution.

We stare down into our bowls and begin to eat. We're too hungry to care, maybe even hopeful that if we start to die all at once instead of slowly, they'll have to let us out.

"Shit," Park says a few spoonfuls in because the noodles aren't noodles, they're roots.

"Beets," Campbell announces, examining the white strings hanging off her spoon. "The taproots."

We polish it all off before we look at the farm. The beet patch is nothing but a morass of ants swarming freshly turned dirt.

"Well," Campbell says. "No more beets."

Inside, I have to cheer.

★　　★　　★

Day 565: Esparza has been talking to his wife for hours, trying to get her to reconsider, and in the slivers of phone time he leaves everybody else, we organize a lawsuit: wrongful imprisonment. We watch on the webcam as the papers get served. Karpov's lawyers call later in the day and make it clear that this won't be a speedy solution.

Before dinner that night Bhatnagar plays logic games with Mission Command. "What if there was a flu epidemic that wiped out everyone on Old Earth and left us sealed inside?"

"Old Earth?" Mission Command asks, and I think despite myself how proud Igor would be that even Bhatnagar was using his vocabulary, accepting this distinction.

"What about an earthquake? A natural disaster? What would be the protocol then? What if one of us died?" Bhatnagar asks, and there's a pause. He's onto something. "What *if* one of us died? What happens then?"

"If we see a body..." they say. "If one of you dies we can input the missing code."

"Then Igor's dead," Bhatnagar says. "He left us root soup and died."

"We need to see the body."

"He drowned. In the ocean. You'll just have to trust us."

"Your ocean's not that deep. You can fish him out."

"Okay," Bhatnagar says. "Fine. I'll bring you a body. I'll fish his body right on out." He stalks from the room, a hunting look in his eye.

249

"Someone should warn Igor," Park says, and everyone turns to me.

He isn't in the desert or the savanna or the ocean or the beach or the rain forest. I check the North and South Lung. I walk all the tunnels: filtration, air monitoring, storage. I check the provisions room, the squat grain bins, and the dangling chain nets that were supposed to hold bananas, coconuts, papayas. They've been empty for a year. The chains rustle as I walk beneath them.

I climb a ladder up a fake armadillo burrow as the sun sets, a halo of light above the desert. The stars come out behind the beams that gird our sky. We've complained about the graph-paper view, about being guinea pigs in a cage, but tonight it makes me feel safe. If we're leaving soon, I can allow myself to love this little disaster of a world. Maybe even love my fellow Terranauts. Tonight we're special, in our beautiful glass box beneath the galaxy. I sit on a real boulder, not fiberglass, and wonder if this is what my parents feel, if this is *illumination*. If I could feel this all the time on any Earth, Old or New, I'd go there. I'd go to Idaho and eat mine tailings. I'd go to Romania and swim in the cyanide-laced Danube. I'd stay in NovaTerra. I wonder if this is what Igor feels, why he's so frantic at the thought of leaving. But eventually hunger howls in me, rises up and gnashes its coyote teeth. I climb back down the ladder to walk to the habitat pod. *If you still had God,* my parents whisper, *hunger would find no purchase.*

In the dining room there's no food, only panic. Bhatnagar never came back from his Igor hunt, and now Park is missing too. In her unlocked room Campbell and Esparza find something brown and small and scaly balled up on the bed. It unrolls and sniffs at them. An armadillo.

On the phone with Mission Command, Campbell starts to cry. It's unsettling to see her get emotional. I bring her her blue-striped towel and she pulls it around her shoulders. Karpov's people finally seem to feel her urgency, but it's almost morning before there's any kind of plan. One more day, they promise. Twenty-four hours for Karpov to get his press releases and PR people in order, ready to spin NovaTerra into something other than disastrous. We'll be allowed to come out if we handle this in an "orderly fashion," sign all their forms, take down our complaint posters. There's even talk of consolation money, twenty-five thousand each for our distress. Someone just has to stand by in the command center for further instructions.

I offer to stay. Campbell has pulled her towel so tightly around her that I can hear the fabric start to tear. Esparza's been staring at the wall since his last unanswered phone call to his wife. No one's in any shape to attempt a search-and-possible-rescue mission for Bhatnagar and Park, and the first documents the Karpov lawyers e-mail over are non-self-endangerment agreements. *We don't want this problem to get any bigger,* they write, *and we don't want you coming out tomorrow in front of the cameras looking any worse than you already do.*

I tell Campbell and Esparza the two of them should try to get some sleep, and they walk down the short passageway to the habitat pod. At lunchtime Campbell brings me the last of the hummingbirds, a small group of them arrayed on the plate like plucked peanuts, and all I can think about is how beautiful they once were. I tidy the room, line up the cans of mud we've been writing with, watch the first ten minutes of six different movies on streaming video because I can't concentrate. Every hour I receive some new Karpov demand and I agree, on behalf of the remaining Terranauts, to various nondisclosure statements, to the wardrobe choices for our first post-departure press conference.

In the late afternoon Campbell knocks on the door. Her hair's wet, her towel's pinned around her neck like a superhero cape, and she's holding a butcher knife. "Esparza's missing. Not taken," she adds before I can ask. "He spelled out GONE OCEAN with all the silverware while I was in the shower."

"It's Friday. His wife."

"Hope springs eternal. I'm going after him. The last thing we need now is to find him belly-up."

"You're sure that's a good idea?" All of a sudden I'm terrified of being left alone, but I don't want to show it. I don't want to look afraid and I don't want Campbell to cry again and I want us all back the way we were, pissed off and petty and safe.

She gives me a long, appraising look. "What do you think is actually going on?"

"What do you mean?"

"You knew him best."

"Esparza?"

"Igor." She runs her thumb against the edge of the butcher knife. There's no blood, no cut, no line in her skin. All our blades are dull.

"He's a hard person to know," I say.

"So are you."

"I don't try to be."

She looks at me with what might be sympathy, fingers the safety pin fastening the towel at her throat.

"I don't know what's going on," I say. "I really don't."

"He's a scrawny, spacey little shit. Let him try something." She whooshes the butcher knife in an arc, speeding toward an invisible neck, but when she stops the blade mid-air, her hand is trembling. "I'll be back with Esparza before you know it," she says, sure she can convince us both. The cape ripples as she strides down the hallway, ready to fight crime or fly away.

That's the last I see of her. Night falls. NovaTerra stays dark. I click the switches in the command center on and off. I click them in the hallway, the dorms, the kitchen. All the interior lights have been shut off. When I return to the command center, the computers are down. There's no power anywhere in the habitat pod. I pick up a paring knife from the dining table, the last leg of the N in Esparza's OCEAN.

From the ridge, the desert sky outside the roof is an impossibility of stars. The ocean is a square of soft, lapping black. I can just make out the bobbing dinghy, spinning slowly like a clock hand. I climb down, carefully, to the beach. I don't have a flashlight, but I know every inch of this world by now. The trail down the fake cliff is already smooth, eroded by footsteps. Then I go across the beach, into the sea grotto, and down the hallway to the electrical substation. I know this is probably a bad idea, but it doesn't seem like there are any good ideas left. The paring knife is sweaty in my hand. I have no clue what I'm supposed to do with it.

An orange light spills from a doorway at the end of the hall. I wait for my eyes to adjust and stand just beyond the light. "Hello?" I ask softly. To shout feels embarrassing, even though I know we should be far beyond embarrassment.

At first there's only silence, and I wonder if I'm wrong. Then Igor steps into the doorway. He's naked, and I can't help but notice that his torso and legs aren't much paler than the rest of him, the parts that peek out of his jumpsuit. He's been spending a lot of time like this, nothing between him and the sun that NovaTerra shares with Old Earth.

"We're leaving," I announce. "Tomorrow morning. They're letting us out."

Igor is expressionless—*Illuminated*—as if this news changes nothing, as if the decisions have already been made.

I ask him where the others are.

"I dug up all the beets for you."

"I never asked you to do anything for me. Where are Park and Bhatnagar? Campbell and Esparza?"

"You've been hungry for a long time. Old Earth won't fix it."

"June and Vikram and Elizabeth and Hector. Where are they?"

"That's why you came here. That's who you are." He looks up and raises his arms as if the ceiling, the dirt and fake rock and glass above us, might have an answer. "This wasn't about the money for you either."

"You can tell yourself that if you want. You can believe anything you want to."

"This world can provide, given the chance. This world—"

"This world is crap. The beets are dead, the lemurs are dead, the fish are dead. The *hummingbirds* are dead, the—"

"The people are dead."

I can't quite make out Igor's face, can't search it for sincerity or bluff. "We're not dead," I say automatically, as if this is an argument we can have, as if logic still has some purchase.

"We're Terranauts," he says. "The only true ones."

"I don't believe you." My voice shakes. My right hand shakes so badly, the knife handle bounces against my thigh.

He tilts his body in the doorway, and the orange emergency light floods across his profile. I realize I've never seen anything less than sincerity on his face, can't even imagine what a lie might look like. He raises his hands again and this time I can see that they're filthy—darkness jammed under the nails and smeared down his wrists and arms.

"What did you do?"

"The provisions room. You can look if you want."

"Please. I just want to leave."

He shakes his head, ducks back into the room, and there's a whooshing, a high whine, and a sound like a balloon wheezing empty. For the first time in 566 days, everything is silent. No filter for the ocean, no scrubber for the air, no condensers drawing moisture from the savanna. His footsteps return to the hallway and the only sound is our breathing. I expect the flare of a flashlight. My fingers curve themselves involuntarily into shapes: a lemur, an armadillo. My grip becomes an open, blinking eye, and the knife clangs to the floor. When he steps toward me, I run.

We're the only two people who could do this, who know the tunnels well enough to race flat out in the dark. I lead us aboveground, flying up the stairs to the North Desert fast enough to lock the door behind me before he catches up. I emerge into stars, the jagged, looming shapes of the mountains, the grid of bars. From the ridge, the boat is still visible, drifting. The waves have stopped. I call out but nobody answers.

There's a smell of smoke from the ventilation shaft. A coyote howls. Startled, I trip backward and cholla needles pierce my calf, rip my jumpsuit as I tear myself away. Blood runs down the back of my leg. The coyote howls again and sounds so close it's as if he's in here with me. The last lemur in the rain forest shrieks. Something is rising up the air shaft, a chink of metal against fake stone, an approaching slither. Nylon rope and crampons, or a pair of claws and a body that has shed its clothes.

"Igor?" I whisper, because it seems useless to hope he won't find me.

"Eve," I hear. "Eve."

I want to ask him if he's getting what he wants, if this is what he's believed in all along. I want to ask him how *illumination* comes, how certainty tastes and fills the body, heavier and happier than doubt. I want to know how fear feels when it stops.

It is night on New Earth. It is a shift in the homeostasis. It is the beginning of whatever comes next.

Acknowledgments

Thank you to the editors who originally published these stories and made them better in the process. Editing short stories is often a labor of love, and I have benefited from both the labor and the love. I have also benefited, as a reader and a writer, from the magazines and anthologies that help sustain and celebrate the short story. May they survive and thrive.

The story "On the Oregon Trail" owes inspiration to the computer game The Oregon Trail, originally created by the Minnesota Educational Computing Consortium. Other stories owe less obvious but profound debts to the friends and fellow writers who read various early versions, or accompanied me on visits to biospheres, arcologies, or backyards. I'm grateful for the company of those who wrote their own work alongside me, or who simply commiserated with me afterward. I've learned a great deal from all the writing communities I've been a part of, especially Grand Valley State University, the MFA Program for Writers at Warren Wilson College, the *Kenyon Review*, the *Kenyon Review* Writers' Workshop, and Arizona State University.

Enormous gratitude to Jim Rutman and Ben George, without whom this book wouldn't exist. I am also pleased to be in the good hands of the entire team at Little, Brown, including Bruce Nichols, Craig Young, Pamela Brown, Evan Hansen-Bundy, Jayne Yaffe Kemp, Gregg Kulick, Gabrielle Leporati, Lena Little, Pamela Marshall, Marie Mundaca, and Tracy Roe.

Thank you to my husband, W. Todd Kaneko, who makes all things possible. Thank you to Leo for the joy. Thank you to my sister and father and mother. And welcome to the two littlest terranauts, here at the beginning of whatever comes next.

About the Author

CAITLIN HORROCKS is the author of the story collection *This Is Not Your City* and the novel *The Vexations*, a *Wall Street Journal* Top Ten Book of the Year. She is a recipient of the O. Henry Prize, the Pushcart Prize, and the Plimpton Prize. Her fiction has appeared in *The New Yorker*, *The Atlantic*, the *Paris Review*, *Tin House*, and *One Story*, among other magazines, and has been reprinted in *The Best American Short Stories*. She lives with her family in Grand Rapids, Michigan.